To Shannon, David, Donald and Patrick... to the original gang and the dream that was (and is) Blue Inferno. Fifteen years later and still kick'n.

PORTAL HUNTERS: BOOK THREE

JUSTICE FOR ALL

By

David Furr and Shannon Smith

PROLOGUE

A steady breeze blew in off the ocean, carrying with it the smell of salt. Waves lapped gently against the rocky shore of the small peninsula known as Shoreline Aquatic Park. Other than the squawking of gulls, it was the only sound that could be heard for a mile around.

The normally packed and busy downtown that stood behind the park was closed and quartered off as a precaution. The rows of boats that berthed at the marina to the east sat empty, leaving Hollywood all by herself. She let out a sigh, wishing she were there under different circumstances. It was a beautiful day in Long Beach, and the deep blue Pacific waters were inviting. The temperature was in the mid-seventies and there was not a cloud in the sky. It would have made for a great day on the beach. She made a note to herself to come back sometime soon, preferably when the city wasn't about to be destroyed by a giant sea monster.

The afternoon sun hung high in the sky, casting a bright glare off the Pacific's shimmering surface. The glare didn't bother Hollywood, though. She was accustomed to lights far brighter than any normal human could withstand. It was one of her unique gifts. She had others, but as impressive as they were, they wouldn't be enough for the crisis at hand. Until backup arrived, all she could do was scan the horizon—watching and waiting—and hope the others would make it in time.

What's taking them so long?

Her gaze panned from left to right. Across the harbor sat the *Queen Mary*. Once a proud naval vessel, it was now a popular hotel and iconic landmark. Unfortunately, its size and position would make it a prime target. *Everyone better be off that thing*, she thought to herself.

Hollywood turned her attention out to sea. Still nothing. The water was calm. With luck, the peaceful scene in front of her meant that Nemo Jones had done his job, though most likely it only meant he'd bought them a little time, nothing more.

A familiar hissing sounded to her right. She glanced back to see a gold and silver portal form next to the small, whitewashed lighthouse that sat at the end of the tiny peninsula. A large, burly man emerged and marched toward her. A sudden chill filled the air as he approached.

"Just you, Tundra?" she asked, disappointed.

"Not quite," a woman's voice sounded out of nowhere. There was a popping sound, and the trim, thin figure of Fast Track appeared next to her.

In the warmth of the late California spring, Fast Track seemed at home. She wore sleeveless, black and red tights and a pair of dark shades that covered her eyes. Her long, jet black hair was pulled back into a ponytail. If not for her golden belt and the International Department of Justice emblem embroidered into her tights, she would resemble a water skier more than a superhero.

In contrast, Tundra looked entirely out of place. Where Fast Track's complexion was olive-brown, Tundra's was pale. His hair and full beard were white with only a hint of gray. Thick, bearskin hides were draped over the plated battle armor that covered him from his neck down. Despite his garb, Hollywood knew that he was not uncomfortable. The aura of cold that surrounded him kept his body at the same unnatural temperature regardless of the environment.

"Good of you to come," Hollywood said with a wry smile. "I'd hate to take all the credit for this one, myself."

Fast Track returned the smile. "Sorry to disappoint, but don't worry, I'm sure you'll find a way to hog the spotlight even though we'll do all the work." Her smile disappeared as she looked out across the waters. "Speaking of... You see anything, yet?"

"Nope. All's quiet here," she answered. "Whether or not that means anything—well, your guess is as good as mine."

Tundra strolled past her and over to the rocky peninsula edge. He squinted and shielded his eyes as he stared out across the seas, obviously not taking the glare as well as Hollywood, but refusing to complain.

"Are we sure it is the Sea Hag?" Tundra asked.

"That's what Nemo's message said," she replied. "He was trying to lock her up before she could make it to shore, but I haven't heard from him since."

Fast Track frowned. "I don't like this. How did the Hag escape in the first place?"

"A very good question," Tundra said in his usual deep, growling voice.

Hollywood shrugged. "Does it matter? She's free. I mean, did we really think we could keep a ten story sea monster locked in a makeshift underwater prison forever?"

"We could try," Fast Track responded. "Nemo was certain it would work."

"Obviously it didn't. So where's everyone else?" Hollywood asked. "You're the only ones the Department could spare?"

"Mr. Black is following a lead on Mr. White and Gabriel's off planet. It looks like it's just the three of us," Fast Track answered.

"Great, just—great," Hollywood muttered. "A crisis breaks out and everyone decides to take a vacation."

"Your United States Air Force has also scrambled two F-16 fighters to aid us. I am sure it will be enough, Holly," Fast Track said, reassuringly.

Hollywood turned back toward the waterfront. "I hope you're right."

"What is that?" Tundra asked, pointing out across the water. Next to the *Queen Mary*, what appeared at first as an unusually large wave formed and then gave way, as something stirred just beneath the surface.

"Uh-oh," Hollywood muttered.

The massive form of the Sea Hag rose out of the water. She was gigantic, there was no denying that, gigantic and pathetically hideous. Her frame was thin, too thin. Green skin sagged against her bones. Her hair was nothing more than a mass of seaweed that hung over her shoulders and covered most of her face. Her teeth were yellow and crooked, and her left eye was bigger than the right.

Standing there in the bay, she towered over the *Queen Mary*. With an evil grin, she reached out to grab the front of the ship. From across the harbor, the three heroes could hear the sound of panicked screams.

Guess everyone didn't make it off, Hollywood thought to herself. "Those jets better get here soon."

"They won't be long, but we can't wait," Tundra announced. "Hollywood, can you get its attention?"

She gulped. She knew it was the right call, but she wasn't eager to draw that beast any closer to their position. It could step on and crush them without even noticing. "Yeah," she admitted, all the same. "You'd better cover your ears."

A single, piercing note blared from Hollywood's lips. Fast Track threw her hands over her ears, but even that was not sufficient protection against the agonizing volume at which her call sounded. As Hollywood sang out, she lifted her right hand into the air. Sparks of blue, green, and red formed around her fingertips and shot into the sky. Twenty yards overhead, they exploded in a dazzling display of color.

It had worked. The Sea Hag had already turned away from the ship and was heading straight for them.

"Looks like she's a fan," Hollywood jested.

"What!?!" Tundra shouted at her.

"I said—! Ah, heck, I told you to cover your ears, Peter!"

"Tundra! See if you can slow her down!!!" Fast Track shouted into his ear.

Tundra responded with a curt nod. The air around him began to stir, blowing with it an unnatural chill. Fast Track shivered and Hollywood pulled her thin, gold jacket close against her. There was a sudden burst of frozen wind and Tundra went flying across the harbor and toward the giant.

Even as big as he was, Tundra was no bigger than her nose, yet as he flew up to her face, he hauled back and punched her, full force. The Sea Hag let out an angry, gargling cry and staggered from side to side while flinging her arms around her head as if to ward off an annoying fly. Tundra darted in and out of her flailing limbs, then closed in again and delivered another solid blow. The cracking sound it made echoed across the water.

"That should keep her busy," Fast Track said. "My turn."

Faster than the human eye could register, she darted off across the water. In less than a second, she was at the base of the *Queen Mary* and then with a loud pop, she disappeared. Three seconds later there was another pop and Fast Track materialized next to Hollywood, holding two shaken hotel porters.

"Some of the staff decided to stay behind," she said. "There's about a dozen more."

"I'll make sure the Hag doesn't notice anything," Hollywood responded. "Go on and get the rest."

Fast Track zipped back out across the water and disappeared with another pop. The two porters stared at the scene in disbelief, then turned and ran back toward the city.

* * * *

Dr. Mutt sat bent over the control of the International Department of Justice's central computer as he watched the battle unfold. On the immense oval-shaped plasma monitor that loomed in front of him, Tundra traded blows with the monstrous Sea Hag. The satellite image gave Mutt a bird's eye view, which meant that Tundra was the most noticeable member of the team, being higher in the air, but not the only visible member. Mutt periodically adjusted the controls to better see Fast Track as she teleported on-and-off the ship, rescuing the last of the crew. Hollywood was escorting the hotel staff off the peninsula and to a waiting police van. All and all, his fellow I.D.J. agents were doing well.

As he leaned forward to adjust the view settings, Dr. Mutt's long brown ears brushed against a set of keys and the image flickered and then went black.

"Doctor," the tall, ebony woman standing next to him said, her tone carrying with it a mild rebuke.

"Sorry," Mutt responded in a gruff voice. He pulled his ears back behind his head and turned the screen back on.

"Doctor, you're drooling on the controls, again," the woman pointed out.

Mutt sucked his tongue into his mouth and brought his jaws tightly together. "Sorry," he muttered again. "I just get excited watching the team at work. Sure wish I could be out there with them."

Dianna, Mistress of the Portals, looked down at her companion and smiled. "You're not as young as you once were, Geoffrey."

Mutt looked up at her and gave her a toothy smile. His already wrinkled face seemed to wrinkle even more in the process. "Yeah, but being around you makes me feel young."

"Doctor, please," Dianna responded, blushing. She was indeed a stunningly beautiful woman, as Mutt would often remind her. Unusually tall, she stood at six feet and two inches. Her hair was knotted into long rolls which were fastened by a golden clasp and hung down her back. She wore a long, black, single-piece dress that left her shoulders bare. On each wrist was a series of golden and silver bracelets, each a different tint that would periodically glimmer in the light as if glowing. Some believed they were the source of her powers, but no one dared to ask. She was the only human alive that could summon portals at will, and the International Department of Justice was just thankful she chose to share that ability with them. They didn't press their luck by inquiring into matters that she did not wish to discuss.

"I still have to wonder," she said, drawing attention away from the doctor's flirtations and back to the matter at hand, "how did the Sea Hag break free in the first place?"

The doctor shrugged. "The cage should have held. Nemo and I spent months designing it. If he followed my instructions to a tee, then there's no way she was able to break out on her own."

"Which could only mean—" Dianna began.

"That someone helped her," a deep, elegant voice said from behind the two.

Dr. Mutt and Dianna spun around and simultaneously gasped with surprise.

* * * *

The Sea Hag lay slumped over the top of the *Queen Mary*, her large, watery eyes only half opened. Tundra wrapped the enormous anchor's chain around her wrists, tying her hands together behind her back. Hollywood and Fast Track stood on the shore of Shoreline Aquatic Park and waited for Tundra to finish.

"That went remarkably well, if you ask me," Hollywood said, smugly. "Not that I was worried, mind you," she added.

Fast Track gave her a sideways glance and grinned. "Oh, right, you *weren't* worried."

"Of course I wasn't!" she protested. "We always get the job done, don't we? I just thought it would've been nice for the others to show up for—you know, a little bonding time, build up team spirit and all that good stuff, ya know."

Fast Track opened her mouth to respond, but a loud electronic beep cut her off. Hollywood and Fast Track both looked down at their belts. The IDJ communicator each member carried was flashing red. That could only mean one thing.

"More trouble," Fast Track said. With her lightning fast reflexes, she jerked her communicator off her belt and keyed it on. "This is Fast Track."

"Elizabeth, we need you back at headquarters, ASAP!" a man with a deep, British accent said over the comm.

"Mr. Black?" she responded. "What's wrong?"

"I'll explain when you get here," he said.

"Okay, no problem. Have Dianna open a portal and we'll come right over," she answered.

"We can't," he answered. Black sounded panicked. That wasn't like him. Fast Track and Hollywood exchanged worried looks. "You'll have to get here on your own. And bring Tundra!"

"Okay, sure thing," she said, "Fast Track out."

Hollywood shot a brilliant red flare in the air above her to signal Tundra. Having finished securing the Sea Hag, he flew over and landed between the two heroines.

"I think that will hold her," he said. "We should contact Nemo and have him return her to her cell."

"Holly will take care of that," Fast Track said. "We're needed elsewhere." She took hold of his arm. "Hold on."

She took off running, with Tundra in tow. It was an odd sight to see such a small woman dragging such a large man, but they didn't go far. After three steps there was a loud pop and the two were gone.

* * * *

With another loud pop, Fast Track and Tundra rematerialized in the main control room of the International Department of Justice's headquarters. She released Tundra and took a single step forward. Her jaw dropped, alarmed by what she saw.

"Oh my—" she began.

Tundra muttered an obscenity in Russian.

Lying before them was Dr. Mutt, his face bruised and his white lab coat stained with blood. The oval-shaped screen that stood behind him was cracked and the control board smashed. The room was filled with the smell of electrical smoke.

Bending over Dr. Mutt was Mr. Black. Black was tall, with a thick muscular frame. He wore suit coat and tie, both a solid black that was so pure they reflected no detail or texture and seemed to drink in the surrounding light. His shirt was as white as his skin both, like his suit, too perfect and likewise without any visible detail. It made him appear as if he were a made of gloss-cover wax and not an actual person at all. Despite his unnatural appearance, he was formidable to behold. His shoulders were broad, his gaze hard and intimidating and he towered over every member of the team including Tundra. Yet at this moment, he seemed neither formidable nor imposing, but… helpless.

"What happened?" Tundra demanded. The words boomed through the cavernous space that was the main control center.

"Mr. White," Black answered. "We were tricked—played."

Fast Track shook her head. "I don't understand. You were tracking Mr. White. I thought he was in Europe."

"I was tracking him and the trail lead me back here, but too late," Black explained. "He was in league with Dr. Vamperic, that much I knew. I thought he was hiding in Vamperic's secret lair in Transylvania, but I quickly discovered the two had set out for the Pacific. That's when I realized the truth."

"The Pacific?" Fast Track was puzzled.

"They released the Sea Hag," Tundra said, understanding.

Black nodded. "It was a diversion. With Gabriel off planet and myself distracted by following a false trail, our field team was reduced to only four. They knew it would take all four of you to deal with the Sea Hag, leaving Headquarters only lightly defended. While you were at Long Beach, White and Dr. Vamperic broke in, assaulted Dr. Mutt and took their prize."

"Their prize? Wait—where's Dianna?" Fast Track asked.

"Dead," he answered. "Vamperic created a device that would suck the powers out of any gifted human allowing him to harness it for his own use. Unfortunately, the process disintegrates the intended victim. Dianna's gone. I'm sorry"

"Oh, Dianna," Fast Track covered her mouth and fell to her knees.

Tundra was unmoved, yet his facial features hardened. "So, Mr. White now has control over the portals."

"For all practical purposes, yes," Black answered. "But he doesn't grasp how to use them, fully."

"How can you be sure?" Tundra asked.

Black gestured to a metal door parallel to where they stood. It led to the Headquarters' server room. "Simple, see for yourself."

Tundra put an arm around Fast Track, and escorted her toward the door. "Come, my dear." As the two heroes approached, the doors swung open. Tundra took a quick step back. "How is this possible?" he muttered.

In front of him, blocking his way into the room, was a shimmering gold and silver portal.

"I caught them trying to access our network," Black said. "It wasn't their primary reason for coming, merely a sort of *coup de grais*, a little bonus to their already substantial victory. When I confronted them, White opened this portal, allowing Dr. Vamperic to escape. He and I fought for a bit, but seeing that he would have no quick victory over me, he made his escape through the portal, as well."

"But what does this prove?" Tundra asked.

"If he had true mastery over the portals, he would have closed his escape door behind him, insuring we could not follow."

"It could be a trap," Tundra pointed out.

"Maybe, but my instinct tells me no," Black said. "In either event, it is irrelevant. We must go after him. If he does gain complete control over the portals, he will be unstoppable."

Tundra ran his fingers through his beard. "I am afraid you are right." He patted Fast Track on her shoulders. She continued to weep for her fallen comrade with her face buried in her hands. "Pull yourself together, my dear. The day, I am afraid, is still in need of saving, and there must be vengeance for the blood spilt."

"No, not vengeance, Peter," Black said. "Justice."

CHAPTER ONE

The words 'Liberty for the Innocent, Punishment for the Guilty, and Justice for All' were carved into the granite wall that loomed behind the high justice's bench. Ivan Jast had always liked the phrase, but today the words had an ominous tone. Where before it had always seemed so clear, today innocence and guilt seemed less concrete and more abstract, and the words 'justice for all' carried with them a hidden threat instead of a reassuring promise.

He directed his gaze away from the carving and turned his attention to the high justice's bench. The bench itself towered over the rest of the room, standing five meters off the ground. It was wooden, unlike the glass and metal furniture that composed the room. Draped across the front was the symbol of the United Earth.

The judge—an older man from Nigeria, with deep brown skin that contrasted against his pale white hair—glared down at everyone else. Next to him were two other benches, only half as tall. On the right hand side sat an Egyptian woman, wearing crimson and black robes and a hijab. Ivan didn't know her age, but she couldn't have been younger than forty, he guessed by her appearance. On the left-hand bench, sat a much younger judge, also wearing the red-and-black robes that were traditional in the higher courts.

The other two judges sat in silence as the high justice began to speak. "Sergeant Ivan Allen Jast, you stand accused of two counts of disobeying direct orders, one count of falsifying data, and one count of high treason against the Civil Union of the United Earth. How do you plea?"

Ivan took a breath before responding. He could feel the sweat on his palms and moisture on his forehead. Hopefully it wasn't showing, he thought to himself. There was nothing like a nervous expression accompanied with a statement of denial to make a man look guilty. Worse, he knew he *was* guilty, as a matter of technicality. He had allowed three unauthorized personnel into the heart of the Portal Command, to the Portal Matrix itself—the heart and soul of the technology that had, more than once, brought the galaxy to a point of crisis. But as a matter of principle, he was not guilty. To be guilty of high treason meant to stand against one's government in the most extreme way. This he had not done. On the contrary, he had saved all of humanity from the worst possible fate, and for that he might be labeled a traitor and sent to his death.

Out of the corner of his eye, he could see a small group from Portal Command sitting along the far corner of the long judicial hall. At the end of the row was his longtime friend Sergeant Gregory Mortan and, next to him, his commanding officer, Lieutenant Kayla Marro. It warmed his heart to see her sitting there, though the cold, blank expression she wore did not reassure him. It wasn't that he feared what she thought as his commanding officer. Kayla knew he was innocent. She had been there with him the moment a possessed Éva Katona had tried to unleash a hostile, alien presence onto the world. No, he wasn't worried about their professional relationship, but rather their personal one.

He and Kayla were lovers in secret, or had been before this. It pained him to think what this meant for their relationship, even if he was acquitted. It had been two weeks since she had spoken to him, right after the death of his older self. Their last conversation worried him almost as much as the charges he now faced. He faced death every day as a Hunter, so the prospect of dying wasn't as terrifying to him as it might be to others, but the thought of losing Kayla was not one he could bear.

You've already lost her, the rough voice of Whrongtt floated through his head. He shook off the memory. *No, I can't accept that*, he told himself. He had to believe her presence here today was reassurance of her love and support, although in truth he knew it was probably a requirement of her duty as his superior and as a witness to the crimes of which he was charged.

"Your plea," the high justice reiterated

The harshness of his voice snapped Ivan back to his present situation. The weight of it hit him again, as it had so many times that morning. He felt almost sick.

"To the charge of falsifying data—" he hesitated. "I plead guilty. I plead not guilty to the rest."

"Let the defendant's pleas be noted in the records," the high justice said, with a nod to the clerk on his left. "We will now review the matter of bail. In cases of treason, bail is traditionally denied. However, I have received a request from the Gaoro Embassy that we reconsider the matter. I understand there are several here who wish to speak on your behalf." He paused and squinted at a tiny view screen resting in front of him. "We will first call Sergeant Gregory Mortan."

* * * *

"I don't like this," Vice Minister of Defense Samuel Kadam said, sourly. He sat reclined in a large leather seat just to the right of the floating holographic broadcast of Sergeant Jast's hearing. "Having your government request leniency against Earth policy makes the Civil Ministry look bad. Isn't it bad enough that we're trying a renowned war hero for treason? This would be a good time to show the solidarity between our two governments, Ambassador, not flaunt our differences."

Next to him, Ambassador Ruthr Humrun sat in an identical chair with his legs crossed. While Vice Minister Kadam scowled in irritation, Humrun's own expression was docile in comparison. He watched the proceedings with a look of mild interest. To Humrun's left were two other chairs. Closest to Humrun were Malena Ibsen, the Prime Minister's chief of staff, and sitting beside her Gafa Al-Falahi, the Minister of Justice.

"On the contrary, Vice Minister, that would be exactly the wrong thing to do," Humrun said, his tone direct but not unpleasant. "You are right, some will resent the fact Sergeant Jast is on trial, regardless of whether he is guilty or not. We need a way to dispel that resentment, and a voucher for leniency is the best way."

"That doesn't dispel it, it deflects it onto us," Kadam retorted.

Humrun shook his head. "I don't believe so. High Justice Gowon is a reputable figure within the Civil Union, and several members of his family fought in the Resistance. He will not be viewed as biased against Sergeant Jast on any political basis. If anything, by making my government seem more compassionate on the matter, we assure that the public views this as a truly fair trial."

"But isn't that just a lie?" Malena Isben interjected. "It was your people who put the pressure on us to move forward with a trial in the first place, and your people who continue to put pressure on us to see that he's not found innocent. So, you're neither lenient nor fair."

Humrun's bemused expression darkened. "I take it when you mean 'my people' you are referring to Fleet Commander Borxos."

Malena didn't say anything for a second, then – "Yes."

"Mrs. Isben, you will find that, as it is in your government, we Gaoroes have a wide range of political ideals and a wide range of people who position themselves behind them. The fleet commander represents the views of *some* in my government, but not all, and definitely not mine."

"Be that as it may—" she began.

"Be that as it may," Humrun cut her off, "if the Prime Minister is unhappy, he could pardon the sergeant, at will. He has that power."

Malena shifted uneasily in her seat. "The Prime Minister himself has not voiced his concern on the matter."

"Ah," Humrun began with a smile, "so this concern is not shared with everyone in your government? Then, you see my point. We both suffer from the conflict on opposing political views where unity would best serve all interests. But there is never unity in politics."

"So it was your idea to request bail for Sergeant Jast, then?" Malena asked, raising an eyebrow. This time, it was Humrun who hesitated to respond. His delay was all the answer she needed. She looked over at Minister Al-Falahi—who watched the proceeding with seemingly no interest in the conversation at hand—then back at the ambassador. "Why?"

"Borxos' approach is typical of a military mind. He wants an example made of the sergeant. I had to interfere," a troubled expression came across Humrun's face for a moment and then faded into his usual diplomatic calm. "The commander is a capable military officer, I do not doubt, but he lacks the subtlety necessary for politics. Yet I fear he will try his hand at it, all the same, throwing the weight of his office around like a club. You should not let him intimidate you," Humrun glanced over at Kadam, "any of you."

Kadam flushed with anger. "You suggest that we would?"

"Perhaps not you, Vice Minister, but I worry about others. Take, for instance, Minister Gramont. The minister and he have spent a lot of time together since his arrival, ever since the incident with Sergeant Jast and Corporal Katona. There is talk the commander and he are discussing ways to dismantle the Matrix and move it off world."

It was Kadam's turn to look uncomfortable. "The minister is just exploring options."

Humrun leaned toward Kadam. "A dangerous option to consider. As I said, the commander lacks the subtlety. Pushing for this now will only inflame your people."

"Some would disagree," Malena said. "Some would be glad to get rid of the thing. Moving it might end the Crisis."

"There is no scientific evidence to say that it would," Humrun countered. "If the Matrix is moved and the Portal Crisis continues, you will have civil war, and if you lose, Gaoro and Earth will be at war again. And if war broke out while the Matrix was in Gaoro hands—"

Malena squirmed uncomfortably in her chair. "If that happened, humanity would not have—" the words hung on her lips, as she finally understood.

"—A chance," Humrun finished for her. He glanced over at Kadam. The sour look on his face told the ambassador that he'd already come to the same conclusion. "I did not accept the role of ambassador to Earth to see your world oppressed by my own people. This situation, which could arise if rasher minds prevail, is counter to my purpose here."

"And what is your purpose?" Malena asked, her voice measured and suspicious.

"To foster peace, of course," he said, innocently enough.

"You'll pardon me if I doubt your sincerity," she responded. "An ambassador's loyalty is always to his own world first. If the Matrix were in your hands, wouldn't it be better for your own people?"

"Would it?"

Kadam glanced over at the ambassador, still scowling, but said nothing. He turned his attention back to the broadcast. Malena ran a finger thoughtfully across her lower lip.

"I see. You want to avoid a second Crisis, one that might have a more direct effect on your nation," she said.

"I simply don't want rash action to disrupt peace," the ambassador answered. "We still don't know why restoring the Matrix hasn't stopped the Crisis when all evidence says that it should. We have no idea why dimensional portals are opening on their own when the Empress' top minds were unable to create such portals deliberately. My point is that there's much we don't know, and moving the Matrix while so many mysteries remain could be disastrous—just as another war between our two people would be. All of this should be obvious, my dear Ms. Isben. However, to my colleague Commander Borxos, it is not."

Humrun's serious expression melted away as he returned his attention to the broadcast of the trial. "Ah," he said, in a jovial tone. "I see Director Ferrgerr is taking the stand, now."

* * * *

Corporal Devon Hwang fiddled with the holo-tuner, trying to get a better signal. The broadcast of the trial faded in and out, but the image was never clear. With all the interference coming from the Matrix's core it was difficult to get reception. Even though the core was dozens of meters below, shielded by thick layers of titanium, concrete, and lead, the frequencies it radiated throughout the Compound were powerful and disruptive. It took specialized hardware, based on Gaoro technology, for their communicators and inner-channel network to function seamlessly, but the pod-receiver Devon was using was not military issue, and not up to the task.

The door behind him opened with a swish. Devon instinctively shoved the receiver hastily into his pocket out of sight—too hastily. He missed the pocket's lip and it fell to the floor with a clang.

"Tisk-tisk, Dev," said Corporal Hammed Azari as he entered. "Playing with toys when you're supposed to be working?"

"Oh, it's you," Devon said, feeling slightly embarrassed. He reached down and retrieved the receiver. "Close the door, will ya?"

The door slid shut, as if on cue. "It's the trial," Devon explained, "I figured out what channel they're broadcasting on, but heck if I can get a clear signal."

"It's not a trial, it's a hearing," Hammed corrected. "I doubt anything exciting is going to happen until the actual trial starts. Seriously, Dev, you shouldn't be fooling around on duty. Assistant Director Flupd's been cracking down on discipline ever since Sergeant Jast went bonkers."

"So you think the sergeant is crazy?

"Got to be," Hammed said. "He let a bunch of whack-jobs into Portal Command to stop the end of the world because 'his future self' told him so. Does that sound to you like a sane thing to do?"

Devon placed the receiver onto the control station and began adjusting the light frequencies once more. "Well, if he was crazy, what about Éva? What was she doing in the core, and what about those people they say she killed?"

Hammed smirked dismissively. "Come on. If she killed anyone, it would be her on trial. Who says she even went into the core?"

"Stefan was on duty when she arrived that day. He said there was something weird about her, something unnatural. Scamardo went with her and ended up shoved in a waste bin. Doctors still aren't sure how he died, but it wasn't by natural causes."

"Stefan likes to exaggerate," Hammed replied. "You should hear him talk about his time in the war. You'd think he was Sergeant Traush himself, just to listen to him."

"Right, there's Sergeant Traush. What about him?"

"What about him?" Hammed asked. He sounded almost bored.

"They say Éva killed him, too. We haven't seen him since, have we?"

Hammed chuckled. "You really think that skinny tramp could kill Sergeant Traush?"

"Hey!" Devon retorted, obviously annoyed. "All I'm saying is there are more to these portals than most people think. How do you know Sergeant Jast isn't telling the truth? Look at what happened in Madrid and Debrecen."

"Those were flukes, and no one really knows what happened anyway," Hammed said. "Really, you've been hanging out in the bays by yourself too long. You should ask for reassignment—maybe try for Hunter yourself—then you'll see there's nothing to these rumors. They're just spatial holes. All they're doing is dumping space junk into our atmosphere, that's it." Hammed motioned to the empty space in the room's center reserved for incoming portals. "Nothing super natural or super human is going to come bursting out. Trust me."

A sudden spark of energy flashed in the room's center. Hammed lurched back. Devon leaned over the control board. "Someone's trying to activate an incoming portal."

"No kidding," Hammed answered sarcastically. He was recomposed and slightly flushed with embarrassment at being so easily startled.

"You don't understand. Nothing's scheduled to come through, and I'm not receiving proper security encoding," Devon explained. It was not uncommon for a Hunter or a military official to make a quick, unscheduled jaunt back to the Compound, but every summoner was set to transmit a security key the moment they accessed the Matrix, identifying who they were.

"Maybe something's wrong with their summoner," Hammed ventured.

"Maybe, but I'm not taking any chances." His hands flowed over the controls as he began activating the security protocols. There was another flash in the room's center. Devon frowned. "It's not working."

"What do you mean?" Hammed asked, less composed than a moment before.

"I'm trying to block it out of the Matrix, but it's not taking. We may have a rogue, here."

"Come on, Dev. Rogue's can't form this close to the Matrix's core."

An oval, gold and silver portal formed. In and of itself, it resembled every other portal that opened in the bay throughout the day. Devon drew his pistol and took a step around the control panel and toward its mouth. Hammed glanced nervously from Devon to the portal then drew his pistol.

"Maybe it's a malfunction," Hammed offered.

Devon said nothing. He edged closer.

A silver, gauntleted hand shot out through the opening and grabbed hold of Devon by the neck. Instinctively, he dropped his weapon and began clawing at the metal hand that held him, with no effect. It lifted him off the ground and tossed him back across the room.

Hammed stood wide-eyed and motionless as a monstrous metal shape stepped through the portal's opening and into the bay. The man (or creature) that emerged wore plated body armor that covered him entirely. Over the armor, it wore a black and purple suite, the style of which Hammed had never seen. There was something archaic about its design, the way the shirt collar was turned up, the broad cut of the shoulders, and the signs of rot and tattered ends of the sleeves. The helmet was more of a mask made of steel like the armor, but fashioned in the shape of a man's face. The features of the face, however, were barely human. The nose and eyes were right, but the mouth was too wide and bore long fangs that protruded over the bottom lips and the ears were long and pointed.

The only part of the intruder that was visible beneath the armor were two bloodshot eyes that glared back at Hammed with a burning contempt.

"Ho-hold it right there," Hammed said. From behind him, he could hear Devon pulling himself to his feet. "You've gained illegal access to Portal Command and Control. I'm placing you under arrest."

The metal creature regarded him for a moment longer, then threw its head back and laughed. "Puny mortals! Do you really think your toys are any match for Dr. Vamperic!?!"

Hammed glanced back at Devon. His comrade appeared to be fine, a little shaken, but unharmed. He came up alongside Hammed. "What did he just say?"

"Yield now and I may be merciful. Resist me, and you will feel the full force of my wrath!" Dr. Vamperic threw back his head and began laughing again. It was a deep, mirthless sound that echoed behind his metal mask.

Hammed and Devon looked at each other. "Is this guy for real?" Hammed asked.

Devon shrugged. "Must be some kind of a nut job. One heck of a strong nut job, though," he added as he massaged his neck.

"Okay, final warning!" Hammed called to Vamperic. "Get your hands in the air, turn around, and get on your knees. Do it or I will shoot!"

"Enough!" Vamperic snarled. He threw his hands out in front of him. Beams of light flew out of the ends of his fingers. From his right hand, red lights struck Hammed. The young man's entire body began to glow red and, in an instant, he was gone. Nothing remained except a small pile of ash. Blue lights from his left hand slammed into Devon's chest and threw him across the room. He smashed into the same wall Vamperic had thrown him against moments earlier, bounced, and then rolled onto the floor with a groan.

The second attack left Devon disoriented and weak. It wasn't just the impact against the hard, metal wall. The energy from the beam had drained him of his strength. The room was spinning and try as he might he couldn't rise into a sitting position.

The sound of steel against steel echoed throughout the dome-shaped room as Vamperic marched over to where he lay. Reaching down, Vamperic grabbed him by his shirt and hoisted him off the ground. He pulled Devon close and glowered.

"You begin to understand my powers, little man?" he growled. Devon grunted, but offered no distinguishable answer. "Good," Vamperic continued. "Now, tell me, where am I, and where is Mr. White?"

Chapter Two

"This may sting," the medical technician said without a hint of interest or compassion. Ivan flinched as she jabbed the needle into his outstretched arm, but the pain was mild and passed almost instantly. Withdrawing the needle, the technician swabbed his arm with alcohol a second time and stowed the syringe back into her small, black briefcase. "All right," she said, "you're good to go."

"Thanks," Ivan mumbled. He flexed his arm, measuring the lasting soreness of the injection, and then turned to face the others.

Director Ferrgerr, Kayla Marro, and Judicial Sergeant Tam Zayed stood at the open cell door. The medical technician filed passed the three without as much as a glance.

Sergeant Zayed stepped forward. "The chip implanted in your arm will allow us to track your movements." she explained. "You will have free roam of the city, but should you attempt to leave Cairo, or access a portal for any reason, we will know at once. Officers will be sent to retrieve you, place you back under arrest, and you will face additional charges of parole violation. You will report here at 8 AM every other morning, starting tomorrow, and check in with your parole officer," she continued. "Failure to do so will qualify as a breach of your parole, and will result in your arrest." She prodded his recently injected arm with a nightstick. "We'll know where you are, don't forget."

Ivan rubbed his arm and nodded, doing his best not to appear annoyed. He'd secretly hoped that the police would show him a degree of favoritism—after all, he was a renowned war hero—but Sergeant Zayed was like any other judicial officer he'd encountered since his arrest: hard, practical, and unsympathetic. She wore a tightly fitted dark gray uniform that buttoned up the front, a leather weapons belt, and a sash bearing the insignia of the Civil Ministry. The uniform and her stern attitude reminded him too much of the New Moon's judicial enforcers, a group he'd had many unpleasant dealings with before the war. In fact, if he had to guess, he was certain Zayed had served as an enforcer. It would not be a stretch to imagine. The Civil Ministry had kept many of the New Moon's various regional infrastructures in place in order to make the transition of power smoother. As Ivan thought about it, he started to suspect that the court had deliberately assigned former New Moon officers on his case to prevent the favoritism he'd otherwise receive—not that it mattered. Prejudiced judicial offers were the least of his worries right now.

Zayed pulled herself up to her full height and loomed over Ivan. "Is there any part of these conditions you do not understand?"

"No. I understand, and don't worry. You'll have no trouble from me," he answered.

She regarded him, seeming unconvinced then motioned toward the door. "Then you are free to go," she said.

"Thank you," he said as he stood and crossed the room. Director Ferrgerr and Kayla fell in step beside him. No one spoke until they were outside the correctional facility. "Director," Ivan began, "I appreciate what you said at the hearing."

"I only offered the facts as I saw them," he said.

That was true. During his hearing both Greg and Kayla had recounted his heroism in the war and praised his personal character. While touching, the testimony came off as exaggerated and personal. Ferrgerr, on the other hand, detailed specific behaviors Ivan had demonstrated since joining Portal Security in quantifiable terms. He offered not a hint of praise, but listed specifically what he had done. The approach came across very matter-of-fact, and Ivan could tell it was just that sort of unbiased information the judges were looking for.

While the director's testimony had done him the most good, it was Kayla's words he'd appreciated the most. It was reassuring to hear her defend his character so strongly and passionately. He could tell from the way she'd spoken in the hearing that all his doubts about their relationship were unfounded.

As they approached the street, the director continued. "You understand that you will have no access to the Compound during the duration of the trial."

Ivan pulled his thoughts away from Kayla. "Of course," he replied.

"I have to tell you Sergeant, that regardless of the outcome, your career with the Hunters will most likely be over," he went on.

Ivan glanced up at the tall Gaoro and then over at Kayla. Ferrgerr's expression was calm but unreadable, as always. Kayla offered no visible expression either, but he could detect a sense of anxiety all the same.

"But sir, if I am cleared—" he began.

"Sergeant, you admitted to altering records," Ferrgerr went on. "You will not be found innocent of all charges. Not only that, but an incident like this has raised too many questions and brought too much unwanted attention into the Project."

Ivan glowered. "You're going to discharge me even if it's proven I saved all of our collective behinds?" Ivan immediately regretted such a direct and unprofessional response, but his anger at the thought of being dismissed outright kept him from offering an apology.

"I may not have a choice," Ferrgerr said. "All the same, you shouldn't worry about that now. You haven't been found innocent yet, and you face very serious charges."

An understatement, as always, Ivan thought. If found guilty on all counts he would be executed. That was a certainty.

The three came to the end of a sidewalk leading away from the correctional facility. Along the sidewalk a busy road branched off in two directions.

"This is where I will leave you," Ferrgerr said, reaching for the summoner tucked away in his front pocket. "I sincerely hope you will be cleared, Sergeant Jast." He pressed the tiny button on the end of his summoner and a small portal formed in front of him. Ferrgerr began to step through, then paused and looked over at Kayla.

"Coming, Lieutenant?"

"No thank you, sir," she answered. "I'm taking the afternoon off. I'll just—walk."

He nodded and then stepped through. The portal closed immediately. Kayla turned toward Ivan and offered an outstretched hand. "Sergeant, as the director said, I do hope they find you not guilty."

For a moment, her formality confused him, but then he remembered they were still in eyeshot of the courthouse. There were probably listening devices staggered around the grounds. He took her hand. There was something in her palm; metal and flat. She slipped it into his as they shook hands. "Thank you, Lieutenant. Perhaps we'll run into each other again before the trial."

"Perhaps," she said. With that, she headed toward the east end of the street. He watched her go.

Once she was out of sight, he turned and tried to hail a passing cab. It took a few minutes. Most of the cabbies weren't eager to pick up someone just being released from prison. Eventually, a heavyset man in a small, silver glider swooped down. The passenger side door opened to admit him.

"Where to?" he said in a thick Egyptian accent.

Ivan looked down at the object in his hand. It was a pass card. There was a name and address written on the back. "Hotel Ramora," he read aloud.

* * * *

The tiny light on the touchpad turned from red to green and the door slid open. Ivan tucked the pass-card back into his pocket and stepped inside. He was greeted by a waft of cold, recycled air that tasted of cleaning solution and ozone. It gave the place an impersonal, artificial feeling. All the same, as the lights came on, he could tell the place had class. The outer sitting room was lined with baseboards and crown molding of dark, polished wood. The walls themselves were made of tan marble. A long, red and orange couch adorned with silk tassels and a gold lining sat next to the bedroom door.

Warm colors, Kayla's favorite.

Reserving the suite must have been tricky, he surmised. She'd registered the room under a fake name, which was no small task in-and-of itself. This was one of the few luxury hotels in Cairo, recently restored from the Siege. Many of the hotels in town would forego the need for reliable government ID—given that most citizens had lost theirs in the Siege—but not this one. A place like this would only accept identification that they could validate, and somehow she'd managed to provide them with a fake one without raising any suspicion. It was a good thing she had, though. Meeting him in the clandestine fashion as they often did was risky enough under the best of circumstances, but the pending trial only made it more precarious for them both—more her, though, than him.

Ivan opened the bedroom door, half hoping to find Kayla waiting for him. No such luck. It was dark and quiet inside. Dim lights kicked on, barely enough to see by, but just right to project a certain, desirable mood. As Ivan entered, the door slid shut behind him.

It was as stylish as the sitting room. A large, king sized bed lay in the room's center with another red and orange couch off to the side. The dressers and cabinets were of the same dark wood. Ivan went up to it and felt the smooth surface. *Hand carved if I had to guess.* He turned and strolled over to the edge of the lavish bed, tucking his hands into his pockets and wondering to himself what exactly Kayla had in mind. For the last week he'd been worried that she didn't even want to speak to him anymore. Now this?

The sound of the suite's main door opening came from behind. Ivan waited at the foot of the bed as the echo of soft-toed boots crossed the outer room's floor. The bedroom door slid open.

"Hey there," Ivan said with a subtle, yet warming smile.

Kayla stood in the door, the light from behind her spilling in around her, giving her a glow, or perhaps it was just Ivan's wishful imagination. She was dressed in a sky-blue shirt that fit perfectly about her frame, black bell-bottom pants that had a glossy sheen about them, and leather high-heeled boots. A brown leather belt hung around her waist, dropping down on her left side and resting against her thigh. It was a nice outfit, Ivan had to admit—casual, but classy. Her bangs were neatly parted so as not to hang in her face, and her hair was pulled into a ponytail draped over her right shoulder.

"Hey," she answered Ivan.

In the dim light of the bedroom, Ivan couldn't tell for sure if she was smiling. Her lips seemed slightly upturned, but she had a lost look about her, the same confused and tired expression he'd seen on her face ever since the incident with the possessed Éva.

Ivan wasn't sure what to say. Instinctively, he wanted to reach out and embrace her, yet a deeper, perhaps wiser instinct told him to play it cool.

"You found the room," Kayla said, an odd statement of the obvious.

"Yeah. It would be nice if they'd put room numbers on these things," he fingered the pass card, "but whatever. I kind of figured you wouldn't use your real name, so when I spoke to the guy at the front desk, I figured I would try a couple of the code names you used in the Resistance, starting with your favorite—"

"Chloe Mathus."

"—and got it right." He rocked forward and back on the toes and heels of his feet, feeling awkward just standing there. "Ah, good old Resistance. Those were the days, weren't they?"

Kayla came into the bedroom and walked over to Ivan, stopping half a meter away. With her heels, she was almost as tall as Ivan, yet still he felt as if he was looking down into her glassy and watery eyes.

"Ivan—" she began. Without warning, she threw both her arms around him and pulled herself tightly against his chest, her head resting on his shoulder.

It took Ivan a second to register a reaction. He reciprocated, placing both his arms around her. The warmth of her, the softness of her touch, the subtle smell of her perfume—it was Heaven. As he held her, he could feel her tremble and the moisture of tears soaking through his shirt. Gently, he stroked her back, running his fingers up and down her spine.

"Hey, now, it's all right," he said. "It's all right."

She looked up at him, her eyes red and face wet from the tears, yet still the picture of loveliness. He could see fear in her though.

"No, Ivan, it isn't all right. It couldn't be less all right," she answered.

"Oh, I dunno," he replied with a teasing grin. "I could imagine a few worse situations."

"This is serious!" she retorted.

"Hey now, of course it is," he ran his fingers through her hair as he spoke. "Trust me. No one knows it better than I. Think about it, though. I've got a top attorney, the truth is on my side, and best of all the judges were favorable enough to grant me bail. If they were so convinced I was a dangerous traitor, they wouldn't let me go wandering around."

"It isn't that simple. This trial is too high profile. It's become political."

"Political?"

"The director confided in me," she went on. "He's worried. The new fleet commander wants to divert funds away from the Project, but he can't do it without an excuse."

Ivan drew away from Kayla and sat on the edge of the bed. "An excuse? Why on God's green Earth would he even consider pulling away from our funding? That's crazy!"

Kayla took a seat next to Ivan. "Like I said, it's political."

"But it doesn't make sense!" Ivan retorted.

She took his left hand into hers. "Being the daughter of a politician, I can tell you that politics rarely makes sense. If you're found innocent, that means you really did save Earth, which also means the portals are more dangerous than we realized. The Gaoro council and the Civil Ministry would have to increase our funding. But if you're found guilty... well, they can discredit anything you said about the incident, or any of the bizarre evidence."

"Like another me lying dead in a morgue."

"Yes," her voice grew more quiet, "like that."

Ivan stood and paced back and forth in the narrow space between the couch and the bed. "Great, so I've become a pawn of intergalactic grandstanding. That's just great." He stopped pacing and shook his head. "Aah, but that doesn't matter. Borxos represents the Gaoroes' military interests in this sector. Sure, the Project is run jointly between the Ministry and the Gaoroes, but the Gaoroes handed my case over to Ministry. It's an internal matter. They have no say."

Kayla's gaze wandered to the floor. Ivan could see tears welling in the corner of her eyes. "I'm—not so sure," she said, her voice nearly cracking.

"Oh, come on. I've heard all the conspiracy theories about the Gaoroes secretly running our government, but you and I both know there's nothing to them. It's just xenophobia from paranoid people who're still upset about the Siege."

"I—" she paused.

Ivan knelt down, rested his arms on her lap and looked up into her eyes. They stared at each other in silence then she reached down and touched his cheek.

"I just know it's a dangerous situation. There's a real chance I could lose you, and I can't do that. I just—can't." Her voice was stronger, but the fear was still evident in her tone. "You're everything to me, Ivan. Everything."

Ivan reached up and took the hand that stroked his face. Their fingers intertwined. "Hey, you haven't lost me yet. Let's not worry about things we can't change. Right now, we're together. Let's just enjoy the moment. It's all any of us has, really."

"Yes, and—that's why I asked you here."

"Oh?" Ivan responded.

"You know that I was in the room when the other you, the one from the future, died. He held on long enough to speak to me, and then he just faded away. When I left that room that day, I suddenly realized I had just watched you die. The realization was more than I could bear, and it got me thinking."

"About?"

"About you, about me, about what could have happened, and about what may still happen. Having you here is almost like a second chance, and it's a chance

I don't want to waste." Her other hand came up and she stroked his temple. "I've had to make some tough choices in the past. One of those choices cost the lives of my parents. I can't change that now, and I can't change what may happen to you, but I can change how I spend my future, and—uhm," she seemed suddenly nervous. "What I'm saying is— I want to marry you."

Ivan's heart leapt. "Marry?"

"Yes, I want to marry you now."

"N-now? Right here?"

The seriousness of her expression broke and she grinned down at Ivan. "No, silly. I have friends in the Department of Civil Affairs. I already spoke to them. They can cut through the red tape and have us a marriage license in a day or two. We can be married before the trial begins. For however much time we have left, whether it be weeks or years, we can be together. We can be a family."

"You're serious." He released her hand, but remained kneeling in front of her.

"Yes! Yes, I couldn't be more serious," she responded. "I'm tired of the crises of the universe standing between myself and the life I want. I've given it a lot of thought. I want to be with you. I want to be a part of you, body and soul. Marry me, Ivan."

Ivan got up from his knees and sat on the bed next to her, putting both arms around her and drawing her close. His face was just two centimeters from her.

"Kayla, are you certain?" he asked. "You know what this could mean for your career.'

"Careers are replaceable. You aren't," she answered, her voice strong and giving no hint of uncertainty.

He brought her even closer, until their noses touched. "I love you so much, Kayla. You have no idea. I do want to marry you, and I'd marry you right here if I could, but I won't put you in a dangerous position."

She pulled back, to better see his face, and looked into his eyes as they spoke. "Ivan, they're not going to execute me for violating codes of conduct."

"You may not be tried as a traitor, but if I am convicted as one you could find yourself with more troubles than you can imagine. You'd be the wife of a traitor. Like you said, this has turned political. Guilt by association can be as bad if not worse than actual guilt."

"Guilt by suspension?"

"Yeah, think about it. You were in the Core with me. Granted, everything you did was by the book and no one is questioning your presence there, but if I'm found as a traitor, they may start to wonder if it was by mere coincidence that you were in the Core the same time I was. They could brand you a traitor simply because they believe it, even if they can't convict you in a court of law." Ivan sighed. "I want nothing more than to marry you, but I can't tell myself I love you and put you in that kind of position."

Kayla's eyes began to water, and Ivan felt a sudden pang of guilt. Why did there seem no way not to hurt her? "Let's do this..." he said, "if I am found innocent of treason, we'll get married, even if the rest of the charges land me in jail for a time. We can get married before or after I serve my time, your call, but only if I am found innocent of treason. All right?"

Kayla nodded slowly. "Okay, okay. Just know that I'm yours, and if you change your mind, I'm willing to risk it—even risk my life if that's the price I have to pay. I'll have my friend hold the paperwork on standby in case you do, or for the day you're found innocent, whichever comes first."

Ivan pulled Kayla to him and kissed her deeply. They held on to each other for several long seconds before taking a breath. When their lips moved apart, Ivan kissed her on her cheek and then worked his way down to her neck. Kayla sighed wrapping her arms even tighter around Ivan. Gently, he lowered her to the bed as he moved his lips to the front of her neck and then to the other side.

"What are you doing?" Kayla asked, abruptly.

Ivan stopped. His right hand was on the buckle of her belt and his fingers had just begun to work at the strap. She released Ivan and propped herself up on her elbows. Ivan rolled to his side, feeling a little confused.

"I'm sorry," he said, blushing. "I just thought, you know, asking to meet me in this room and considering your proposal that you were ready for this."

She gave him a reproachful yet teasing look. "We've talked about this. You know I want to wait till our wedding night. I asked to see you here because I wanted to propose in a romantic and private setting. I didn't want anyone to know about us until the marriage was done."

"Right, okay." Ivan felt both flushed and frustrated.

She moved closer and put her arms back around him. "Of course, if you change your mind and want to get married this week, I'll book this room again and we can—" her fingertips moved playfully up his back, "—pick up where you left off."

"Fair enough," he said with a smile. "I love you, you know that."

"Yes, and I love you, with my whole being."

She leaned against the bed, pulling Ivan with her and resting his head against her chest. He closed his eyes and relished the sense of her warmth, softness of her touch, sound of her breathing, and even the pleasant smell of her perfume. She stroked his neck as the two lay there in silence and in bliss.

* * * *

"WHERE—IS—MISTER—WHITE!!??!!"

Dr. Vamperic held Devon high and slammed his head into the wall with each syllable he spoke. At the first impact there was a loud snap and Devon went limp, but still Vamperic shouted his question and thrust the man repeatedly against the solid metal wall. A circular blood stain formed on the spot behind Devon's head, growing darker with every blow. His legs and arms flopped at his side like those of a stuffed doll.

"We entered the portal together, but only I came out!" Vamperic stopped bludgeoning the man. "What have you done with him? Where is he!?! WHERE—IS—HE!?!" He smashed Devon's head into the wall three more times and then glared into his face. Blood trickled out of his mouth and his pupils stared off into nothingness.

"Naarh " Vamperic flung the corpse across the room. "The humans of this planet are pathetically frail!" He marched over to the bay's main console. "These machines are very bizarre, but there has never been a device that Dr. Vamperic could not master!" he said aloud, as if speaking to someone, but there was no one there except for Devon's corpse.

He placed his metal hand flat on top of the controls. A series of thin copper wires emerged along the joint-ends of his gauntlet and crept onto the panel. One by one they inserted themselves into the controls by working their way through the narrowest of spaces, between the control's plasty-shield covers and the metal lining. After the last wire penetrated, they each began to glow, blue at first and then white. From inside his armor, Vamperic could see a holographic image appear in front of his visors, displaying bits and pieces of data as it downloaded.

"Fascinating," he continued aloud. "I have never seen technology so advanced, except for my own. Very impressive for such a weak-bodied people. Perhaps this is why they are so feeble. With technology this impressive, they no longer have to rely on physical strength, or so they believe."

The door opened behind Vamperic. He glanced over his shoulder and growled at the lone person who entered.

"What the—?" Gregory Mortan blurted. He stood in the doorway and gawked at Vamperic in disbelief.

"Leave me, or I will destroy you as I did your friend!" Vamperic snarled at the Hunter.

"Uh?" It was just then that Greg noticed Devon's bloodied body lying on the other side of the bay. "Holy—!!"

In a simultaneous motion, Greg reached over his shoulder and pulled out a half-meter, light gray rod with one hand while slamming his fist into a small, yellow panel next to the door. The yellow panel lit on contact and a series of alarms rang out. The rod immediately extended once, twice, until it was as long as Greg was tall. The top end expanded into what resembled a wide-mouthed gun barrel. As the staff took shape, a translucent shield sprung out of Greg's left wrist and covered his arm from the elbow to the ends of his fingers.

"You defy me? So be it!" Vamperic ripped the wires free from the console, spun toward Greg and fired two red beams, one from each gauntlet.

Greg ducked low and held his arm-shield high, covering his face. One of the beams shot passed, but the other struck the shield dead on. The translucent surface erupted with a hot flash and sent searing fragments flying in all directions, some embedding in his arm while others bounced off his helmet. Greg bit his lip, but managed to choke down a scream.

"Very good!" Vamperic said with a chuckle. "I can see you will pose more of a challenge than your two comrades."

He fired another beam, blue this time. The beam flew passed Greg as he dove to the side. Bringing the weapons end of the staff up and around, Greg retaliated, firing a beam of his own at Vamperic. His shot was well aimed, but useless. The energy bolt stopped centimeters from Vamperic and dissipated against an unseen force field.

"Muhahaha!!!" Vamperic laughed maniacally. "You see now how useless it is to resist me!"

Greg gritted his teeth and felt a helpless sense of frustration swell up in him. Stubborn determination took hold. As Vamperic fired another red beam, Greg darted out of its way and then threw himself forward. He spun his staff around and then brought it down hard on Vamperic's head, hoping the invisible shield only worked against energy-based assaults. The end of the staff connected with Vamperic's helmet knocking him off balance. Greg brought the other end of the staff up and fired point-blank into his face.

"Rrraaahhhhh!!!" Vamperic shrieked. He threw one hand over his face. His other arm swung blindly at Greg with surprising strength and speed. It caught Greg on the side of the helmet and sent him sprawling backward.

"What the heck is going on!?!"

Greg looked up, a little dazed from the blow. Sergeant Jonah Spears and three armed guards stood in the doorway, their weapons trained on Vamperic. Vamperic lowered his hand from his face. His helmet was blacked and cracked, but still in one piece. Blood red eyes glared through his visors at the new arrivals, full of hate and venom.

"You all right, Greg?" Jonah called out.

"Yeah, I think so," Greg responded as he pushed himself up.

"Who is this guy?" Jonah asked.

"Heck if I know, but he killed Hwang," Greg answered.

Vamperic threw his head back and cackled. "Who am I? I am your doom!!" He fired two more red beams. One beam exploded against the door while the other hit a guard in the chest. His body erupted into red sparks and he was gone.

Jonah swore loudly and opened fire with his staff. The two remaining guards followed his lead and unloaded their rifles at the armored intruder. Each bolt vanished into a spray of blue sparks as it got within centimeters of Vamperic.

"This isn't working!" one guard blurted.

"Don't stop! Keep firing!" Jonah ordered.

The more shots they fired, the brighter the sparks. The force field began to ripple, becoming visible for the first time.

"His field is weakening!!" Greg shouted.

Vamperic backed away. "Fools! You win this round, but this is far from over!" He touched the bay's console and activated the summoner. A portal formed in the room's center next to where he stood.

"Greg!!!" Jonah shouted.

"I'm on it!" Greg switched off the weapon's component, activated the disrupter, and fired at the portal... too late. Greg's discharge hit the portal and collapsed it with a loud pop, but Vamperic was already gone.

"Ah, blast!" Jonah muttered. "How did he know how to operate the controls?"

"Couldn't say, but all we need to do is check the log and see where he went," Greg said as he hurried over to the controls. "Oh, snap! I don't believe this!"

Jonah ran up beside him. "What?"

Greg pointed at the readout on the console's screen. "He scrambled the log. Not only did he know how to summon a portal, he knew how to make sure we couldn't track him."

"Looks like we got ourselves a new problem," Jonah said. "I'll contact the director and—"

The console's main panel lit up. Jonah and Greg both leaned forward and read the text that popped onto the screen.

"Someone's coming through," Jonah said.

"Someone without proper access!"

Greg backed away and held the weapon's end of his staff aimed at the room's center. Jonah and the two guards fell in step, all pointing their weapons in the same direction. Golden sparks appeared first, followed by a bright flash as the portal materialized.

"You think it's that same guy, coming back?" Jonah asked Greg.

"Not unless he brought help."

The outline of three humans could be seen in the shimmering silver surface of the portal. The first stepped out. He was a large, muscular man in his fifties—or so he appeared—dressed in armor and bearskins. A woman with an olive complexion wearing red and black tights came out and stood next to the first, followed by a man wearing a suit and tie of a black so solid and complete it hid all detail and skin so white it reflected the glow of the portal.

"Lower your weapons!!!" the large man boomed. "My name is Tundra, the Siberian dreadnought, and I've come for justice!"

CHAPTER THREE

The electrical current came at Michael Traush from all directions. It was blindingly bright, searing his vision as it cut through his flesh and filled him with incredible agony. He hung twitching in the air, floating just above the floor. In as much as it was possible, he did his best to hide the effects of the pain, but the current triggered impulses in his nerves and caused muscles to spasm. Even with his Rensha training, there was nothing he could do to counter that, so he bore it without a cry or complaint. After all, it was no worse than a sayder probe at level four.

There were three Gaoroes in the room with him. A shock trooper carrying a large assault rifle flanked the door. A second Gaoro, an officer of unknown rank, sat at a control panel. His attention was entirely on the readout in front of him, paying Traush no mind—not directly, at least. The third Gaoro was dressed as a naval officer with the rank insignia of second commander. This one Traush knew, or had come to know in the last week of his imprisonment. His name was Thish Vhast.

"Are we feeling talkative yet, Sergeant Traush?" Commander Vhast asked, as he paced just outside the force field that held Traush in place. "No? Perhaps a slightly higher setting, then."

Vhast glanced over at the other officer and nodded. The officer pressed another button on the panel and the electrical current intensified. Traush flailed as a fresh spasm rushed through him. Air escaped his lungs, but still he did not cry out. He took a deep breath and quieted his mind.

The device they used on him was known as a whaf shield. It was not much different than a sayder probe. Like a sayder, the pain inflicted was not actually real. There was no electrical current surging through his body. Holographic imagery combined with a mind feed gave the device every illusion of inflicting real harm onto a person's body. Since Traush was trained to withstand a sayder, he found this no more challenging to endure. The only real difference was that it used a gravity and energy field to immobilize its victim, which meant he would not be able to slip free and kill his tormentors, as he had when strapped to General Rourke's sayder.

Since there was no hope of escaping, the best way to deal with torture was to focus his mind on something else, to disassociate the conscious from the body. Traush let himself breath steadily, forcing the process against the twitches and spasms of his muscles. After a few minutes of controlled breathing, the pain lessened and his mind was finally able to wander. His thoughts went back in time.

A week ago he'd been serving as a combat trainer at Portal Command. It was his sole responsibility until one morning, in response to an emergency, he was authorized for field work and sent out on assignment. His orders were to track down a Hunter by the name of Éva Katona. Very little information had been given to him as to why there was need to track Corporal Katona, but Traush had a habit of following orders, not questioning them. This time, however, such a habit had proved nearly fatal.

Something had happened to Éva. As Traush had learned in the recent days from Ivan, she had been possessed by a creature from another dimension known as the Darkness. The force that inhabited her gave her supernatural powers. Traush had experienced those powers first hand, and barely survived.

Éva tried to kill him by bludgeoning him with her portal staff. While possessed, her strength was superhuman. Traush had managed to parry the blow, but the impact of the two staffs had caused an eruption of rogue portals. One had opened up directly beneath him and, before he could respond, he fell through into a spiral vortex.

Rogue portals could lead to anywhere. The possibilities were endless. Until recently, it was believed that 'anywhere' simply meant anywhere in the physical universe, but the incident in Debrecen had taught the world differently. Still, Traush had not anticipated the possibility that portals could take a person to another place *and* time, but that is exactly what happened to him. He was deposited, unharmed and unconscious, aboard a Gaoro cruiser in orbit of Earth, three years after his battle with Éva.

Three years wasn't all that long and Traush wouldn't have expected radical change to occur in such a short span of time, but a great deal had changed. The alliance between the Civil Ministry and the Gaoroes had failed and a war between the two had broken out—if it could really be called a war. The Gaoroes military presence in the system combined with Earth's devastated economy and utter lack of naval forces made the conflict very one-sided. The only humans who opposed the Gaoro were a small but resourceful band called the New Resistance. Many of Traush's former colleagues from the old Resistance and the Portal Hunters were members, including Ivan Jast.

Ivan had been captured shortly before Traush arrived. When the Gaoroes found Traush unconscious in the battle cruiser where Ivan was being held, they assumed Traush had come to rescue him. In what they believed to be an ironic gesture, they locked the two together.

Another wave of pain surged through Traush as the whaf shield increased in intensity. He took a deep breath and slowed his pulse.

The state of galactic affairs had deteriorated far more than Traush would have thought possible. It wasn't just the war. It went deeper than that. He had plenty of previous dealings with the Gaoro, both as friend and foe, and he'd never heard of them using torture before now. Their sense of civility was too high. Yet something in the last three years had eroded their moral conduct. The whaf shield wasn't even a Gaoro device. It was invented and used by the Krarno. This made him wonder if there was a possible connection. Had the Krarno put aside old grudges and formed an alliance with the Gaoro? That seemed unlikely, on historical basis alone. Besides, Ivan told Traush that they were using sayder probes as well. It seemed that the Gaoroes were trying to play catch-up on the latest torture technology by salvaging what they could from other races.

The pain continued to increase. Focusing on the past week wasn't distracting enough, so his mind took a different approach. It began to view the last seven days as an equation that needed solving. No, more than that, he told himself, it took in the last three years—or what he knew of it—as an equation that needed solving.

It should never have gotten this far. The Portal War had been devastating for both the Gaoro and humans, even if more so the latter. The only way the Gaoroes would even go against Earth would be as the result of desperate circumstances and with the certainty they could neutralize, or counter in some way, the humans use of portal technology.

When Traush arrived in this future, he was eager to try and understand what had happened, but the Gaoroes had taken Ivan out of his cell for interrogation, and he had not returned for two days. When he did, he was hardly the man Traush remembered. Whatever they had done to him—sayder probe or whaf shield—it had been brutal. Ivan wouldn't speak for a whole day, and when he started speaking his sentences were fragmented. On the fourth day, the Gaoroes had taken him again, and for another day Ivan was silent. Finally, yesterday, Ivan was able to pull himself together and the two had talked. He began by explaining what had happened to Éva, of the arrival of the new fleet commander Borxos, and what that meant for the Project.

"The Defense Minister was disturbed at the reports of what happened to Éva, and what had almost happened to all of us as a result. His concerns were compounded quickly."

"How so?" Traush asked.

"The Guardian and the Darkness weren't the only strange and unexplainable things to come out of the portals. Those were only just the beginning. Commander Borxos pushed the Defense Minister hard, telling him it wasn't safe for the Portal Matrix to exist on an inhabited planet, and eventually he caved. But we weren't sure how to dismantle the Matrix. We weren't even sure if it was possible. Borxos kept pushing, though."

"And did they figure out how to dismantle it?"

Ivan shook his head, a smile on his lips, but a haunted look in his eyes. "They thought they did, but when they tried, all hell broke loose. It was the Portal Crisis mach two. A lot of people died. We got it back together and stabilized it, but that was enough for Minister Gramont to lose his nerve. He told Borxos the Matrix had to stay. Borxos wasn't too happy about that. Two days later, Minister Gramont was dead."

"Assassinated?"

"Uh-huh," Ivan nodded.

"By the Gaoroes?"

"We think so. No one knows for sure. The Gaoroes said that human radicals were responsible—someone who blamed the minister for all the deaths that came from trying to take the Matrix apart. But a bunch of people blamed Borxos, saying he needed Minister Gramont out of the way so he could move forward with disassembling the Matrix. Either way, within a week, Borxos was also dead. That, I know, was the Resistance's doing."

"So the New Resistance was around before the current war?"

"Yeah, a few from the old Resistance never trusted the Gaoroes and kept the group together. They were waiting for the Gaoroes to show their hand, and sure enough, they eventually did. When they did, the rest of us from the old days, like myself and Kayla, joined back up."

"Borxos death was the trigger, then?"

"Yeah, when he died, Admiral V'Moreth came back and took over as sector commander. He was determined to find who'd killed Borxos and to oversee the dismemberment of the Matrix. His tactics were pretty heavy-handed. V'Moreth pushed and the Civil Ministry tried to push back, but he would just push twice as hard. He took direct control of the Project and expelled all human involvement. He claimed to have found evidence that a Hunter conspired in Borxos' murder, but it was just an excuse, and we all knew it. When he did that, the Civil Ministry tried to retake the Compound by force. That didn't go so well. That's when most of us went underground and reconnected with the Resistance."

Traush took it all in. It made sense, and now that he knew the truth, all the signs that this was coming were there. But the question is could it have been avoided, or was it inevitable? Traush found it interesting that he thought of events that had already transpired as if they were part of the future. He supposed that he still thought of himself as belonging to those three years past, but he had no idea if he would even be able to return to that time, especially if the humans had lost control of the Matrix. No, those three years were over and done with—years lost. It made more sense to focus on what to do about the current predicament.

The first step, naturally, was to escape. That wasn't as easy as he'd hoped. It was impossible to open the door to his cell from the inside. Whenever it did open, there were always three or four shock troopers present. Traush sized them up. These soldiers were top of the line. He had no doubt he could defeat any one of them, but they had the advantage of being armed and he wasn't sure he could defeat three at once while he himself was unarmed. It was possible, but if he miscalculated it would mean his death, and Ivan's, too. It wasn't the idea of death that bothered him—he was Rensha—it was the idea of pointless death. There was no need to hurry and make a rash move. He'd lost three years already. What were a few more days or weeks? He'd bide his time and find the ideal opportunity. It would reveal itself eventually.

"Had enough, Traush?" Vhast asked, pulling Traush away from his wandering thoughts. "I'll ask you again, how did you gain access to the Matrix? How were you able to port yourself to this cruiser? Is there a traitor among the Gaoroes, someone who helped you? If so, who is he?"

The pain tripled suddenly, then went back to the level it was a second before. It was done for emphasis, Traush knew. Vhast circled the force field, his hands folded behind his back as he waited for a response. When Traush didn't answer, Vhast motioned to the Gaoro at the controls, and the pain tripled again. This time it stayed at that setting.

Traush fought to maintain consciousness. He quickly recalled battles he'd fought in, remembering wounds he'd received. *I overcame those. I'll overcome this, too. Pain is an illusion, the body's way of testing ones soul. I will persevere.*

There were no secrets Traush was withholding, but he didn't dare admit this. He knew the cell he and Ivan shared was bugged. They would have heard him recount his story of fighting Éva and falling into the temporal portal, and he knew they wouldn't believe it. They would assume he made up the story as a ploy. If he told them the truth, they would dismiss it as lies, and if he told them nothing, they would assume he held a deeper and more valuable secret. He chose the latter course, because he knew the more torture he withstood and remained silent, the more they would believe whatever secrets he held were of the upmost importance. To that end, they wouldn't dare kill him until they discovered what he knew, and since he didn't know anything he could keep the ruse up indefinitely. He just hoped they didn't accidently kill him in an over-enthusiastic effort to break him.

"Sir, I'm not sure he can hear you," the Gaoro operating the controls said. "These pain readings are well above the normal curve. By all rights, he should have lost consciousness."

"Hmm," Vhast muttered. "Very well. We will pick it up tomorrow. Maybe after a restless night, he'll be more cooperative."

Vhast turned and marched out of the room. The other Gaoro pressed several buttons on the panel, then stood and exited the room. The shock trooper remained.

Traush fought hard against the pain and waited for the shock trooper to release him. *Just one trooper. If I can hold it together, this may be my chance.* But the trooper did not move. He stood at attention, his rifle at his side. The minutes ticked on and still the guard remained at attention.

They're sending for more troopers to escort me. Well, maybe next time. But no soldiers came.

After what felt like an eternity, the door finally opened and another soldier stepped inside. The first soldier saluted the second and then exited the room. The second soldier took up position where the first had been and snapped to attention. He stared blankly at Traush with his rifle slung to his side, and made no motion to release him from the whaf shield.

'*...a restless night...*' *They're going to leave me here with the pain field fully active,* he realized. He fought off a rush of horror. Panic threatened to seize him. *Pain is an illusion. It can only harm me if I let it. I can endure this. Pain is an illusion...*

* * * *

"They left you on the machine all night, didn't they?"

Ivan sat at the end of his cot, picking through the plate of food in front of him. It was Gaoro food and some of it inedible for humans. Traush lay flat against his cot his food untouched, and stared at the ceiling.

"Yes," he answered Ivan's question. "That's what they did to you, wasn't it? That's why you were gone for days."

Ivan merely nodded a reply as he lifted a long, brown, stringing vegetable with two fingers "I'm surprised they didn't keep you longer," Ivan said after he took a bite of the brownish vegetable. He made a face, but kept eating.

"Maybe they will, next time," Traush replied. "They were satisfied enough that I wasn't ready to break, so they didn't waste any more time on me. They probably want to see if the anxiety of facing another interrogation will break me down."

"I guess they're in for a disappointment, since you don't know anything."

Traush sat up. "And what about you?" he asked. "What do they hope to learn from you?"

"Names, places—where our hideouts are and who's in charge these days."

"And did you tell them?"

Ivan shrugged. "No reason not to. They know who our leaders are and the Resistance would have abandoned our hideouts and moved everything after my capture. There isn't anything I know that could help them."

"You mean to tell me you couldn't find the Resistance if you wanted to?"

"No," Ivan answered, a mouth half full of food.

Traush wrinkled his brow. "That could be a problem."

"Why?" Ivan asked, still chewing. "It's not like I'll ever need to. Once the Gaoroes are done with me, they'll execute me as a traitor. The only members of the Resistance I'll ever see again are those who get captured before my sentence is carried out."

"The other day when you were talking about the Resistance, you made a slip. You indicated you were married. I take it you were referring to Lieutenant Marro?"

A faint smile flickered across Ivan's lips. "Yeah, that's right. Sometimes I forget how obvious we were back in those days, trying to be sly and doing a really bad job of it. I should have figured you'd guessed the truth—not that it's a secret anymore."

"And the lieutenant is still alive? Your marriage still going well?"

"Yeah, it was before this," Ivan gestured at the cell walls.

"Good. Hold on to that." Traush lay back against the cot.

Ivan dropped a piece of meat back onto the tray, his expression suddenly forlorn. "I've tried, Michael, I really have, but Kayla and I talked about this. We agreed not to go on a suicide mission to rescue the other person if one of us got captured. If you're hoping she'll come rescue us, you're in for a disappointment."

"That's not what I mean," Traush answered. He folded his arms behind his pillow and propped his head up. "You have something to live for. Hold on to that motivation. You're going to need it."

"For what?"

"For our escape."

* * * *

Golden sparks flared in the center of Al Maadi road. Most everyone wandering close by ran at the sight of a forming portal. A few pedestrians paused and watched as the golden rings formed into a silver glittering oval, curious to see if the portal forming below was the work of the Compound or another rogue. When a hulking figure wearing plated armor from head to toe covered in a tattered, moth eaten suit emerged, the few on-lookers that remained quickly fled

Dr. Vamperic stood in the center of the road and surveyed his surroundings. The neighborhood was in shambles. A third of the surrounding buildings were scorched. Some had even collapsed. The undamaged buildings were all new, but even their newness did little to dispel the bleakness. They were rectangular, gray, and cheaply built. The main road was freshly paved, but the side streets were badly cracked and closed off.

"What a grim place," Vamperic said aloud. "It appears this world has undergone a holocaust. Perhaps that is why the people of this planet are so feeble. Their willpower has been beaten out of them by a superior force."

Vamperic marched down the road, taking broad steps that clanked loudly as his metal boots struck the pavement. "If this planet is crumbling and its people defeated I should have no trouble asserting my dominion over its citizens!!" He threw his head back and let out a loud laugh that echoed inside his steel mask.

"We're not as beaten as we seem," a voice said from behind.

"Who dares—!?!" Vamperic whirled around.

Four men emerged from a nearby alley way. Three were armed with rifles. The forth stood calmly with his hands in his coat pockets. None of them appeared to be soldiers, not in the formal sense. They were all dressed in plain clothing, most of which had visible signs of wear.

The unarmed man took a step forward and removed his hands from his pockets. Vamperic expected him to reveal a hidden weapon, but his hands were empty.

"I apologize if we frightened you," he said.

Vamperic glowered at him. "Frightened, I? No one frightens Dr. Vamperic! I am the terror of the Earth!"

"Indeed you are. Forgive me again. I'm—" he paused, seeming to search for the right words, "—unaccustomed to dealing with someone as—magnificent as yourself."

"Indeed," Vamperic's eyes narrowed. "I might forgive you your slight, but two offenses are too much! You must be taught what it means to anger the dreaded Dr. Vamperic!"

Vamperic lifted his arms above his head and clenched his knuckles tightly together. His fists began to glow orange. The three armed men took a step back and fingered their rifles nervously.

The unarmed man went down on one knee and bowed his head. "If it pleases you, I am at your mercy," the man said. "But I would be of more use to you unharmed, as your servant."

"My servant?"

"Yes, that is why we came to find you, so that we may be of service to you and help in your cause."

"And how is it you knew I was coming?" Vamperic asked, his fists still glowing. "Did Mr. White send you?"

"No, I am afraid I'm not familiar with anyone by that name."

"Then how—!?!"

"We heard that our enemies had attacked you, and we wanted to make common cause with you against them," the kneeling man quickly responded.

Vamperic lowered his arms. "The men with the staffs, those are your enemies?"

"Yes," the unarmed man answered. "They are known as the Portal Hunters, and they have plagued this world for several months. If you will help us defeat them, we will serve you gladly."

"Hmmm," Vamperic took all of this in. Finding Mr. White had been his chief concern. White had the portal sphere they created from Portal Mistress' life essence, and without it he was trapped on this planet. But if White had abandoned him—or perhaps been killed by these Portal Hunters—he would need a force of his own. These four humans seemed willing enough. It was a start. And if he decided later they were no longer of any use, he would have no trouble disposing of them.

"Very well!" he announced. "Rise, and give me your name."

The man rose to his feet and dusted the legs of his pants off. "My name is LeStrange, Major Peter LeStrange of the New Resistance. It is an honor to meet you, Doctor."

CHAPTER FOUR

All the lights were off in the tiny apartment living room, yet Éva had no trouble seeing her surroundings. Every detail was visible, every thread in the carpet, every line on the walls. It wasn't the details, though, that held her attention. It was, instead, the man cowering in the corner and the young girl standing in the room's center—her father and sister.

Attila Katona huddled against the wall, his flesh marked with bruises and his clothing torn in several places. He stared up at Éva in horror, but she did not mind. Instead, she focused her attention on her sister. Greta's face was unrecognizable. Her eyes were black pits and her mouth was twisted into a horrific and diabolic sneer. There was blood on her face and running down her neck.

Éva moved toward the girl. Greta stood there, not acknowledging her older sister's presence. As she came closer, Éva's hands blazed with fire.

What am I doing?

Éva could not understand her own action. It was not by her own willpower that she approached her sister, and it was not by her own ability that she summoned the flames. Something was driving her for a purpose.

A purpose—purpose... Then she knew. *I'm going to kill my own sister.*

Another man entered the room. He was muscular and young, but completely bald. In his hands he held a long staff.

Traush.

Gunnery Sergeant Michael Traush aimed his staff at Éva and fired off a round. She swatted the energy bolt aside with little effort and continued toward her sister. The young girl made no motion to flee. She merely sneered up with a grotesque grin. Éva wanted to shout at her, tell her to run, warn her of the danger she was in, but she couldn't speak. Instead, she continued to advance.

Traush leapt over a chair and landed between Éva and her sister. Éva struck Traush with a casual backhand and sent him flying across the room. He disappeared out of sight, sailing end over end through the air.

At last, Éva was standing directly in front of Greta. Reaching down, she grabbed the girl by the neck, hoisted her up, and with her other hand she punched through her ribcage and ripped her heart out of her chest.

"Noooooo!!!!" Éva cried out, suddenly in control of herself once more. She dropped the bloodied corpse and fell to her knees. The darkness covered the room and she was no longer able to see. Not far from where she knelt, she could hear her father weeping.

"No-no-no-no-no!!!" Éva rocked back and forth. She pressed her hands against her ears to drown out her father's cries. For a moment, she could neither hear nor see anything. There was small comfort in that.

"Is this really what you remember?"

The voice came seemingly out of nowhere. She rose to her feet in a start. It was still black, but she was able to see this man. He appeared nondescript enough: a navy blue business suit, dark brown and gray hair, olive complexion, and no facial hair. His eyes were not shaded, yet Éva couldn't tell what color they were.

"W-what?" she stammered.

"Is this how you remember it?" he asked again. His voice lacked any compassion regarding the tragedy of the scene, but at the same time it was not unkind or unpleasant.

"I murdered my sister," she said, "I don't remember how."

"You don't remember how, yet you're certain that you did?" the man asked.

"I—I remember her face." It came to her in a flash. It was dark, and her sister was on the ground in front of her. Lightning poured out of her and struck the young girl. Greta was begging for mercy—Éva thought, maybe not. Maybe she just screamed. Yes, she remembered her screaming.

"I don't remember the details," Éva went on. There was another flash. Greta was on the ground, still in Éva's apartment. There was a burnt hole in her chest. Éva lowered her head and felt tears welling up. "It doesn't matter how. I killed her. It was my fault."

"Weren't you under the control of an alien presence?"

"I—no… yes, I mean… but I remember it! It was me, I killed her!" Éva protested.

"You just said you didn't remember," the man pointed out.

Éva shook her head. "Why are you asking me these questions? What does it matter to you? This is just a dream. You're not real!" As she said it, she knew it was true.

"Am I not? And does sleep deny the existence of reality? Is truth different to a human when he, or she, sleeps?"

"What?" Éva looked over at the man. It was then that she was able to see the color of his eyes. They were purple, a bright purple that shown in the darkness. And his voice, she recognized it.

"That's what I am seeking to understand. What you perceive is not what others perceive. So what is truth? In your world, who decides it?"

"Get away from me!!!" she shouted.

A rush of adrenaline woke her with a start. The bed covers fell away from her as she hastily sat up. The surreal dream had left her disoriented. It took her a moment, but the ivory-colored walls that were bathed in dim blue light reminded her where she was. It was a small room, only large enough for the hospital bed, a meter wide side table, and the security globes that floated overhead. A meter-by-half-meter window was off to her left and at the foot of the bed was a seamless door.

Éva lay back against her pillow. It had been a dream, she told herself, but that thought was of no comfort. Her dreams—or nightmares more accurately put—were a reflection of reality. Just as it had been in her dream, she remembered torturing her sister and she remembered seeing her lying dead, a hole in her chest, in the middle of the apartment. But the dreams were crueler than the waking reality. When she was awake, she could try to block the thoughts and memories of what she had done, but when she slept, there was no escaping. Each night the same visions came back to her as a brutal reminder. And now he had come back, the man with the purple eyes—the Guardian.

Or was that, too, just a dream, a cruel memory taunting her as she slept? For the first time since falling victim to the Darkness, Éva found herself asking the same questions again. Since the Guardian was a creature of dreams, was seeing him the same as summoning him, or was it merely another trick of the subconscious? Éva was afraid to know.

Closing her eyes, she did the best she could to put those thoughts aside and hoped—prayed—she wouldn't fall back asleep.

* * * *

Attila Katona took the last swig of liquor and then tossed the bottle across the sidewalk. It skidded across the concrete, slid into the sandstone brick walls of First Ministry Psychiatric Hospital, and shattered.

It was well into the nighttime hours and well past visitation, yet he remained fixed in place by the hospital's guest entrance. He'd been standing there for three hours as he slowly nursed the bottle, debating whether he should go inside, and waiting long enough for the visitation hours to expire, thus ending the debate. Even then, he still did not leave.

For two solid weeks he had come directly from work to the hospital, and each time he stood outside until he either lost his nerve or until the visitors' entrance closed and he had no choice but to go home. Often he would stand there for hours at a time, as he had this night, staring up at the outer walls of the hospital, wondering which room Éva was in. Each time he did so, he would relive that horrible night in his mind, over and over again—the night he lost both his daughters.

It was hard for him to accept that it had actually been Éva who committed those deeds. When he saw her in the apartment, eyes blazing with fire and hatred, he knew it wasn't her. He guessed it was a creature that came out of a portal, like in Debrecen. When Director Ferrgerr told him the truth, his mind wouldn't accept it, not until he learned they had committed Éva to this hospital.

"Your daughter was not in control of her actions," the director said in an effort to reassure Ati. "Something took over her body. We don't know what exactly. The investigation is still ongoing."

He tried to take comfort in that. But knowing it had been her physically, even if not mentally, was still too much. When Ati went to the hospital the first time, all he could see in his mind's eye was the evil grin she wore as she tortured him—him, her own father. He'd left without seeing her.

On his second visit, he thought of Greta, and of what Éva—possessed or not—had done to her. It was bad enough she tortured her father, but torturing her sister and exposing her to the black ooze—could there be forgiveness for that? *It wasn't her. It wasn't her.* But it was. It was her hands that opened that portal and called forth the creature and her voice that laughed as Greta twitched and flailed at the touch of the dark ooze.   And again, as he mourned his murdered daughter, he left without passing through the hospital's doors.

A wave of nausea came over Ati as the alcohol took effect. He swayed from side to side, but kept his balance. The dizziness passed after a moment.

"I need a drink. I'll see Éva tomorrow. I will," he lied to himself, "I will. I will."

He staggered down the street, block after block, until he saw the familiar brown rectangular building he came to every night after his failed visits. A softly glowing sign that read 'Saloon' was the only marking on the building. It wasn't large and it was definitely not clean, but it was one of the few bars in Cairo so it was usually packed with people. Ati liked that. Somehow in a crowd of strangers he felt the most isolated, which is exactly what he wanted.

The clientele was a stark contrast to the main populace of Cairo. Despite the large number of Egyptians and English men who had died during the Siege, both nationalities were still the most predominate. But even though they no longer answered to a New Moon government most natives still held on to the New Moon faith, which had strict rules against the use of alcohol. A few took advantage of their new liberties and would frequent bars, but not this one. The clientele was almost exclusively Europeans.

Since the establishment of the Civil Ministry and the Hunter Project, more and more Europeans came to Cairo looking for a better life, ironically leaving behind one bombed-out city for another, just as Ati had. At least Cairo was being rebuilt with all due haste. Unlike Ati, most of the men and women who came did not have contacts in Portal Command, which meant for them, jobs were harder to come by. Ati could tell that the people who came here each night were not people who'd lost wealth during the Siege. They were people who had nothing before, and even less after. They were desperate, angry, and possibly dangerous. Even so, he was comfortable here. He shared their anger, if not their desperation.

There were two empty stools at the bar. Ati took a seat on the one next to the wall and motioned at the barkeep for a beer. The barkeep sat a bottle in front of him without a word and then went to wait on other customers.

Just over his head a holographic broadcast was playing, recounting the news of the day. Ati tuned out. His thoughts went back again to that night. He remembered Greta, standing there in front of the bald Portal Hunter. He remembered seeing the bolt of hot energy punch through her chest and the shocked look on her face as she slumped dead to the ground. He remembered the Hunter staring down at her, devoid of compassion, as if he'd murdered dozens of children before.

Ati signaled for another beer. His head was swimming in an alcoholic haze, but as long as he could remember that night, he wasn't drunk enough. He would drink until he could forget, but the second bottle didn't help. He signaled for a third.

"You think they'll let him off?" a voice said next to him.

Ati glanced to his side. The stool that had been empty was now occupied by a middle-aged Caucasian man. He had a shaggy brown beard and shoulder length hair mingled with gray. He wore a dark gray work jacket that had once been black. He fingered an untouched glass of beer in front of him.

"Huh?" Ati responded.

The man nodded at the holo-broadcast. Ati looked up. A well-known reporter, Denise Brewen, stood in front of a court house there in Cairo. Next to her was a holo-image of Sergeant Ivan Jast. Ati didn't know the Sergeant well, but he'd seen him around, even once or twice with Éva. They were in the same unit, if his memory was correct.

"Sergeant Jast, do you think they'll let him off? They granted him bail, you know. Some think they're just being nice before they drop the hammer, but most people think it's a sign they'll go easy on him, maybe even find him completely innocent."

The bartender gave Ati his third beer. He gulped down several mouthfuls before saying anything. "Dunno. Why should I care?" he answered finally, doing his best not to slur his words.

"If anyone would, I figured it would be you," the man said, still watching the screen.

"How would you know what I care about?" Ati growled at the man before taking another swig.

"He tried to kill your daughter, didn't he? Your older daughter, that is," the man said.

"What do you know about any of my kids!?!" Ati gritted his teeth at the man. His knuckles went white as they wrapped around his bottle. He was more than half tempted to smash it over the man's head.

"You're Attila Katona, right?" he said nonchalantly, seeming to have no clue how angry he was making Ati. "I know some people who work at the Compound. That makes me a little knowledgeable on the gossip. You look like her, you know. It was an easy guess."

"You know Éva?" Ati's anger lessened, turning instead to extreme discomfort.

"Not personally, but I've seen her a time or two, and of course she was on the news a while back." The man took a sip from his beer and went on. "Word is your daughter entered a restricted area, the same one that Sergeant Jast supposedly broke inside. When the sergeant found her there, he tried to kill her."

That wasn't the way Ati had heard it. Ferrgerr had told him that Éva had broken into the Matrix core, under the influence of whatever it was that possessed her. "No, no Sergeant Jast tried to stop her," Ati said. "She—she wasn't herself, ya see."

"Maybe not," the man said. "But I don't think the sergeant cared. You know he brought three unauthorized people into the Compound and took them all down to the Core. That's why he's up on treason charges. Whoever those three were, they were some kind of covert hit squad. They were all trying to kill your daughter, not stop her. Now *that* I have on a good source."

"Yeah, well, maybe he did. Doesn't matter. They'll fry him good for what he done." Ati looked away and stared down at his half-finished bottle. Suddenly, he didn't feel like drinking anymore.

"So you don't think they'll let him off, then?" the man asked, inquisitively.

"That's what I said, isn't it?"

Ati threw his money down on the bar. He had to work in the morning and he knew he'd feel like hell as it was. All he wanted to do was leave this conversation behind with all its painful memories.

"See, I don't think so," the man replied. "They're going to circle their wagons. He'll get off. Just you watch."

"Yeah, well, maybe," Ati said as he stood. He tried to turn and walk away, but a wave of vertigo hit him and he was forced to sit back down.

"Yeah, you watch," the man went on. "The sergeant's a well-connected man. The rumor is he's been banging his superior officer, Lieutenant Kayla Marro. During the war, she had important contacts in both the New Moon and the Resistance. Sure, she's a big time war hero, but that doesn't mean she doesn't know whose palm to grease. Yeah, she's sitting pretty with all the right people on all sides of the fence. She'll call in favors and make sure her boy toy doesn't get wasted.

"Besides, the Ministry won't want to face the heat that would come from locking the sergeant away. If one of their own is convicted of a high crime, people might start asking questions about the Project, and they don't want that. So he'll walk. It's the same reason they didn't look too deeply into the death of your other daughter."

Those last words struck Ati like a fist in his gut. His pulse raced and his head swam with rage. "What'd you say!?!"

"Your youngest daughter, wasn't she killed by the famous Michael Traush?"

Ati stood quickly, too quickly. The alcohol ran to his head all at once and he lost his balance. Staggering sideways, he stumbled directly into a tall, heavyset man with short, spiked hair and a tight, black leather shirt. The tall man shoved Ati back against the bar.

"Get off me!!!" he blared.

"Hey, hey, easy!" the man sitting next to Ati said. "My friend's just had one too many. He didn't mean anything"

The tall man glared at Ati, his nostrils flaring with each breath. Ati leaned against the bar, his anger forgotten for a moment and replaced with fear.

"Better not touch me again," he muttered and turned away.

Relieved, Ati sat back on the stool. For a second he even forgot why he'd been so angry, and then it hit him. He leaned against the bar and felt as his heart raced, unsure if it was from adrenaline, the rush of fear, or from anger.

The man sitting beside him patted him on the shoulder. "Hey, you all right? Need me to fetch you a cab?"

"Don't—touch me, just—leave me alone," Ati answered under his heaving breath.

"Okay, sorry if I upset you," the man replied, turning back toward the broadcast. "I was just making conversation."

The two sat there in silence, the man watching the news and Ati staring at the unfinished beer in front of him. Finally, after two minutes had passed, Ati spoke up.

"What did you mean—" he started, and then stopped. The man looked over at him. "What did you mean it was the reason they didn't look into my daughter's death?"

"Well, did they?"

"Nobody knows where Sergeant Traush is. Probably dead."

"Are they sure? How hard have they tried to verify that fact?"

Ati didn't answer at first. He remembered what he'd seen in the apartment. "He fell into some kind of a portal. I think it was a rogue," Ati replied. "Sergeant Jast said he was dead, said he had it on a good source."

"Ah, the sergeant again, the same sergeant who's up on treason charges," the man said. There was a hint of mirth in his voice that Ati didn't like.

"You saying you know something about Traush?"

"I'm saying I don't think he's dead," the man explained. "Think about it. Sure, he fell into some kind of portal. So what? For that matter, did he really fall? Maybe it was a clever getaway. The man's infamous. People thought he died during the Siege, and as it turns out he went half way across Egypt while the planet was under heavy fire, killed the Empress and then fled the planet. Is it so hard to believe he's still alive today, without any hard evidence to the contrary?"

The thought had not occurred to him, but as the man spoke, Ati knew he was right. He offered no reply. He simply sat there, trying to come to terms with what he was hearing.

"Just goes to show," the man went on, "there's no justice these days, not unless we make it ourselves."

* * * *

"Oh, slap me!' Greg blurted.

He and Jonah held their staffs at the ready, the weapon's end pointed at the three intruders. Next to them, the two guards glanced from the intruders to Jonah, waiting for instructions. "This isn't possible!" Greg went on. "There's no way these freaks hacked into the Matrix!"

"Don't tell that to me," Jonah answered. "Tell it to them!"

Tundra, Fast Track, and Mr. Black exchanged glances.

"What are these men babbling about?" Tundra asked Fast Track.

"I don't know, but I don't think they're happy to see us. That ugly mug of yours must be frightening the locals," Fast Track answered with a smirk.

"I'm certain it is not my face that intimidates them," Tundra retorted. He cracked his knuckles together for emphasis.

"Let's be careful," Mr. Black added in. "We don't know anything about this place or these people. They are wearing uniforms. Perhaps they're the local authorities."

"You got that right!" Greg shot back. "Let's see some hands. Put'm in the air. And no sudden movements!"

"Are those supposed to hurt us?" Fast Track asked the two Hunters, gesturing at their staffs.

Greg pointed his staff above his head and fired a single blast. Fast Track flinched and took a step back. "Does that answer your question?" he asked. "Now, hands in the air. Last warning!"

"Certainly," Tundra said.

Slowly, he lifted his hands above his head and turned his palms out, facing the Hunters. A violent blast of cold wind shot across the room. Greg and Jonah were blown backward. Greg lost his balance and flew into one of the guards, but Jonah thrust the end of his staff against the ground and kept himself from falling. The icy blast threw the second guard up and into the wall. He struck it with a thud and slid back to the ground, unconscious.

"Well done, Tundra," Black said. "Fast Track, your turn."

Greg was back on his feet in an instant. Jonah had his staff out and ready to retaliate just as quickly, but neither one got a chance. A red blur swished across the room. Greg and Jonah felt the staffs leave their grips. Before they realized what was happening, Fast Track was standing next to Tundra, two staffs under one arm and the two rifles tucked under the other.

"What? How—?" Jonah stammered.

"Let's just say I'm faster on my feet than you are on the draw," she answered. "So, you guys want to play nice, now?"

The remaining guard drew his pistol and opened fire at Fast Track. Tundra dove in front of her. The pistol's discharge hit him in the chest, leaving a blackened spot on his armor, but doing no other harm. The guard fired again, higher this time. Tundra shielded his face.

"Aarh!!" Tundra cried out, sounding more annoyed than hurt. The round struck ribbed metal covering his arm, leaving another charred mark, but failing to penetrate.

Next to the door, Greg caught sight of the rifle belonging to the guard Vamperic had slain. He dove, grabbed it, rolled across the floor and came out of the roll firing. He hit Mr. Black twice in the chest. The energy caused his suit to ripple with each bolt, as if it were made of black ink. Mr. Black looked at the spot where he was hit and then over at Greg, seeming unimpressed.

"What is it with all these portal freaks? Don't they know how to die!?!" Greg blurted, throwing in a few choice curses under his breath.

"Let's get out of here!" Jonah shouted as he rushed for the door.

"You'll get no argument from me!" Greg called back.

Covering for the others, Greg laid down suppressive fire, aiming most of it at Tundra. Tundra blocked the bolts as if swatting away annoying flies. As soon as Jonah and the guard were clear, Greg ran out the door and closed it behind him, leaving Tundra, Fast Track, and Mr. Black alone in the portal bay.

"Well, I think we made a good impression," Fast Track said sarcastically. "Don't you think so, Peter?"

In response, Tundra merely brushed the charred ends of his bear skins and gave an irritated grunt.

* * * *

Jonah and the guard stood outside the door panting.

"What was *that*!?!" Jonah asked.

"Heck if I know," Greg answered. "Whoever they are, this is a major security breach. They're in a portal bay and have both our staffs. That gives them almost unlimited access to the Matrix."

"We've got to alert the lieutenant," Jonah said.

"Forget that! We've got to tell the director!" Greg handed the rifle to the guard. "Stay here. Shoot anything that comes out of that door," he looked over at Jonah. "Come on!"

The two ran down the corridor. The area around the bay had been empty, but the further into the heart of the Compound they ran, the more people they passed. Everyone gave them strange stares as they sprinted along at full speed. If anyone got in their way, they shoved them aside and hurried on despite the angry shouts of protest that trailed in their wake. They rounded another corner just as Assistant Director Flupd stepped out of a restroom door. Jonah ran straight into him. His helmet collided into Flupd's snout. Flupd covered his snout with both hands and let out a muffled roar.

"Aaah! *Dtas thudd roff!*" he swore in Straffies,. "What's going on here!?!"

Jonah was able to quickly compose himself and snapped to attention, but it was Greg who responded.

"Assistant Director, we've got a major, major problem!" Greg said, his words almost blurring together. "We've got an intrusion into one of our bays."

"What!?! What are you babbling about?" Flupd demanded, speaking through his hands as he cradled his snout.

"It looks like a rogue. We saw it open in the middle of the bay and these three people wearing costumes came out," Greg went on. "They look human, but they can't be."

"Rogue portals can't open in the Compound. It's impossible!" Flupd snapped.

"Sir, if it isn't a rogue then someone's hacked in," Jonah interjected, "but either way, these three were—well, like Sergeant Mortan said, they had superhuman abilities."

Flupd was dumbfounded. "I—wha—where are they now!?!"

"In the bay, I think, Bay 12. We posted a guard," Jonah said. "Sir, they took our staffs."

Flupd yanked the communicator off his belt. "Seal Bay 12!" he shouted into it. "Now! And lock down the Matrix. Yes, that's what I said. Stop all traffic, coming or going. What? I don't care, they'll have to wait. JUST DO IT!"

Flupd snapped the communicator back onto his belt. "You two," he said to Jonah and Greg. "Get as many Hunters as you can and get back down to Bay 12. I want those intruders neutralized. I'll notify the director."

"Uh, sir—" Jonah began apprehensively.

"Get to it, NOW!"

"Yes, sir," Jonah answered, unconvincingly.

Greg looked over at Jonah as soon as Flupd was out of ear shot. "You have any idea how we're going to take those three down?"

"Not a clue," Jonah replied.

"Great," Greg sighed.

The two hurried back the direction they came. Everyone they passed continued to gawk at them, increasingly confused. They signaled every Hunter they came across to follow them. Curiosity kept anyone from refusing. They all fell in step as the two continued jogging back toward Bay 12.

At one point, they stopped at a weapon's locker and started to grab everything they could find, passing rifles, staffs, even grenades out to the Hunters who were tagging along.

"Grenades!?! What is this about?" one finally asked.

"Hey," another Hunter called to Greg as he wandered by. "I can't access the Matrix. There's a mass lockdown going on. You heard anything about that?"

"Yeah, you might say so," he answered as he passed another heavy assault rifle to the Hunter next to him.

"All right, everyone listen up!" Jonah called out as the last rifle was distributed. "We're heading around the corner to Bay 12. We've got three intruders pinned inside."

"Hopefully," Greg muttered.

Jonah gave him a sideways glance before continuing. "We'll give them one chance to surrender and come with us peacefully. If they as much as think about refusing, hit them with everything you've got."

"Everything?" asked a Hunter holding two grenades and a staff.

"Everything!" Jonah replied. "Okay, let's go."

* * * *

Mr. Black gently rubbed the smooth surface of the bay's main control panel. It was covered with cracks and burn marks from an earlier confrontation. Across the room, Fast Track and Tundra studied a series of computer banks that were affixed to the wall.

"The people of this world are very advanced," Black said. "Dr. Vamperic is the only one I know capable of reproducing anything like this."

"You think these people work for him?" Fast Track asked.

"Hmmm, no," Black replied. "I have not been able to decipher these controls, but from the looks of this room alone, I would say we are in an elaborate complex. If Dr Vamperic had such a base, we would have discovered it by now."

Fast Track strolled over next to Black. "So where are we?" she asked.

"Perhaps not where, but when," Black countered.

Tundra's eyebrows rose. "When?"

"Consider; the people we encountered seemed human enough, so we are not likely on an alien world, yet their technology surpasses ours."

"We couldn't have traveled to the future, if that is what you are suggesting," Tundra retorted. "Dianna was only capable of opening portals from one place to another. If White is using her life essence to create portals of his own, he would likewise be limited."

"Dianna kept many secrets from us," Black replied. "I suspect she was capable of more than she let on. As much as she trusted us, I don't believe she trusted anyone enough to grant them the ability to travel through time, not even herself. Mr. White and Dr. Vamperic, however, would have no such inhibitions. If they could travel through time, it makes sense that they would go to the future, learn the secrets of its technology, and then return to our own time and use it to enslave all of humanity."

"That makes sense," Fast Track admitted. "And if that's true, then we'd better find them fast!"

"Fast is your specialty, my dear," Black smiled and gestured for the door. She led the way as the other two followed. Stopping at the door, she reached for the handle and found none.

"Very odd," Tundra said.

"Not very conventional, at least," she said.

"Perhaps one of the buttons," Black suggested, motioning toward a small control panel.

Fast Track pushed the largest button and waited. When nothing happened she pushed the next and then the next. Each one beeped, but produced no other results.

"We may be in some kind of a prison," Tundra observed.

"I don't think so," Black answered. "This doesn't look like a prison cell."

Tundra flexed his muscles. "Prison or no, we can't waste time. Move aside and I will make an opening."

Fast Track stepped to the side. "Be my guest."

Mr. Black stroked his chin thoughtfully. "If the people we encountered are the local authorities, they may not appreciate—"

BAMM!!!

Tundra's fist punched directly through the titanium door. The upper half of the door hung loose, but the lower half was still tightly sealed.

"Yes?" Tundra waited for Black to finish.

"Uh, never mind."

Tundra grabbed a torn edge of the door and pulled with all his might. A loud creaking sound echoed throughout the bay as the door slowly began to tear. Then, with a pop, the door ripped free of its frame. Tundra tossed the ruined metal across the room. Mr. Black placed a hand on his shoulder.

"Peter, until we know more about where we are, I suggest we do everything possible to avoid further confrontation."

Tundra made a thoughtful sound under his breath, but offered no other reply. He merely glared down at the hand on his shoulder. Black released him and the three marched into the outer corridor with Tundra in the lead.

"Freeze!!!!"

A dozen men and women, each wearing the same off-white and blue or red uniforms stood surrounding the door from the outer hallway. Each one carried either a rifle or a long metal staff pointed directly at the three heroes. One even had a grenade in a free hand ready to throw.

Tundra looked over at Black. "You were saying something about avoiding confrontation?"

CHAPTER FIVE

Ivan got back to his apartment very late. Even though Kayla and he had done nothing licentious, Kayla had fallen asleep in his arms as he held her. Unwilling to disturb the moment of bliss, he let her sleep and in doing so, fell asleep himself. It was past midnight by the time they left the hotel.

It was worth it, in Ivan's opinion, even though he had an early morning and a busy day ahead of him. After checking in with this parole officer he would spend the rest of the day meeting with his attorneys and going over their case.

Ivan found it strange to be back in his apartment. It was a relief to be out of jail, but the last time he'd entered his apartment he was ambushed by four people from the future, one of whom turned out to be his future self. They meant him no harm and had only accosted him so that he would hear them out, but all the same, he felt jittery walking about into his apartment's living room. He moved quickly through each room, turning on all the lights. He paused in his living room's center and glanced at the spot where Ester Katona, Éva's mother from the future, had stood invading his refrigerator. The kitchen was empty this time, as was his apartment.

All was not as he'd left it, however. There were obvious signs that his place had been searched: drawers open, furniture slightly out of place, and a small decorative statue laid on its side. None of that surprised him, though. When he told Director Ferrgerr the truth of what had happened, he also mentioned Father Kim and how he'd stayed behind in his apartment until the others were finished. The director had dispatched men to Ivan's place hoping to find Kim, but he was not there. Undoubtedly, the authorities had taken advantage of their access to his apartment and searched for any evidence that could condemn him. They had not found that, either.

As much as he disliked the priest, it irritated him to know that Kim was gone. With his older self and the future Mrs. Katona dead and Whrongtt refusing to help, that only left Kim as a witness to the truth.

As Ivan plopped onto his bed, his thoughts centered on Father Kim. In the last week, he hadn't given it much thought. He was gone, and that was that. Now, however, his curiosity was peaked. What *had* happened to Father Kim, anyway?

* * * *

"The darkness is everywhere! Everywhere! I don't mean the darkness that you perceive with your senses, either, but the darkness that lurks within the souls of men"

Peter LeStrange flinched as he heard the voice of Father Kim echoing down the dust and ash filled corridor. He hated carelessness, especially in matters of security. The Indigo Towers were supposed to be abandoned and it was up to each member of the New Resistance to help maintain that illusion. Even though this region of town had been vacated, patrols, prospectors, and scavengers made their way through the empty streets daily. If someone heard the shouts of a deranged preacher coming from inside, they might decide to investigate. Of course, twenty stories in the air, Peter knew no one would hear. If he was honest with himself, he knew the real reason he cringed at the sound of Kim's voice wasn't because he was worried about security, it was because the man really, really irritated him.

Kim's voice grew louder as he reached the open door at the end of the hall. Boss Raspin stood in the entrance way, his arms folded, watching the scene inside. Peter came alongside him and peeked in.

"We think it's the shadows in the corner or the poorly lit alley way that we should be frightened of," Kim went on, "but what hides there is no more dangerous than what hides in our souls, and we cannot lock our doors against that! That is why it is everywhere, because we carry it wherever we go."

Father Kim marched back and forth on top of a scratched and scorched office desk that he used as a stage. The desk was pushed against the far wall of a long, rectangular room that had once been a nondescript conference hall. The Indigo Tower was full of otherwise useless space. This was just one of many. But for Kim it served as an ideal place for his own mini-chapel.

"We can only push the darkness out of our souls by turning toward God and letting His light shine on us. But how do we do that?" Kim asked.

He stopped his pacing and glared out into his audience. There were eight in attendance, all hardened men who'd fought in the old Resistance save for one young teenage girl, the daughter of a veteran from the war. Not one of them, though, appeared the least bit interested in what Kim had to say. Two of them were asleep, one even snoring loudly. The others sat restlessly, staring at the wall or their feet. Only the girl kept her attention on Kim, but her glassy-eyed stare was vacant.

"I will tell you," Kim went on, either tired of waiting for a response or oblivious to the fact no one really heard the question. "No man can look on God and hope to live. Scripture teaches us that. So we must look on the face of those to whom God has spoken and let their light fill us. I am such a person. Listen to me, and God will deliver you from the darkness."

Peter touched Raspin lightly on the shoulder. Raspin glanced over at him and gave him a short nod. The two turned and headed back down the corridor toward the stairwell and away from the conference hall.

One of the men sitting in Kim's service got to his feet and followed close behind. Peter didn't know the man's name, but he was seeing increasingly more and more of him over the last two weeks. In fact, now that he thought about it, these last two weeks were the only times he'd ever seen him at all. Whoever this was, he appeared about the same time as Father Kim.

He was a muscular, Caucasian man, not particularly tall, but formidable just the same. Even though he was obviously of European descent, Peter detected a hint of Egyptian blood in the man. He wore a tan cloak made of a course fabric that resembled sackcloth. The hood of the cloak was always up. He often wore a red scarf around his neck that covered his mouth. Because of that, Peter never got a good look at his face and couldn't see his hair. Still, the man looked familiar. Peter wasn't sure where, but he was certain he'd seen him during the war.

Despite the eerie familiarity, Peter did not like this man. He was leery of all the motley lackeys Raspin kept close around him, segregated away from the rest of the Resistance, but this was more than that. There was something about the way the man carried himself and his cold, blank expression that unnerved Peter. He was too detached, too emotionless, and yet, at the same time, very alert.

Peter glanced back at the man as he shadowed them down the hall. It was Peter's guess that Raspin had made him his top bodyguard, though why just in the last two weeks he wasn't sure. It might have had something to do with the Seven Seals. Security had tightened up in the Indigo Towers ever since the nuclear missiles were brought into storage.

Peter was just about to ask the man pointedly who he was when Raspin finally spoke up.

"I take it you found Vamperic?" Raspin's voice was deep, yet it cracked as he spoke. Peter sometimes wondered if that was how he got his name; 'Raspin' for the guy who always spoke in a 'raspy' voice. Maybe, maybe not. He didn't for an instant think it was his real name.

"*Doctor* Vamperic," Peter corrected. "You can't forget to call him that. Jones made the mistake of calling him 'doc' and he killed him on the spot before anyone had a chance to react. He just—vaporized him, for the lack of a better word."

"I warned you not to rile him," Raspin replied.

"But you didn't tell me the guy was a psychopath. After he murdered Jones he ranted on about his 'superior nature', and then blabbed on about how he'd 'crush his enemies' and enslave all of humanity in a world of 'eternal night'.

Between rants he would laugh incessantly. Whoever this guy is, he's *waaaay* off the sanity chart. I was sorely tempted to put a round in the back of his head and leave his body for the vultures, and I can tell you I was *not* comfortable bringing him here."

"It will be fine," was all the reassurance Raspin offered.

Peter frowned, not satisfied with the answer. "How could you know he was going to be there, anyway? When we found him, even he didn't know where he was."

"Like I said, I have sources in the Compound," Raspin answered.

"But that doesn't explain it. If Dr. Vamperic really did break into a portal bay and use it for his escape, the Hunters would have backtracked the log and gone after him. They didn't, which means the doctor really did scramble the logs as he claims."

"True, or I would never have sent you there. You would have been captured, for sure," Raspin said with a nod.

"Right, which means no one in the Compound has access to that information, which means your contact is full of it, only—" Peter paused.

Raspin looked over him and smiled. "Only he was right."

"Yes, he was." Peter's frown deepened.

"Don't concern yourself with the details, Peter," Raspin replied. "The Hunters will clear up the logs soon and then they'll know where Vamperic went. Of course, thanks to us, it won't do them any good. It's enough to know that my source was able to get me the information first, and thanks to him we have Vamperic, not the Hunters."

"And what does that matter?" Peter asked. He already knew he wouldn't like the answer.

"Wait and see," Raspin smiled, "wait and see."

The two continued down the stairwell, with the hooded man close behind.

What an odd sight the three of us must make, Peter thought, trying to distract himself from the uncomfortable silence. *Me, a once-proud military commander, now living no better than a vagrant, this hooded monster behind us, and Raspin, the oddest of us all.*

Peter had never before seen anyone like Raspin. Raspin had received severe wounds during the Siege, and the process that had saved his life had left him with a truly bizarre appearance. Raspin wore a scratched and dented golden helmet that covered his entire head and his face down to the end of his nose. It was said this helmet was all that kept his skull together. Judging from the mass of burns and scars that covered his face (what little that showed) Peter had no doubt this was true—partly, at least. His eyes were hidden behind a red visor that would glow softly from time to time. It was impossible to tell where he was from. His skin was dark, but it was only visible on his face and neck. He wore long sleeves and gloves at all times. All the same, he was certain he was of African descent—perhaps descending from American refugees or from Africa itself. The scratchy sound his voice made masked any hint of an accent.

They continued on in silence, listening to the clacking of boots against the steel steps echo off the walls.

"Eight people tonight at Father Kim's meeting," Peter said after a few minutes, trying to find something to break the uncomfortable silence. "I think that's a record."

"Sala volunteered to go tonight. I think she was curious."

"No doubt she regrets it," Peter responded.

"No doubt," Raspin added with a slight laugh.

"I don't get it," Peter went on. "Nobody's buying his crap, you have to force people to attend his meetings, half of whom sleep through them, and yet he acts as if you made him king of the universe."

"He has what he wants, an audience," Raspin answered. "It doesn't matter if they are forced to attend. What matters is that he believes they come willingly. He's like a kid with a new toy. For now, that's all we need to do to keep him happy."

"And why are we trying to keep him happy?" Peter did not try to hide his disdain as he spoke.

"Because he's an untapped fountain of information."

"Raspin—" Peter began, then paused. "Look, don't misunderstand me. I appreciate everything you're doing for the Resistance. You kept us together after the war when most of us abandoned ranks, and you've kept everyone inspired and hopeful, but I don't understand your fascination with collecting lunatics. First Kim and now Dr. Vamperic."

"Kim is deluded and self-indulgent, but he is not insane."

"He says he's from the future," Peter pointed out.

"You don't believe that he is," Raspin observed.

"Why should I? There's no evidence the portals make time travel possible."

"But they do," Raspin's head bobbed up and down as he spoke. "They do, and soon you will have the evidence you need to know that they do. For now I need you to trust me. Kim is from the future, but he's from a different future."

"Okay, let's just say you're right, and he's from this alternate timeline," Peter said. "If your future is going to be different than his, how can he know anything that would help us?"

"Throw a stone into a pond and you'll see the water ripple. Throw a second stone into the water and you'll notice the rippling patterns change. But there are similarities in the two different patterns. It is the same with time. Kim may not know how our future unfolds, but we can use him to uncover the similarity of patterns."

Peter offered no reply. It was the best answer he'd gotten out of Raspin in weeks, but it didn't tell him much.

The three reached the bottom of the stairwell and came to a set of metal doors guarded by two men. Seeing Raspin coming, the two guards pushed the doors open and stepped aside.

The tower's massive basement warehouse was lit as bright as day. The trucks that had delivered the nuclear weaponry were long gone, but seven crates remained stacked neatly against the east wall, each one holding one of the deadly missiles. Flanking each door within the warehouse was a pair of guards armed with assault rifles. In the center of the warehouse, a series of tables were lined together in a long row. Strewn along the top were a wide range of tools, most Peter didn't recognize or know what they were for. Next to the row of tables was a stack of small metal boxes. There was writing on the side in an Asian script Peter could not read. Standing in front of the tables, with his arms folded behind him, was Dr. Vamperic.

Raspin took several steps forward then stopped and bowed low. Peter decided to stay back. Vamperic turned slowly toward Raspin and stared down at him with his blood-red eyes. He regarded him for a few seconds before speaking.

"So you're Boss Raspin, the leader of this army?"

"Yes, most excellent doctor, it is an honor to meet you at long last," Raspin answered.

"You know of me?" The menacing edge seemed to leave Vamperic's tone for a moment.

"The legend of the great Dr. Vamperic has traveled far and wide," Raspin answered.

"And just how far? Where am I?"

"Cairo, my magnificent doctor, but not the Cairo you know. This is a different Earth than the one you left behind."

Vamperic put his hands on his hips and turned his head upward. "So, it is true, alternate realities do exist! Ah, think of the possibilities! Not only could I rule Earth, I could rule a dozen Earths!"

"Or hundreds," Raspin said. "I do not doubt there are an endless number of such realities"

"Yes, yes! There will be no end to the conquest! I will plunder a million worlds, century after century! MUHAHAHAHA!!!!" Vamperic's laughter danced off the concrete walls of the warehouse. For twenty seconds he continued to laugh. Raspin remained kneeling the whole time. Finally, his cackling ceased and he began to pace.

"Where to begin? Where to begin?" He mumbled. "I should start by finding every reality where the International Department of Justice has a headquarters and eliminate them, just to be safe. Once they are all out of the way, no one can stop me!"

"A clever plan, but I see one problem," Raspin interjected.

Vamperic's eyes flashed with anger. "Problem! What problem!?!"

"It is the portals that make your plan possible, but—unless I am mistaken—you have no access to the portals. Mr. White has the Mistress' sphere, does he not?"

Vamperic marched straight toward Raspin, almost running. Three of the guards pointed their weapons at the armored man, but Raspin waved them off. Vamperic came right up to Raspin and loomed over him.

"So, you know of Mr. White! These others would not share any information with me," Vamperic's hands balled into fists. "Where is he!?!"

Raspin remained cool, keeping his posture low and making no indication he was afraid. Peter fingered the hilt of the pistol in his pocket.

"We're not sure, your Excellency," Raspin apologized. "I know he has abandoned you. He wants the power of the Mistress for himself."

Vamperic clinched his fists. "If that fool believes he can cross Dr. Vamperic and survive, I—I—" His whole body shook with rage. "Naaah!!! He will pay for this treachery!"

"I am sure your vengeance will be swift and cruel, but if it's portals you want, we can help."

Vamperic stopped shaking. His eyes narrowed. "How?"

"My man here, Major LeStrange," Raspin gestured back toward Peter, "he told you about our common enemy, the men who attacked you when you arrived?"

"The Portal Hunters, yes, he spoke of them. They, too, will feel my wrath for their insolence," Vamperic growled.

"And nothing would please us more than to help you defeat them, but you can go a step further. Like your enemies, the Hunters are the masters of portals, but unlike your enemies they do not rely on mystical forces to control them. They have achieved it through science. There are not many alive who understand the inner workings of this technology, but with your vast and, of course, superior intelligence, you could easily discover their secrets and use it to suit your own needs."

"Yessss," Vamperic said with a hiss, "yes, I could at that."

"And I know you downloaded several files from the Compound's main computer," Raspin went on.

"Yes, I—wait, how did you know that?"

"The Hunters have very good security guarding their network. It wasn't enough to prevent you from accessing their files, but it was enough to detect your breach."

"Bah! That's of no concern. With the information I took, there will be no stopping me! MUHAHAHAHA!!!"

Vamperic cackled on for a solid minute. Peter shifted uneasily from foot to foot, waiting for him to finish. Raspin remained in his kneeling position. Finally, Vamperic's laughter grew quiet. Raspin cleared his throat and continued.

"Very true, Doctor, very true. With portal technology, the whole multiverse will lay at your mercy. You would only need the proper equipment to begin your work. We could provide that for you… for a small price."

"Price!?! You would barter with Dr. Vamperic!?!" He reached down and grabbed Raspin by his collar and hoisted him up. "You will do this for me as my slaves, or I will destroy you! I will destroy you all!"

Peter wrapped his fingers around his pistol's hilt and was about to draw. Raspin remained calm and stared back at Vamperic—centimeters from his face—with a placid expression.

"Please, Doctor, there is no need to be forceful," Raspin said. "You will find our price to be reasonable, I assure you. There is no one else on this planet that will help you, not for such a simple fee as we would ask. Without our help, you'll find yourself trapped on a world with no allies or resources and you will never unlock the secrets of the portals."

"It is not help I need, it is obedience!" Vamperic snarled. "I will rip this world apart until I find what I need! I will unlock the secrets of the portals, with or without your help!"

"How certain of that are you?" Raspin replied. His expression of humility and hospitality was gone from his face, replaced by a self-assured grin.

Vamperic's breath was heavy. He continued to hold Raspin by the collar and glare at him with his blood-red eyes. Every guard in the warehouse now had their weapons trained on Vamperic. Even Peter had his pistol out and at the ready. Raspin's confident smirk remained, unflinching.

"What is this 'price'?" Vamperic asked in a cold voice.

Raspin pulled himself out of Vamperic's grasp, and straightened the collar of his coat. He started off toward the other end of the warehouse, heading for the stack of crates. Vamperic turned and watched his every step, but made no move to follow.

"While our society has made great strides in certain areas of technology, we have fallen behind in others. One of the sciences we've forgotten over the centuries is nuclear science, primarily in the manufacturing of nuclear powered weapons," Raspin said. He came up in front of the crates and placed a hand on the nearest one. "We've recently come into possession of seven nuclear missiles. Combined, they have enough destructive power to kill every man, woman, and child on the planet."

Raspin turned back toward Vamperic. "My organization has no desire to destroy an entire world, so that much raw power is overkill, pardon the pun. We would like to disassemble these missiles and build smaller, more practical weapons, such as tactical warheads or briefcase nukes. Four of these alone could make a hundred such devices, and we would have missiles to spare.

"You're welcome to our surplus and to whatever supplies and assistance we could provide. I imagine it would come in handy when replicating your own portal summoning devices. All we ask is that you teach us how to tear down the other four for our purposes."

Peter couldn't believe what he was hearing. Raspin couldn't seriously consider letting this lunatic have access to the Seven Seals? The thought of putting such unbridled power in the hands of a madman made his blood run cold.

Vamperic crossed his arms and made a grunting sound. "That is your 'price'? A small child could accomplish that with little effort!"

"Then it would not be too difficult for you?" Raspin asked in an innocent tone.

"Of course not!!" Vamperic barked back. "Very well! I will build you a new arsenal, one more powerful than you could possibly imagine, but I expect your complete obedience once the task is complete. Your COMPLETE obedience! Is that understood? The portals will be mine! They MUST be mine! MINE!!!"

Raspin's grin widened. "Of course."

* * * *

"Please, there's no need for violence," Fast Track pleaded. "Just lower your weapons and we'll talk this out. 'Kay?"

"You can talk to your attorney, your all under arrest for trespassing and gaining illegal access to the Portal mainframe," Jonah ordered. "Now, face down on the ground, hands behind your heads, or we will open fire!"

"This isn't going well," Black stated.

"Thank you, Captain Obvious," Fast Track retorted. "So what do we do now?"

"Might I point out that any one of us could take out these men with little effort?" Black pointed out.

"He's right," Tundra replied eagerly.

"I thought we agreed to avoid a confrontation," Fast Track answered.

"But the confrontation has found us," said Tundra.

"Hey!" Greg shouted. "Enough chatter! Get down on the floor, or we'll put you there!" Greg dared a step forward and jabbed his rifle in Fast Track's face. "Believe me, you don't want that!"

Mr. Black took a step back. "As fascinating as this conversation is, I'm afraid I must go. The longer we spend here, the further Mr. White gets from our grasp."

Greg jerked the rifle in Black's direction. "Stop right there!" he demanded.

"Black, what are you doing?" Fast Track asked.

"I'm leaving you two to sort this out. I'll find Mr. White and come back for you when I've located him."

Black took another step backward. His back was pressed against the wall. His foot moved to take another step. As he did, his features became a blur of shadow and then melted into the wall

"Stop him!" Greg shouted.

Two Hunters opened fire, but their blasts merely struck the wall, leaving dark burns against the white metal surface. Black was gone.

"It seems we have no choice. Black has made the decision for us," Tundra said with a sigh. He lifted his hands in the air. "Very well, gentlemen, we surren—"

Greg's head jerked around as Tundra's arms rose above his head. "Oh, snap!" he swore. "Drop him!!!"

Every Hunter opened fire. A solid rain of energy bolts and plasma discharges slammed into Tundra. One blast caught him full in the face. The rest landed dead center in his chest and a couple struck his shoulder. The force of the assault shoved him into the wall.

"Peter!" Fast Track called out in alarm.

One of the Hunters spun his staff toward her and opened fire, but it never found its target. With a blur of red motion, Fast Track went into action. Five Hunters were down within a second as she rushed by and struck each one in the back of the head with a well-aimed blow.

"Snap!!!" Greg swore as three more Hunters hit the ground.

One of the Hunters swung his staff around and over his head instinctively. The blur of red flew directly into it. There was a loud grunt and Fast Track went rolling across the floor, grabbing her chest where the staff's end had caught her.

"Good work, Marcus," Jonah said as he came up on Fast Track. He shoved the end of his rifle against her forehead and planted one knee on her abdomen, pinning her down. "Don't' even think of moving, not even a millimeter. Don't even breathe."

"So I guess this is out," she replied.

Her hand moved faster than he could comprehend. One second he was holding his rifle against her, ready to pull the trigger in a heartbeat, the next it was in her hands. Jonah sat there, his knee still digging into her, stunned by what had just happened. Before he could react, she shoved the butt of the rifle in his gut with surprising speed. The breath left his lungs and he found himself tumbling backward.

"Jonah!" Greg called out.

He lifted his rifle and took aim at Fast Track.

"A-hem!" a thunderous voice came from behind.

A massive, gauntlet covered hand grabbed him by the back of his neck and hoisted him off the ground. Greg kicked wildly, searching for solid ground. The next thing he knew he was flying through the air. The wall at the opposite end of the hall rushed up to greet him with a thud. Everything went white and he felt himself freefall. A second later the ground came up to meet him as well.

"Uuuuuh," he moaned before passing out.

"Nice one, Peter," Fast Track said with a nod. The Siberian dreadnaught grinned back at her and dusted off his hands.

A single Hunter remained standing. He shifted his rifle between the two heroes and eased gradually away.

"I think your boss—" Fast Track began, pointing down at the unconscious Gregory Mortan, "said something about surrendering. You want to continue the discussion?"

"Uh," he stammered, then dropped his rifle and took off running.

He got about three meters and then skidded to a halt as a series of green, crisscrossing lights formed in front of him. The lights filled the hall, cutting off his escape and weaving their way up to the ceiling and down to the floor at the other end of the hall.

"What is this?" Tundra asked, scowling at the green grid that encircled them

There, on the other side of the barrier, stood Director Ferrgerr and thirty heavily armed marines. A door on the opposite end of the corridor opened and Assistant Director Flupd marched out leading another two dozen marines.

"Yes," Director Ferrgerr said to Fast Track. "We would like to continue that discussion."

Chapter Six

The Gaoroes waited four days before sending food or water to Traush and Ivan's cell. During the first of those four days, the Gaoroes took Ivan for another round of interrogation, leaving Traush alone. When they brought Ivan back, he merely lay on his cot for hours, not sleeping but not speaking either. After a while, he finally pulled himself together and tried to engage Traush in conversation, probably in an effort to lift his own spirits, but Traush just sat there, his legs folded underneath him, staring off and offering no sign that he even heard him Eventually, Ivan gave up on him, rolled over and went to sleep.

The next morning when he woke, Traush was still sitting in the same position, not having moved a centimeter and still staring off. Ivan complained about the lack of food and asked Traush if he thought the Gaoroes were trying to starve them to death. When Traush said nothing, Ivan lost his temper.

"What is wrong with you? Have you already cracked? Huh? Have you? I thought you Rensha were the toughest around! What, you think I don't know how hard this is? Well... do you?"

Traush blinked, but nothing more. Ivan went on for almost an hour before finally giving up and lying back down.

The third day Ivan paced constantly. From time to time he would stop and ask Traush if his pacing bothered him. He hoped to goad a response, to find some way of striking a nerve. But if his pacing did bother Traush, he wouldn't say. Instead, he continued to sit there, not speaking, not moving.

After three days of denying them food, the fourth morning a thin slot in the cell door opened and a single plate of a gray mash appeared. It wasn't much, but it was food.

"Thank God," Ivan said, hopping up from his cot and descending on the meager meal.

Before he could reach it, Traush leapt up, snatched the plate, and emptied its content into the cell's toilet.

"What the—? What is your flip'n problem!?!" Ivan bellowed.

Traush gave Ivan no reply. He placed the empty plate next to the cell door and sat on his cot, his legs folded underneath him. Ivan yelled at him until he was utterly exhausted. After that he lay back on his own cot and mumbled loudly for the rest of the day.

On the fifth morning, another plate, just like the one before, appeared. Ivan woke groggy from his slumber and stared at the food for a second before he realized what it was. He started to move toward it, but Traush was too fast. Once again, he grabbed it off the floor and headed for the toilet. Ivan grabbed him by the shoulder.

"Noooo!" he roared at Traush, pulling him away from the toilet.

Traush thrust his elbow into Ivan's ribs and knocked him off.   Ivan fell onto his cot and leaned forward with both arms wrapped around his ribs as Traush unceremoniously flushed the tray's contents.

"You—crazy—!" Ivan sputtered between coughs. "I don't care if you are a friend, a former comrade-in-arms, or a flip'n Rensha. If you do that again, I will kill you!"

Traush looked back at him, saying nothing, and then took a seat on his cot.

The cell door opened with a loud swish. Commander Vhast stood there, flanked by four Gaoro shock troopers. Two troopers held heavy assault rifles at the ready while the other two carried stunning spears. Vhast was not happy.

"I realize our cuisine doesn't appeal to humans, but I would have thought after five days you would have been a little less selective," Vhast said. "If you wish to starve yourself and your companion, that is your business, but you will not die until your secrets are mine."

Vhast motioned to the troopers beside him. The two armed with stunning spears moved into the cell and advanced on Traush. He looked up at them with the same dull, unconcerned expression he'd worn for the last several days. The troopers raised their spears and brought the electrified ends up toward his chest.

Traush's hands darted out, grabbing each spear just below the electrified head and then pulled backward, hard while sliding toward the floor. The two troopers fell forward, their spears' ends crashing against the metal wall with a loud hiss. Traush brought his knees up as the two soldiers tumbled on top of him, catching them both in the gut and then, kicking out, he forced them back across the room. Both soldiers released their spears and crumbled to the ground.

The two remaining troopers brought their rifles up and opened fire. Traush rolled off the cot as a wave of plasma showered down and set it ablaze. He snatched one of the spears from the ground, spun the electrified end toward the two shock troopers and flung it through the air. It soared toward the closer of the two. He tried to get out of the way, but its tip caught him in the shoulder. There was a loud crackling sound and the Gaoro went into involuntary spasms.

The first pair of soldiers crawled back to their feet and reached for their sidearms. Traush leapt sideways, putting the two between him and the fourth soldier before he could retaliate. The soldier closest to Traush took a swing at him with his left hand as he pulled his pistol free with his right. Traush dodged the blow, grabbed the Gaoroes right wrist and twisted. The soldier cried out as his wrist snapped. The pistol fell from his hand and into Traush's.

Traush backhanded the broken-wristed Gaoro, knocking him out of the way. The second soldier already had his pistol drawn. He squeezed off a round. Traush dropped to his knee just in time. The blast brushed his ear instead of blowing off his head. Traush fired at the second soldier's knee. The Gaoro let out a loud wail and went down, but Traush caught him before he could hit the ground. Putting the soldier in a headlock, he spun him around to face the door, and leveled the stolen pistol at his head.

"Drop it," Traush said to Vhast and the one remaining trooper.

"What do you hope to accomplish, Traush? Surely you don't think you can get off this ship. I have a hundred armed Gaoro aboard," Vhast lifted a small rectangular device. Traush wasn't sure what it was, but it resembled a summoner. "All I have to do is press this button and—"

Traush whipped his pistol out and fired two shots before either Gaoro had a chance to respond. His aim was true, hitting each one in the center of their forehead. They collapsed dead to the floor without as much as a whimper.

The second Gaoro withered in his grasp, trying to break free. He elbowed Traush hard in the ribs. Traush released him and shoved him forward. Unable to speak from the strain of the chokehold, the soldier let out a weak cough and dove for the closest weapon. An energy blast caught him in the back of the skull before he could reach it.

Hot steam poured out of the barrel of his stolen pistol. He shifted his aim between the three dead and the one unconscious Gaoro, and then turned toward the one remaining soldier who sat huddled against the toilet, cradling his broken wrist. The injured trooper pulled himself to his feet, saying nothing, but meeting Traush's gaze with equal intensity and a hint of hatred. The two stared at each other for a moment longer and then—

CR-RAA-KK!!!

The energy blast passed through the Gaoro's neck and killed him instantly. Traush shoved the pistol through his belt and went over to the cell's door where Vhast's body lay.

"I—I don't believe it," Ivan gasped. He was standing on top of his cot, pressed against the wall. "You took them all out in under a minute. Why the blazes didn't you do that before!?!"

"Up to now, every time they came to extract one of us from the cell, they were always careful in all the right ways," Traush said flatly. "Not so today."

"What was so different about today?"

"The food ploy. That's what tipped me off. They were getting desperate. Starving us for three days? No one starves anyone for such a short period of time and hopes they'll crack," Traush said as he riffled through Vhast's pocket.

"Felt pretty blasted effective to me," Ivan grumbled.

"If that was their intent, they would have started with a week, not three days," Traush replied. He continued to search Vhast as he explained. "They merely wanted to make sure we were weakened and hungry enough to eat whatever they gave us."

"Yeah, so?"

"There was poison in that mush, most likely some kind of a neurotoxin. After three days our digestive system would've been completely flushed out, so the toxin would've been especially effective."

"Why go to that much trouble? Why not flood the cell with gas or just shoot us in our sleep?"

"They weren't trying to kill us," Traush lifted up a spherical device from Vhast's pocket and then threw it aside. "The neurotoxin would have made us extremely vulnerable, psychologically. We would have offered up the most sensitive information gladly and with little prodding. They still would've put us under a whaf shield or sayder probe, just to make sure. By discarding the food I not only avoided the poison, I also provoked them into action. They got frustrated and they got careless."

Ivan slid off the wall and onto the cot, seeming more confused now than frightened. "Huh?"

Traush shoved Vhast's body aside and moved over to the corpse of the closest soldier. "They were angry, that made them sloppy," he went on as he riffled through the soldier's pockets. "They wanted to break me and I wasn't playing along. But it was more than that. They thought—not having eaten anything for five days—I was weaker than I was. What they didn't know is that Rensha must fast for two weeks without sleep and then defeat another fully rested Rensha of a higher rating before we can be assigned to the royal palace. I feel fine, a little thirsty, but fine."

Frowning Traush shoved the soldier aside and went to the next.

Ivan leaned over and grabbed the closest weapon that lay on the ground, one of the assault rifles the soldiers had carried. "So, I take it this is only phase one of some master plan to get us off the ship. What comes next?"

"I'm working on that part," Traush said, digging through the tunic of the last dead soldier.

"You're working on it? Michael, you're looting dead guards!" Ivan fumed. "We've got maybe another minute before the entire ship realizes what's happened!"

"I can't find their summoners. They must have known it was a bad idea to bring them into the security block," Traush stood up. "We'll have to find where they're kept. Any ideas?"

"Aarrh!!" Ivan threw the rifle on the ground and collapsed onto the cot. "This is just great. We're going to die. We're really going to die!"

Traush frowned. "Ivan, is there something you're not telling me?"

Ivan glowered up at Traush. "The Gaoroes don't use hand held summoners, you idiot! A hand held device is too easy to steal, and they guard portal technology twice as tightly as the Empress ever did! The only summoner on the ship is the ship's own summoner. The controls for it are on the bridge!!"

"That could be a problem," Traush admitted.

"A—A problem!?!" Ivan stood and leaned toward Traush, putting his face two centimeters from the former Rensha. "There are over a hundred soldiers on this ship, half of which are probably already on their way to this cell right now! The other half stand between us and the bridge!!! This is more than a problem, this is a flip'n disaster!!! We're dead!!! We're flip'n dead!!!!"

Traush bent down and retrieved the rifle from the floor. "In that case," he said, handing the gun back to Ivan, "you're going to need this."

He shoved the pistol in his waistband and went over to get the other rifle. Ivan stared at the rifle in his hands—an empty, stunned look in his eyes.

"It was a good run, I suppose," he muttered. "I—I knew I'd never get off this ship alive, anyway."

"In that case, you've got nothing to lose," Traush said, heading toward the open cell door.

Ivan looked up from the rifle and over at Traush. Traush stood in the entrance, stone-faced, and waited. "Ah, to heck with it. At least I'll get to die killing Gaoroes," he said as he hit the charger on the rifle and fell in step behind Traush. "Could be worse."

* * * *

"This is a dandy plan, Peter, just dandy," Fast Track said. She stood with her hands on her hips in front of the sealed, electrified titanium door. "Yep, just dandy."

"You speak as if it were my idea," Tundra replied. He sat behind her with his arms crossed on a narrow bench that was barely large enough to hold his massive frame. "You were the one who suggested we try and reach a peaceful solution."

She turned to face him. "Well, you agreed to it, so—that makes it your fault as much as mine," she countered.

"That hardly sounds fair," Tundra scowled.

"Doesn't it?" she glanced back at him with a grin. "Ah, but seriously, Black's probably hot on White's tail. I suppose this isn't as bad as it seems. If these... what did they call themselves?"

"Hunters," Tundra answered.

"Yeah, if these Hunters will just hear us out, maybe we can get their help finding White. I mean, we don't know anything about this world. Where would we even begin?"

"Neither White nor Vamperic know anything about this world, either," Tundra pointed out.

"Don't they?" Fast Track countered. "It was their idea to port here. God only knows why. We could really use these Hunters' help to give us an edge in finding them, and maybe even help taking them down."

"Perhaps, but if they insist on holding us here much longer, we will have to take matters into our own hands," Tundra replied, his voice low and threatening.

"And make another enemy in the process?" Fast Track asked, her eyebrows raised.

"We may have already done that, my dear. We may already have."

* * * *

"Incredible, just incredible," Major Hammad Mubarak muttered as he peered up at the image of Tundra and Fast Track looming above him on the large overhead monitor. Standing beside him Lieutenant Kayla Marro, Director Ferrgerr, and A.D. Flupd watched as Fast Track began to pace. The major looked down at a smaller screen in front of him and continued to shift through the incoming data.

"And you said they both exhibited super human abilities?" Kayla asked.

"Yes, but they varied," Ferrgerr replied. "For instance, the woman is unusually fast while the man is unusually strong."

Kayla shook her head. "Why does this always happen when I'm not here?"

Mubarak paid the conversation no mind. His attention was focused entirely on the incoming data. "Fascinating. They speak the same language as us only their accent sounds a bit—well, dated."

"Dated?"

"Yes. This accent was common roughly one hundred years ago, but it's definitely one of Earth origin, which is extremely odd."

"How so?" Ferrgerr asked.

Well, they speak our language and appearing as human as they do, the natural assumption would be that they are human. But if they are, they are not from Earth—not our Earth. So why do they have such a quaint accent, or for that matter, any accent of Earth origin?"

Ferrgerr's ears seemed to perk. He came up alongside Mubarak as he worked. "What exactly do you mean they are not from our Earth?"

"It's the portal, the one they used to enter the Compound," Mubarak replied, his attention fixed solely on the screen in front of him as he spoke. "To begin with, it's just a reoccurrence of the portal the armored assailant used."

An image of Dr. Vamperic appeared on his monitor, next to the incoming data. Vamperic loomed over the portal bay's controls, coils coming out of his armor and into the panel.

"This man, robot, or—whatever it is, he didn't just stumble through a rogue portal. This portal was created from his end."

Kayla's eyes went wide. "Are you certain?"

"Yes," Mubarak said. "The signatures on this portal are unmistakable. It was manufactured independently of our own network."

"Then our worst fears have been realized," Flupd shook his head. "Someone's built their own Matrix."

"In a way, but not what you think," Mubarak went on. "Its signature also has an unusual frequency I've only seen three times before."

"In Madrid, Debrecen, and in the Sahara."

The three turned toward Kayla.

"Come again, Lieutenant?" Ferrgerr asked.

"It was a guess," she answered. "Only three times? It's dimensional. That's what you were about to say, wasn't it, Major?"

Mubarak hesitated. "Yes. Yes, it was."

"So what you're saying is that someone from another dimension built their own Matrix and used it to travel to our own dimension." It was Ferrgerr who spoke.

"From what I have been able to examine so far, that would be my guess."

Flupd leaned against the wall. "Then it's worse than worse."

Kayla walked over to the larger screen. The two prisoners continued to pace. "You may be right, Assistant Director."

Ferrgerr headed toward the door. "I think it's time I spoke with our guests."

* * * *

Another pair of Gaoro shock troopers hurried down the corridor, heading toward the detention block. Traush and Ivan crouched low behind a set of metal crates, just out of sight. The Gaoroes' heavy footfalls echoed down the passageway then fell silent as a door slid shut behind them. Traush motioned for Ivan to keep quiet. Slowly, he leaned closer to the crates and listened.

"It's clear," he said in a voice no more than a whisper.

The two stood, each clutching their stolen rifles.

"They sure were in a hurry. I'm surprised they didn't stop and check the crates. It was an obvious hiding place," Ivan thought aloud, keeping his voice low, as well.

"Right now they're just combing the ship for us and sealing off sensitive areas. There's nothing here of value, so it wasn't worth their time to stop. But once they've finished with their initial sweeps, they'll be back," Traush answered.

"Then we'd better move," Ivan said.

Traush remained in place. He stared thoughtfully off to the side, stroking his rifle like a pet cat. "Aside from the search parties, they will have divided all their remaining troops into pairs and stationed them as guards throughout the ship. They're probably at every major junction by now."

"Fine—yeah, great. So they're everywhere. Am I supposed to be surprised?"

Ignoring Ivan, Traush strolled down the corridor and surveyed their surroundings. The corridor was long and wide. Boxes and steel pallets of all sizes lined the hall along one side. On the wall opposite were five doors, each three meters by two meters with inscriptions posted in Straffies.

"Hmm, I wonder," he muttered. He strolled over to the closest of the five doors. It opened at the press of a button. The space beyond was like a cave. There was no light, and the environmental controls ran only on half capacity, making it very cold. Traush stepped inside and disappeared into the shadows.

"Hey!" Ivan called out. "What are you doing? I thought you said there was nothing of value here?"

"Aha!" Traush's voice called back.

A loud, mechanical hum roared out of the black.

"Holy—! Traush?" Ivan took a quick step as something stirred within the shadows.

* * * *

"YEEEE-HAA!!!" Ivan shouted as the doors to the adjacent hallway burst open.

The two Gaoroes that stood flanking a wide, arch-like entrance halfway down the corridor spun in the direction of the exploding doors. Two graviflux cargo lifts came flying toward them, one piloted by Ivan and the other by Traush. Both lifts had a solid metal frame and were as tall as a Gaoro. They had a transparent windshield that separated the person who drove it from the cargo itself. The shield on Traush's lift was already blackened and cracked from weapons' fire.

A ten-centimeter wide tube jutted out the front of each lift, serving as the gravity grip by which they were able to nullify the ship's artificial gravity and carry even the heaviest cargo effortlessly. At top speed, the lifts could make forty kilometers an hour. On an open road, that would hardly be impressive, but in a cruiser's enclosed corridors, it was plenty fast.

For a split second, the Gaoroes were too shocked by what they saw to react. That split second was all Traush and Ivan needed. Traush fired a single shot through the crack in his front shield, hitting the Gaoro on the left directly between his eyes.

The other Gaoro fired wildly at the two oncoming vehicles. Traush swerved hard to avoid a plasma bolt while another struck Ivan's lift on the side. The lift shuttered, but Ivan threw it into top gear and flew straight for the guard.

"Yeee-haa!" Ivan cried out again as he switched on the lift's gravity grip. A translucent white beam shot out and grabbed the guard. He flailed his arms wildly, losing hold of his rifle in the process. Ivan jerked the lift to the side and slammed the breaks as he rammed the opposite wall. The guard impacted against the metal surface with a sickening thud. The white beam went dim and the guard's bloodied body slid to the floor.

Traush pulled up alongside Ivan. "It would have been faster and safer just to shoot him," he pointed out.

"Ah, but less fun!" Ivan laughed as he spoke.

Traush drew his lips into a thin line, obviously not amused. "You'd better pull it together, Ivan. We got this far on luck, but we're entering the main level now and luck isn't going to cut it. There will be a lot more personnel wandering around. We probably won't get another ten meters before someone—"

A shrill, animal-like cry cut Traush off. In the far end of the corridor, a Gaoro crewman stood cradling an armful of data pads and staring wild-eyed at the two humans. Traush whipped his rifle around and fired a single shot. The blast cut through the crewman's neck, severing his head from his body.

"—spots us," Traush continued, without missing a beat. "If we hope to succeed, we'll have to hit them hard and fast and not waste a second of time. Understood?"

"You're kidding? Sure, I'll hit'm hard and fast if you want, but you really don't think it will make any difference?" Ivan jabbed his finger in the direction of the arching doorway. "They'll be a least a dozen, if not more, well-armed Gaoroes down that corridor. We'll be blown to pieces before we can take out even half."

Traush sat at the controls of his lift with a sullen yet thoughtful expression. Suddenly, he jerked the controls and turned the lift sharply around. Making a u-turn, he drove up to a wall panel and started typing away at the controls.

"Hmmm, yeah, that corridor is too wide and intersects with several major hubs. It'll be teeming with Gaoroes. But this passageway here," he gestured to something on the screen that Ivan couldn't see, "yes, that would work."

Pulling the lift's controls in the opposite direction, he turned back around and headed toward the decapitated body at the far end. "Come on," he called back to Ivan. "I've got a plan."

* * * *

Ivan laughed the whole way down the corridor. He sat pressed against Traush in the tiny cabin of the graviflux lift, leaning forward with a broad grin. Traush wondered if perhaps the former Hunter's sanity had finally snapped. Whether it had or hadn't, at least he was no longer complaining. For that Traush was thankful.

It was difficult to steer with Ivan sitting so close. Traush did his best to keep the lift on a straight path, but Ivan kept bumping into him, causing him to veer toward the wall. As annoying and dangerous as that was, there was nothing for it. For Traush's plan to work the two had to share a single lift, and lifts were only designed to carry one Gaoro. At least Gaoroes were generally larger than humans.

Directly in front of them was Ivan's unmanned lift. The corridor was too narrow for the lifts to travel side-by-side, so instead they traveled front-to-back, much like a train. The gravity grip of the rear lift held the front one in place, using it as both a shield and a battering ram.

The front lift crashed through another set of guards, knocking them forward twice before running the pair over with a crunch. Traush had to hold on with both hands to keep from being thrown as the lift leapt and bucked. Ivan started to slide out the side, but Traush grabbed hold of his shoulder and pulled him back in.

The ship's map had marked this corridor strictly for maintenance use. Even though it was less crowded than the main corridor, it still had a great deal of foot traffic. Yet any Gaoro who stood in their way was mowed down. The lifts were sturdy enough to take several rounds of weapon's fire and hold in one piece, and until the Gaoroes could destroy the first lift, they were not likely to hit Traush or Ivan. After a while, the front lift was so charged and damaged from the continual plasma discharges that it was nothing more than a hunk of blackened, misshapen metal, but it still served Traush and Ivan nicely.

The passage did not lead all the way to the bridge, but it would take them to the main junction. If they could survive that, they could board the bridge, but that was a big 'if'.

"I think I see another one!" Ivan shouted over the rush of air, peering out the side of the lift and down the corridor as best he could.

"Careful," Traush said as he pulled him back in.

The sound of a pistol firing rang out, followed by a loud thud. The lift jerked violently.

"Yep, I was right," Ivan said, chuckling.

With one hand, Traush held on to the controls and kept the lift straight and with the other he held his rifle at the ready. *Should be any moment now*, he thought to himself. With the lead lift blocking the view, there was no way to tell when the main junction was coming up. He knew it couldn't be far.

Sounds of angry shouts and words yelled in Straffies could be heard not far ahead. More weapons' fire rang out. The front lift shuddered under the assault. A hunk of the top canopy broke off and flew back at Ivan and Traush. They both ducked instinctively but needlessly. The debris bounced off the front shield and landed somewhere in the corridor behind them.

A bolt of plasma shot out, passing straight through an open space left by the missing canopy and struck the corner of the windshield, directly in front of Traush. His heart skipped a beat as the plasma charred the trans-steel glass, leaving it solid black. Had it not been there, the plasma discharge would have hit him directly in the face, killing him instantly.

The blackened shield made it even more difficult for him to see ahead. He was truly driving blind now. It was time to get creative, he decided. Sticking the rifle out the side, he opened fire into the unseen space ahead. Someone shouted something in Straffies and then there was a loud thud, followed by another. Another Gaoro could be seen ducking aside into the narrow gap between the wall and the two lifts as they raced by. His foot wasn't far enough over, though, and the two lifts crushed it as they passed.

"That makes eighteen Gaoroes in this one hall alone," Ivan said, jubilantly.

Traush merely nodded in reply. His attention was focused on the passage ahead, even if he couldn't see it. Something up ahead sounded different. There were voices, but without the echo that was typical of a narrow metal corridor.

"We're coming up on the junction," Traush announced, realizing in that moment it was true. "Get ready."

The narrow walls disappeared as they came flying out into a circular clearing a dozen meters in diameter. To their left was a large opening which led to the main corridor and to their right was a pair of sealed doors. Behind those doors lay the bridge.

There were seven armed Gaoro shock troopers posted inside the rotund junction. As the two lifts came barreling out of the corridor, they rammed the closest of the seven troopers and killed him instantly. The other six shouted something and darted to the side. Three flung themselves against the sealed bridge doors. The other three ducked to the opposite side of the battered gravity lifts.

It was obvious by their reaction they had no idea what was coming. They were ready for the two escapees, but they weren't ready for a mechanical bullet to come shooting out the side. That had thrown them off balance. They recovered their composure quickly, but to Traush that split second was all the time he needed. He was out of the lift and rolling across the floor before the first trooper could raise his rifle. Coming out of his roll, he opened fire, raining shot-after-shot and swinging the rifle around in a wide arch. Two of the Gaoroes went down. The third flung himself behind Ivan's graviflux lift. Traush rained plasma down on the ruined hulk. It was already so badly damaged that it made for poor protection. One plasma bolt passed through a thin, blackened sheet of metal and struck the soldier. Traush heard him grunt and then saw his limp arm flop out from behind the lift.

From the other side of the two lifts, Traush could hear a heavy exchange of weapons fire. Someone cried out in pain. It was human.

Ivan!

Traush ran toward the one working lift and jumped on top of its canopy. Directly beneath him, Ivan lay on his side. He couldn't tell how badly the former Hunter was hurt. The closest of the three Gaoroes lay face up, his snout burned from his face. Next to him another Gaoro crouched against the sealed door, holding his side. He was badly hurt, but not out of the fight. Behind him, the third Gaoro stood, unharmed, pointing his rifle at Ivan, ready for the killing shot.

Seeing Traush, the third Gaoro whipped his rifle upward, but not in time. Traush fired a round between his eyes then pivoted toward the one remaining soldier. A plasma blast struck Traush in the shoulder as the injured Gaoro fired first. He fell back and rolled off the side, putting the lift between them again.

Traush was back on is feet in an instant. He steadied himself and was about to make his next move when from behind he heard the thunder of feet hurrying toward the junction. The rumble was getting closer and closer.

"Drop your weapon, human, or your friend dies!" the Gaoro called out in Arabic with a thick Gaoro accent.

Ignoring him, Traush ran to the junction's main opening. Two dozen soldiers came rushing up the sloping hallway, less than six meters from the opening. Traush slammed his fist into the junction's access panel. A thick, titanium door slid into place, locking out the oncoming Gaoroes from the main junction. He fiddled with the panel until he found the setting that locked the other door as well.

"I said drop your weapon!!" the injured Gaoro called out again, still on the other side of the gravity lifts. "And open that door!"

With careful, measured steps, Traush walked across the room and around the front, smoldering lift. He leaned over and checked the Gaoro that lay there. *Dead.* Satisfied, he stood up straight and stepped around the lift.

The injured Gaoro had Ivan in a headlock with his pistol pressed against the former Hunter's temple. Ivan was unconscious, a burn wound in his gut.

"Final warning," the Gaoro growled. "Drop it, or he dies."

Calmly, Traush propped his rifle against the wall next to him. He unholstered his pistol, pointed it at Ivan and fired. The plasma blast passed straight through the unconscious man's gut and into the gut of the injured Gaoro.

The Gaoro released Ivan and bent over in pain. Traush fired two shots into his head.

Blood began oozing out of Ivan's mouth. Traush checked his pulse and detected the faintest rhythm. How much time Ivan had left before he would bleed out, he wasn't sure. The plasma had cauterized most of the wound, but he had internal bleeding and it could be bad.

There was a loud thud from the main doors, followed by another. Traush didn't have to wonder at the cause. The Gaoroes were trying to blast their way through. The doors were thick and sturdy, but there were a lot of armed Gaoroes on the other side, desperate to get through.

He began to enact the last phase of his plan. Lifting Ivan over his shoulder, he took the former Hunter and set him on the opposite end of the juncture, as far from the bridge doors as he could. The rear graviflux lift was still operational, thankfully. Jumping into the driver's seat, he switched on the gravity grip, used it to grab hold of the smoldering front lift, deposited the wreckage up against the bridge doors and then parked alongside. He gathered up all the fallen weapons in the room, saving only one rifle and pistol for himself, and stacked them on the driver's seat of the second lift.

The main doors shuddered with a loud boom. Traush glanced back. The door held with no sign of visible damage, but it wouldn't be long before it gave way, he knew. *One minute—ninety seconds, at the most.*

Traush quickly reached behind the second lift and pulled off a small hatch that led to the vehicle's power cell. A faint glow spilled out, showing that the cell held a solid charge. He then moved to the first lift. Even though it had been shredded by weapons fire, the back end was still largely intact. Pulling off the power cell's cover, Traush peeked inside. A warm glow greeted him.

The echoes of weapons' fire filled the junction like a drum as the Gaoro shock troopers continued to blast at the sealed doors mercilessly. Traush took a deep breath and tuned out the sounds of repeated fire. With his rifle in one hand and his pistol in the other, he hurried over to where Ivan lay, took aim at the two glowing power cells, and squeezed the two triggers simultaneously.

A violent explosion roared across the room. A shockwave struck Traush hard, shoving him back into the door. He turned his head and covered his face, but he could feel the heat of the blast searing his exposed skin even at this distance. There was a second, smaller explosion as more combustible material went up in flames.

Everything grew quiet. Traush could no longer hear the sound of weapons' fire against the titanium door. He'd hoped the silence meant the Gaoroes had stopped trying to break through, but there was a faint ring in his ears and he realized he had lost his hearing.

Bits of flaming debris were strewn about the junction. A large chunk of one lift sat in the junction's center, wreathed in flames. There was a dent above it where it had impacted the ceiling.

Traush rose to his feet and squinted, trying to see through the black, billowing smoke that hung thick in the air. There was white light coming from up ahead, but with the smoke he couldn't tell if it was more burning debris, or something else.

The ringing in Traush's ears grew louder, but as it did, other sounds returned. The shock troopers continued to blast away at the door. There was no more time to waste, he knew. He reached down, grabbed hold of Ivan and threw him over one shoulder. With his rifle out and ready, he marched toward the white light. As he got closer the smoke began to clear and he could see it.

There in front of him was a meter-and-a-half by one meter hole in the door with charred and frayed edges from the explosion. From the other side he could see the frightened faces of bridge crew officers staring back at him. He'd done it!

This is it, he thought to himself.

With the weight of Ivan bearing down on his shoulder and the thunderous pounding of weapons behind him, Traush rushed forward into the heart of the Gaoro cruiser.

CHAPTER SEVEN

The underground warehouse made for the largest lab Dr. Vamperic had ever used, but not the most luxurious or even practical. Battered and worn lab equipment stolen from who-knows-where scattered atop a series of cheap folding tables was all he had to work with. It took up only a fraction of the available space, leaving the rest of the room barren.

Despite the vast space, there was no one else in the warehouse except for him. Vamperic knew that there were guards stationed on the other side of the doors, positioned there for his 'protection'. Earlier there had been guards inside as well, and two lab assistants to help him. The lab assistants had proved to be incompetent. When he'd ordered them to assemble a micro-hyper-reverberating-death-ray the two just gawked at him in bewilderment, so he'd vaporized the pair of them and ordered the guards outside. If he couldn't get good help, he'd work alone. He found it all rather annoying, but the meager accommodations did serve his needs, nevertheless. As such, he was willing to tolerate it—for now.

"There—yes!" he said as he tightened one final screw and then stepped back to admire his first creation in this lab.

It was a small cylinder, two centimeters in diameter that was capable of holding four hundred milligrams of fluid. Now, however, it wasn't liquid it contained, but circuits, wires, and a small but potent nuclear core. As innocuous as the device appeared, if detonated it could incinerate everything within a one-third kilometer radius. The shockwave and radioactive waste would go out much further.

With the amount of raw materials he had harvested from one missile, he could produce twenty-five of these tiny bombs. He wasn't yet sure, though, how many of the missiles he would need to disassemble for his own purposes. One of the missiles had already been stripped of its components. Boss Raspin had told him this was done by a rival—someone named Klein—who was working toward the same purpose Vamperic hoped to achieve, and it proved one missile was all he would need.

"'Proof', ha! Does he really believe I am so naïve?" Vamperic said aloud. "If this Klein was able to achieve what I hope to achieve, he would already be emperor of the whole universe! No, I will keep more than one missile for myself."

However, he'd promised the Resistance results before they would help, and he was bound by that promise. He wasn't sure how useful they could be, but they did have a point. They knew more about this version of Earth and the people called Portal Hunters than he did. This knowledge could be useful as would the lackeys the Resistance could provide him. To ensure their cooperation, he would finish converting this one missile into canned-bombs, but after that they would have to do what *he* asked.

Vamperic set the small cylinder back onto the table. "I suppose they will want to test it," he said. His voice was unnaturally deep and echoed throughout the empty room. "I should test it on this place and destroy them all for believing they could treat me as an equal—I, Dr. Vamperic! The fools!!"

"Talking to yourself again, I see," a voice said from across the room.

Vamperic whirled around to see who had dared disturb him.

Strolling slowly across the warehouse floor was a man wearing a white suit and shirt. The white of his clothing was perfectly pure. There was not a trace of discoloration or variation in shades. It was unnatural and uncanny. His skin was equally white, offering no contrast from his clothing. It gave him the look of being made of gloss-covered ivory. There was no sense of detail about him at all, no skin pores, no pattern in the fabric, nothing. His tie, hair, and eyes were equally perfect, only black. He had no pupils or irises, only dark holes in his face. As tall as Vamperic was, this man was taller. Despite his elegant appearance, he was formidable to behold, and though he would never admit it, there had always been something about him that unnerved Vamperic.

"Mr. White," Vamperic said.

"Doctor," he replied with a nod. "You seem surprised to see me."

"How did you get passed the guards?"

"With this," White reached into his coat pocket and pulled out a small glowing sphere. It shimmered with silver and gold light, and fit perfectly into the palm of his hand.

"The Mistress' essence!" Vamperic exclaimed with excitement.

He moved forward and reached out for the sphere. White jerked his hand up over his head, out of the reach of the mad scientist. "Ah-ah-ah!" White chided. "We agreed that I would hold on to this."

"You abandoned me in this strange alter-Earth! Why should I continue to trust you with the sphere?" Vamperic snarled.

"I could care less if you trust me, Doctor," White answered, as he stuffed the glowing, round object back into his jacket. "You'd be a fool to trust me, but you need me as much as I need you. I didn't abandon you here. I was simply delayed."

"Why bring us here to this bleak world?" Vamperic grumbled. "The humans here are fragile, yes, and easy prey, but what advantage is it? Why not return to our Earth and use the sphere to defeat our enemies, once and for all?"

"You already know the answer to that," White said. He folded his hands behind him and strolled over to the work bench. "In fact, I see you're already working toward our goal."

"Our 'goal'? Don't tell me you brought us here to make nuclear grenades! I could have easily—"

White whirled around. "Don't treat me like a fool, Doctor. I know of your alliance with the local freedom fighters, and I know your end game. They have promised to help you build portal devices of your own."

Vamperic gave no immediate reply. His eyes narrowed. "How-?"

"Did I know? Don't underestimate my ability to discover secrets," White began pacing back and forth. "I brought us here because in this timeline humans have learned to manipulate portals without the help of a super powered being. They have something called a 'matrix'. It interacts with a complex array of portals the same way the International Department of Justice's mainframe interacted with the Portal Mistress."

White pulled the sphere back out of his pocket and turned it over in his hand as he spoke. "Her essence gives us the ability to open portals to any time, place, or universe, but it limits us to one portal at a time. Think of what we could do if we could open an infinite number of such portals." White lowered the sphere and faced Vamperic. "If we could build a matrix of our own, we could power it with this," he shook the sphere.

"Yes, yes we could," Vamperic nodded slowly.

"I knew that if I left you on your own, your first thought would be to steal portal technology from the humans so that you could return to our time. You've done just that. Already you've downloaded sensitive files from the portal database and now you've acquired a lab from which to work." White held his arms out. "Brilliant, no?"

"Yes, yes it was!" Vamperic replied with a sinister laugh. "These Resistance fighters thought to play me. They would have me build mere toys for them in exchange for the resources I would need to create a device capable of taking over this portal 'matrix', but now that you have returned with the Mistress' essence, I could use it, the information I downloaded, and what little tools they've given me to finish the job. Soon we will be the masters of portals, and then we will crush both the Resistance and the Hunters, and then conquer the multiverse! Muahahahaha!!!"

White gave a brief smile. "Yes, but let's not crush your newfound allies yet. I have a task for them."

"A task?"

"Yes, we have a—problem," White answered, the certainty gone from his voice.

Vamperic glowered. "Problem? What 'problem'?"

"We are not alone. The International Department of Justice found a way to follow us, even with the Mistress dead. Three of their heroes are here, including my arch nemesis, Mr. Black."

"Impossible!" Vamperic snarled.

"Not impossible. I have seen them," White countered. "They are working to forge an alliance with the Portal Hunters. Together, they could stop us, unless we strike first."

"You have a plan?" Vamperic asked eagerly.

White smiled once more. "Yes. Simple, but effective. These heroes are first and foremost just that, heroes. They would sacrifice themselves selflessly at the first opportunity, so let's give them that opportunity."

"What do you have in mind?"

White leaned close to Vamperic. "Show your newfound allies your first creation," he motioned toward the one ready bomb, "this will give them something to whet their appetite. Then, tell them you refuse to build another bomb until they have met one request."

"And what is that?" Vamperic grew more and more eager as he listened to White's plan unfold.

"Have them acquire a set of valuable hostages from among the Portal Hunter ranks. The Resistance knows their enemies. They will be able to identify and acquire suitable targets better than you or I. Once they do, you will send the Hunters a message, telling them that you will free the hostages if the Justice agents surrender to you. The heroes will agree, unwilling to save their lives at the expense of innocent blood. Once they have surrendered, we will kill them and be rid of them once and for all. Then there will be no one left to stop us!"

"Yes! No one! No one!"

The two villains threw back their heads and laughed, filling the warehouse with the echoes of their dark mirth.

* * * *

Ferrgerr stood in front of a net of tightly woven lasers. The individual beams were very thin, which made it possible for him to stand face-to-face with the imposing, white-bearded man without any risk of his captive lashing out. A security net this tight would shred the strongest metal in milliseconds. If the bearded man tried to touch him, all he'd do is lose an arm.

"You say your name is Tundra," Ferrgerr said.

"Yes, and this is Fast Track," Tundra motioned to the thin woman who shared the cell with him. "We are agents of the International Department of Justice here on a mission to apprehend two dangerous criminals."

"There was another person with you when you arrived," Ferrgerr observed.

"That was Mr. Black," Fast Track interjected as she strolled up alongside Tundra. "He's also a Justice agent."

"And where, may I ask, is he now?"

Fast Track shrugged.

"Undoubtedly, he is continuing on with the missions," Tundra answered, "which my colleague here and I must also be doing. If we have caused you any unwarranted harm or alarm, tell us what you require to set matters right."

"You're human?" Ferrgerr asked.

Tundra and Fast Track exchanged glances.

"Of course," Fast Track answered. "What did you think we were?"

"But you're not from Earth," Ferrgerr stated.

"Uuuuh, yeah, I'm pretty sure we are," Fast Track replied, giving Ferrgerr a curious look.

"Truly?"

"Listen, buddy, it's obvious you're *not* from Earth, so what makes you the expert on who's from Earth and who's not?" Fast Track retorted.

"I am from a planet called Gaoro, that is true," Ferrgerr answered. "But I have resided on Earth for the better part of a year and I work closely with its government. There is no 'International Department of Justice'. If you are from Earth, then it is a different one than this."

"How many Earths are there?" Fast Track asked sarcastically.

"That is the question, isn't it?" Ferrgerr replied. "Tell me, what year is it from where you come?"

"2002 A.D.," Tundra answered. "Our headquarters is located across from the United Nations building in New York."

"New York?"

"New York, the city," Tundra clarified.

"Ah, I see. Let me assure you, there are no governmental buildings in the city of New York, at present," Ferrgerr explained. "In fact, there's not much of anything, other than a few historical landmarks, though few people ever visit them. And the year is not 2002."

Fast Track raised an eyebrow. "When, then?"

"A few hundred years later," was all Ferrgerr offered.

Tundra turned to face Fast Track.

"White and Vamperic have traveled to the future, a time when humans have formed an intergalactic alliance with aliens," Tundra surmised.

"Or the aliens took over," Fast Track suggested. "This guy seems to be bossing all the humans around, and he doesn't seem that friendly. But either way, it fits. Vamperic would want technology from the future to use against us."

Ferrgerr cleared his throat. The two heroes glanced back over at him.

"So, you insist on this story?" Ferrgerr asked.

"Story?" Tundra blinked as he replied.

"In 2002, or even today, no humans have ever manifested the unnatural abilities you two have shown, nor do the historical records ever show there being an International Department of Justice. So, let us start from the beginning. What is it you really want, and how did you get here?"

"Can you believe this guy?" Fast Track balked, pointing her thumb back at Ferrgerr, but turning toward Tundra.

Tundra replied with a stern frown. "You doubt our intentions or our word?" he asked.

"I always doubt what I cannot explain, and even more so that which I can disprove," Ferrgerr answered.

"Then let me give you reason to believe," Tundra replied. With his left hand, he unfastened his right gauntlet and passed it over to Fast Track. Not hesitating, he thrust his bare right hand into the laser net. The lasers hissed loudly as they bore into his skin. There were red marks all along his fingers, palm, and the back of his hand, but they were no more than sunburns. He continued to hold his arm, up to his wrist in the net as the lasers continued to sear his skin. There was a faint burning smell and a whiff of ozone, but nothing more. Tundra's face contorted some, seeming more uncomfortable than in pain. Then, he quickly pulled his hand back and shook it off. Steam rose up from the red whelps on his skin. The injuries, however, were minor.

"I would step right through this force field of yours, but I fear it might singe the beard" Tundra went on, as he took the gauntlet back from Fast Track and fastened it on. "We only stay in this cell as a gesture of good will. Believe me, my friend here," he motioned over at Fast Track, "could escape with even less effort than I."

Ferrgerr folded his arms behind him and stared stone-faced at the two heroes. For several seconds, he and Tundra locked gazes, but said nothing.

A beep and vibration interrupted the uncomfortable silence. Ferrgerr snatched the comm from his belt and held it up to his ear. "Yes?" he answered. "Interesting, very interesting," he said as the voice from the other side spoke. "Yes, I think I should speak to him, send him to my office."

* * * *

Peter LeStrange slammed his fist against the small, wooden table Boss Raspin used as a desk. The loose communicators strewn across its surface hopped at the impact. One rolled off the table onto the floor.

"You can't be serious!" Peter shouted. "Did you actually watch this footage?" He waved a data reader in Raspin's face. The frozen image of Dr. Vamperic and Mr. White standing in the center of the warehouse, their heads angled toward the ceiling as they laughed, was framed across the reader's view screen.

"Naturally," Raspin replied. "I have to admit, I am a little surprised neither one of them detected our hidden cameras. Perhaps they did and didn't care."

"It's so good to hear that *something's* surprised you," Peter shot back. "Of course they didn't care. These two are deranged. Vamperic talks to himself, arbitrarily executes our men, rants on like a simple minded, spoiled child, and yet at the same time knows how to build a nuclear bomb with household tools. This other one—White, or whatever he's called—he seems just as bad. Now, *Doctor* Vamperic is refusing to live up to his end of the bargain and is blackmailing us, and you think his demands are reasonable!?! There's nothing *reasonable* about him!"

"Don't you think you're being a bit dramatic, Peter? I wouldn't call it blackmail," Raspin replied, calmly.

"What would you call it?"

"He wants an advance payment on our end of the deal." Raspin held up a small cylinder. "And he's given us this to prove he can deliver what he's promised."

"One bomb. How do we know it even works?" Peter argued.

"I've had it examined by our own people. From what they can tell, it's the real deal. I have no reason to question them."

"You heard what those two said," Peter jabbed his finger against the data reader's transparent surface. "They have no intention of going further. Once they've neutralized the international agents of—whatever they're called—they'll ditch us and build a Matrix for themselves. We'll end up at odds with them *and* the Ministry. As bad as the Ministry is, these two lunatics are the greater evil, clearly."

"Oh, I don't know," Raspin said, leaning back in his chair. "The greater evil, yes, but I don't think they'll want to be rid of us so quickly, not when they see how valuable we can be. Because of this, I've already agreed to Dr. Vamperic's request."

Peter turned and kicked the communicator that lay at his feet. "What's the point of toppling the New Moon if we end up siding with someone worse? Tell me that!"

"I didn't say we were siding with them. In any event, this debate is pointless. I need you to trust me, as you always have." Raspin took a sealed envelope off the table. "I've identified the easiest targets, two people that are high enough profile to grab the Hunters attention, yet not too high. Even better, they are about to make it easy for us to apprehend them with little effort." He handed Peter the envelope. "You'll find the time and location of where to strike. Four men should be plenty for an assignment like this, but bring people with a little class."

"Class?"

Raspin smiled. "Just read the instructions. You'll understand."

* * * *

"I really can't believe it," the young Hunter said for the third time. "I really just can't believe it."

Ferrgerr took a seat behind his desk and motioned for the cadet to take a seat across from him.

"Oh, thank you—sir," the cadet said, his voice a mix of nervous energy and wondrous excitement. His eyes were fixed on a still image that hovered at the far end of Ferrgerr's desk. It was a holo-capture of the three intruders exiting the portal bay and being greeted by Gregory Mortan, Jonah Spears and a host of other armed Hunters. Lieutenant Kayla Marro took the chair next to the young cadet and studied him with interest.

"I didn't catch your name, Cadet," Ferrgerr stated.

"Oh!" the cadet looked away from the image and met Ferrgerr's gaze. "Sorry, sir, it's Ahmed, Ahmed Akhtar. This picture," Ahmed gestured toward the holo-capture, "it's an actual image? I mean, sir, these three people were really here?"

"Two of them still are," Ferrgerr replied. "We have them detained in a holding cell."

"And they came out of a portal?"

"Yes," Ferrgerr said. "Lieutenant Marro says you recognize them."

"Yeah, I was reporting for surveillance duty in Command and Control, and I saw her studying this image," he explained. "Sir, and I mean no disrespect, is this some kind of a practical joke or—uhm, part of a training exercise?"

Ferrgerr offered no sign of emotion at the cadet's apologetic tone. "No," he answered simply. "Who are they?"

"Well, the big fellow in the battle armor is called Tundra, the woman is known as Fast Track, and the strange guy in all black is called Mr. Black."

"And you knew who these people were before today?" Ferrgerr asked.

"Yeah, they're three of the main characters from *Justice for All*," Ahmed answered, matter-of-factly.

Ferrgerr blinked. "Come again?"

"*Justice for All*. It's a holo-sat that used to be popular with kids."

Ferrgerr just stared at him. Kayla shrugged and shook her head.

"You know, a holo-sat," Ahmed went on, seeming a little bewildered at their response. Then, his face lit up. "Oh, my apologies, you wouldn't know about that, would you? They stopped broadcasting those over eighty years ago, long before your people ever had contact with us. You see, a holo-sat is short for holographic satellite transmission. Not many people remember most of the popular shows from back then. It's really old stuff, very retro. But when I was a kid there was a movement to try and bring them back. Naturally, since the satellite infrastructure for the old networks wasn't in place anymore, it was impractical, but the original holo-files still existed for the more popular series, and you could download them for free. I had every episode of *Justice for All*. I like it the best because it took place in the old nation states. The show's writers were trying to emulate something called 'comic books'. I never figured out what that was, since this was neither a comedy nor a book."

"So," Ferrgerr cut in, "what you're telling me is that we have two characters from a children's fictitious adventure story, one that's been out of circulation for decades, locked in our cells."

"Uhm," Ahmed seemed suddenly very nervous. "Yes, sir, that's about right."

Kayla let out a snort. "Brilliant," she muttered.

CHAPTER EIGHT

The plan had gone better than Traush had anticipated. The Gaoroes had put all their resources into guarding the corridors and junctions in an effort to prevent the two humans from reaching the bridge. Most of their soldiers were scattered throughout the ship and the rest were locked outside of the main junction, trying to blast their way through the sealed door. They had left only two guards on the actual bridge itself, and both were positioned directly in front of the door. Flying debris from where Traush had blasted through had shredded one guard beyond recognition and temporarily stunned the other. Before the second guard could recover, Traush fired a single shot into his chest and then marched to the edge of the command deck.

There were ten Gaoroes stationed aboard the bridge, scattered about at different stations. None were soldiers, Traush could tell at once. Two wore pistols strapped to their belts, but the terrified looks in their eyes told him that they weren't about to try anything. Standing two steps below Traush on a secondary rung of the command deck was a Gaoro officer wearing a uniform almost identical to Commander Vhast's. He glared up at Traush, his body trembling just slightly, though it was not clear if it was from fear or rage. Traush thought he detected a hint of both.

"You're the XO?" Traush asked, matter-of-factly.

"Subcommander Raakox," he replied. "Commander Vhast is dead?"

"Quite," Traush answered. "But you needn't die too, if you'll do exactly what I say."

"This isn't the *Ark Royale*, Mr. Traush. You won't take this ship as a prize for your Resistance. I've set the self-destruct to detonate in—" he glanced at clock, "—four-and-half minutes. The summoners are shut down. You can surrender now, or die with the rest of us."

"No one has to die," Traush replied. "I'm not here to take your ship. I just want off. Give me access to the bridge's summoner and I'll be on my way."

Raakox made a sound like a laugh. "You don't get it, do you? You can port all the Resistance rats you want onto this ship, but it won't do you any good. Only I can stop the countdown. We'll all be blown to a million specks before your little band can unscrew the first circuit on our summoner."

"You're the one who doesn't get it," Traush shot back, his voice hard and cold. "I already know there's no chance of taking the ship or the summoner back to the Resistance, and I could care less. Here, let me explain it this way."

Traush, still holding an unconscious Jast on his shoulder, raised his rifle and shot Raakox in the face. Black ash that a split second earlier had been brain matter spewed out the back of his head and scattered across the bridge. One of the Gaoro crewmen made a startled sound, but no one else moved.

"All right!" Traush announced loudly. "Now the ship is definitely going to destruct. I can't stop it, and neither can you. That should be ample proof I'm not interested in it or anything aboard. All I want is to get off safely. You grant me access to the summoner, I leave, and then the rest of you can port to safety as well. Or we can sit here and die together. What's it going to be?"

One of the armed Gaoroes reached for his sidearm. Traush jerked his rifle to his side and fired. The plasma bolt passed through the Gaoro's chest. He fell face-first against his control panel.

"I certainly hope he doesn't speak for the rest of you," Traush announced, pointing his rifle at the dead crewman. "Well, does he!?!"

"Wait, wait!" another crewman cried out from the far end of the bridge. "Please, don't hurt anyone else."

The Gaoro rose slowly from his station. He was not armed that Traush could tell.

"Can you give me access to the summoner?" he asked. The Gaoro nodded. "All right, get up here and do it," Traush motioned toward the command deck's central console.

"Thadd, no!" a Gaoro sitting at the navigation station protested. The navigator reached out to stop the crewman as he made his way toward Traush. Traush fired a plasma round, severing the navigators arm at the elbow. The Gaoro screeched and fell out of his chair.

"No one help him!" Traush warned, waving his rifle around. "And nobody else move! Thadd, get up here and get this summoner online!"

The crewman, Thadd, paused, shaking nervously as he glanced back at his injured colleague who flopped around on the ground next to his chair, screeching in pain.

"Thadd!!" Traush shouted again.

The crewman started forward again and walked slowly up to the command console next to where Traush stood.

From the outer junction, Traush could hear voices. The Gaoro soldiers had broken through the sealed doors and were just outside. With the hole he had blown in the bridge's door, there would be no way to keep them off the bridge. He only had one advantage.

"Bring it online, Thadd," Traush said as he sat Ivan's unconscious body down into a nearby chair. "You've got ten seconds. Understand?"

Thadd gave a hasty nod and began working.

An energy bolt flew passed Traush. Thadd squealed and ducked low. Traush ducked and rolled out of the way. Coming out of the roll he opened fire and hit the Gaoro soldier as he tried coming through the narrow crack in the bridge's door.

Traush huddled behind a control station that blocked the line of fire, providing him with temporary protection. He peeked around the edge just as a second soldier tried coming through the crack. It was no trick gunning him down. The soldier dropped his rifle and slumped over the body of the first.

Fortunately, Gaoroes were bulkier than humans and the opening was only big enough for one soldier to come through at a time. With two bodies now lying in the self-made entrance, the others would have to pull them away before they could make another attempt

Traush came out from behind the console and fired wildly through the opening. He could hear another soldier cry out in pain, but the bodies blocking the opening and the smoke pouring from the junction made it difficult to see what or whom he'd hit.

"How's it going with that summoner, Thadd?" Traush called back, not daring to take his eyes of the door.

"I think I—yes, it's—EEEEHHH!!!!!"

Weapon's fire from the opening struck Thadd in his thigh. He staggered away from the console before collapsing.

"Thadd? Thadd!!!" Traush shouted at the crewman while raining blast after blast through the opening in a desperate attempt to keep the soldiers out.

Without warning, three of the bridge's crewman gave terrified shouts and leapt up from their posts. There was a swishing sound and a rush of hot air swept across the room.

The bridge door had opened.

One of the crew… Traush realized his mistake instantly, but it was too late to do anything about it. Someone had released the lock on the door. For all he knew, it had been Thadd, and if so, that meant the summoner was still locked down.

Ten soldiers poured onto the bridge, firing wildly in Traush's direction. The scores of plasma that flew across the bridge hit another fleeing Gaoro crewman. Traush hurled himself toward the command console, firing at the oncoming soldiers as he flew through the air. He hit one in the chest and another in the arm. Plasma soared passed him. One singed his right cheek, but did no real damage. Traush landed behind another control station that stood between him and the command console. Directly beside him, Ivan sat slumped forward.

I need a distraction.

A soldier came charging around the station, ready to fire, but Traush was faster. He shot the Gaoro through the neck. The dead soldier's rifle dropped at Traush's feet.

Yes, that should work.

Working as quickly as he could, he grabbed the weapon off the deck, set it to full charge, and then hurled it up over the console into the onslaught of weapon's fire.

A plasma bolt struck the rifle as it spiraled through the air only a meter and a half from Traush. It exploded with a blinding flash. Traush turned his head away. He could feel plasma spray strike the side of his head, searing his ear and cheek. For a moment, he couldn't see anything except for a yellow white light burned into his retina.

The explosion had caused the Gaoroes to cease fire, perhaps because they were blinded, too, or perhaps because they thought the eruption had killed Traush. He could only hope it was the former reason and not the latter. Either way, there was no time to figure out which it was. Still blind, he reached up and grabbed Ivan by the arm and dragged him toward the command controls. He fumbled around until he found a button he knew must be the summoner's activator and pressed it.

The bridge was beginning to come back into focus. The white glare in his retina persisted, but he could make out the oval gold and silver shape of a portal floating next to him. Hoisting Ivan over this shoulder, he rushed toward the glittering silver mist. Weapon's fire roared all around. Something hot blazed across his ribs, igniting his shirt in flames. His foot caught the rim of the portal and he went plunging through, surrounded by glittering sparks and then consumed in darkness.

* * * *

"Hello, Corporal."

Éva's eyes snapped open. "L-lieutenant," she stammered. Seeing Kayla Marro standing in the door way, Éva pushed the bed sheets aside and tried to stand.

"No, please, sit down," Kayla said as she stepped into her room. Éva obeyed. Kayla took a seat next to her bed "How are they treating you? I hear this hospital has a great staff, some of the industry's finest," Kayla commented.

"They're—yeah, they're alright," Éva answered. The strength ebbed out of her voice.

Kayla felt immediately guilty for coming. She hadn't liked the idea of involving Corporal Katona in this matter. Éva had been under round-the-clock psychiatric care ever since the incident in the Matrix's core. It was easy to understand why. Being possessed by an alien entity, forced to indulge her darkest desires and to murder her own colleagues—possibly even Sergeant Traush—and probably her own sister. There was still doubt as to how Greta had died. With Traush gone, her father had not pressed the investigation further. Éva, however, insisted that her sister's death was her responsibility, and that made emotional recovery from her condition challenging, at best.

"How is your treatment coming along?" Kayla asked, gently.

"It's—" Éva hesitated and looked away.

"I'm sorry. We don't have to talk about it," Kayla said, feeling a fresh wave of guilt.

"That's just it, that's all we do is talk about it here," Éva answered, her voice still weak, but flavored now with anger. "What good is that? It doesn't change anything. There's nothing anyone can do. It happened, I committed treason and my sister is dead because of it. My father won't even speak to me, not that I blame him. They could keep me here a hundred years, and it wouldn't change a thing."

"Your father hasn't visited you?"

Éva shook her head.

"I just—" Kayla paused, thinking better than to finish the sentence. She had passed Attila Katona on the way in. It was her assumption he was just leaving, having visited his daughter. Now that she thought of it, he wasn't coming or going. He just stood by the entrance. "Well, I'm sorry to hear that," Kayla went on, wanting desperately to change the subject. "I hate to do this, but I'm actually here on official business."

At that, Éva perked up. Kayla pulled a small holo-player off of her belt and switched the imager on. A crystal clear, life-like image of Portal Bay 12 appeared in front of her.

"I need you to watch this," she said. "We've had a breach in the Compound, possibly a dimensional incursion, possibly a clever hack into the Matrix, though honestly a hack seems less likely. It's been suggested these people could be from the Guardian's dimension. They didn't have the purple glow, but— well, you and Sergeant Traush have the most experience with the Guardian and with the sergeant gone, you're the only one we could ask. Please keep in mind, what I am about to show you is classified. You think you're up to watching this?"

There was a fearful look in Éva's eyes, but after a second she nodded her head slowly. Kayla played the entire footage, everything from Dr. Vamperic's arrival all the way to the interview between Ferrgerr and the two heroes. Éva watched expressionless until it was all done.

"So, what do you think?" Kayla asked.

Éva shrugged.

"Any chance the Guardian might be behind this?"

Éva flinched at the mention of the word Guardian. She shook her head in response. "No. These intruders talk funny, but the Guardian spoke in even simpler sentences and when he spoke it was like you were hearing it in your mind as well as in your ears."

Éva lay back against the hospital bed and placed a hand over her eyes. A deep sigh passed her lips. "Why is it every time we see something new come out of the portals we automatically assume it is the Guardian? I told you already, I came to an understanding with him. He won't attack us as long as we don't attack him."

"We had to check, Éva. We had to be sure," Kayla explained. "The problem with the Guardian is he could look like anyone or anything, and he would take on forms that were fantastical, just like the two in our holding cells."

"And the last time we made that false assumption, I ended up almost destroying the universe," Éva said bitterly.

Kayla had no reply to that. A silence fell across the room as Éva lay there, an anguished expression on her face, her hands still over her eyes.

"Well, I appreciate your time, Éva," Kayla said at last. "Is there anything I can do for you? Anything you need?"

"No," Éva replied.

"Okay, but if you think of anything, the hospital staff knows how to reach me." She rose. "It's good to see you again. Get better, please."

It was dark by the time Kayla exited the hospital. The black sky and dimly glowing street lamps matched her mood. It had been harder to face Éva than she thought. She felt responsible for her predicament.

I should have been on the assignment with her.

She had told Ivan as much, but he reminded her that even if she had gone, she would have fared no better. The Darkness was beyond human comprehension. If she had gone with Éva into the desert, Éva would most likely still have been possessed and Kayla would now be dead. The fact that Ivan was right gave her some solace, but it was a selfish solace, at best.

Ivan…

Kayla looked down at her watch. *Blast! I'm late.* She motioned to a cab hovering near the hospital's guest entrance while fighting off the urge to use her summoner. The restrictions to the Matrix had not yet been completely lifted, and if she tried to summon a portal now, it would draw a lot of attention, attention she did not want.

The cab driver looked back at her and waited for instructions. "Hotel Ramora," she told him.

The cab lifted off the ground and sped through the night.

The hotel lobby was mercifully empty, save for a couple of patrons checking in and the usual staff. Kayla made her way to the lift, trying to be as discreet as she could.

This is chancy, she reminded herself. Up until his arrest, Kayla and Ivan would port to an obscure location for private time together. That way, there was no chance of running into anyone they knew. Given his strict parole, their options were greatly limited. She didn't dare go to his apartment, knowing it would be monitored, and she couldn't risk someone spotting him coming or going from her condominium.

The lift opened into a long hallway with plush, red carpet. Taking quick steps, she marched toward the door marked with the number on her pass card. The door opened with a gentle click and she stepped inside.

The lights were all off. Kayla felt a wave of disappointment. If she was running late was Ivan running even later, or had he not been able to come at all? Her hand moved toward the lights when, from the opposite end of the room, a soft glowing lamp switched on.

"Hello, Lieutenant," an unfamiliar voice said.

On the sitting room's couch sat a middle aged Caucasian man holding a pistol pointed at her chest. Kayla froze and her muscles tensed. At first she thought it was someone from the parole office, but the man sitting calmly across from her was shabbily dressed. He wore a coat that was, at one time, probably considered well-tailored and stylish, but now was faded and threadbare. His slacks were the same color and had a tear on one side that had been mended. This was no policeman, although there was something about him she thought she recognized.

As her eyes adjusted to the dark, his features came into focus and it came to her at once.

"Major LeStrange?"

He responded with a brief smile. "I wasn't sure if you'd remember me. It's good to see you again, though believe me, I am sorry it is under these conditions."

There was movement behind her. From her peripheral vision she could see the shadowy form of an arm reaching for her. She reacted quickly, grabbing the arm by the wrist, bending down and twisting at the same time. With one, solid jerk, she yanked the attacker forward and sent him flying over her shoulder and toward the major.

LeStrange was on his feet, but Kayla's toss had been too well aimed. Her assailant came slamming into LeStrange and knocked him back onto the couch. Before either one of them could recover, she had her own pistol out and pointed at the two.

The two men stood. Her assailant was not someone she recognized. He was a big man with a Middle Eastern look. His eyes were trained on her gun. LeStrange dusted himself off, not appearing the least bit concerned. Kayla leveled her gun directly at him.

"So it's true, you have gone over to the New Resistance," she said, not trying to hide the disappointment in her voice.

"Lieutenant, don't make this any harder than it already is," LeStrange sighed.

"Make what harder? From where I stand, I've got the upper hand."

"Stefane!" LeStrange called, tilting his head toward the bedroom door.

A foot kicked the door and it swung open. Two more men came out of the bedroom, dragging a third by gunpoint. It was Ivan. A man even larger than her assailant held him in a tight headlock and pressed the barrel of a pistol against his temple. The fourth man had an assault rifle out and pointed at Kayla.

"From where I stand, the tables just turned," LeStrange countered. He took a step forward and held out his hand, palm up. "Please, if you come peacefully, you may get out of this alive and free within a day's time."

LeStrange stood a meter from Kayla, his hand still outstretched. She glared at him then turned to look at Ivan. His captor had a hand pressed over his mouth, but there was no fear in his eyes. Kayla couldn't read his expression. She wanted to believe he was willing her to be strong, but when she turned back toward LeStrange, she flipped the pistol, hilt out, and placed it in his outstretched hand.

"See that we do," she said, "or so help me, you'll wish that we had."

* * * *

Traush peered through the tiny window and out onto the street. He didn't recognize the neighborhood, though he could tell they were on the outskirts of Cairo. The city's skyline was visible in the distance. It had changed a lot in the last three years. There were more buildings and the newest ones bore a definite Gaoro design—further proof that the Gaoroes had extended their influence passed that of mere protectors and allies.

The street was empty save for garbage littered about and wisps of blowing sand. From the looks of it, this area had been abandoned. There were fresh plasma burns on the sides of several buildings. There had been a battle here, probably a few weeks earlier. Whoever had lived and worked here had decided not to come back.

A series of weak coughs came from Traush's right. He closed the shutter and stepped over to where Ivan Jast laid. Ivan had faded in and out of consciousness ever since he and Traush ported into this dark, abandoned storage shed. Every time he started to come to, he would black out again before Traush could get a word out of him. His wounds were serious, no questioning that, and there was no telling how much time he had left. If they could get him to a medical facility, he might pull through—except that any decent medical facility would be under Gaoro control.

It was a dilemma without a solution. If the Gaoroes got their hands on Ivan, they would sentence him to death, but if he didn't get proper medical care he would definitely die, probably within the hour. It was doubtful the Resistance would have the means to treat wounds this severe. Given the circumstances,

Traush had already come to accept that Ivan would die. He just had to make sure he didn't die before committing one final act.

"Ivan," Traush called.

"Uuuh," Ivan responded with a moan. His eyes did not open.

Traush slapped him gently and then stopped as he heard the sound of something moving outside. Grabbing his rifle, he pressed against the wall and listened. He heard the sound again, and then again. It was not human, nor Gaoro. Traush felt his tension ease. A small animal, definitely.

Every sound made Traush edgy. He expected Gaoroes soldiers to show up at any moment. It was surprising that they hadn't come already. When he and Ivan ported into this shed, the portal had closed behind them almost instantaneously and no one had followed, but that meant little. The summoner would have a copy of their coordinates stored in memory. The shock troopers would have no trouble reactivating it and continuing their pursuit, and if they were too busy helping to evacuate the ship all they would have to do is transmit the coordinates to Portal Command and let them send someone after Traush.

Yet no one had come. Two hours later, everything was still quiet. Traush could only guess that the summoner's controls had been damaged in the firefight. The Gaoroes either couldn't reopen the portal, or the databanks had been fried and their coordinates lost. Either way, he had a reprieve—for the moment.

Ivan groaned again and his eyes fluttered opened. Traush leaned over him. "Ivan, can you hear me?" Ivan responded with a grunt. Traush gave him a slap. "Hey, stay with me."

"Nu-gub-rraaa…" Ivan mumbled.

Traush slapped him again. "I said stay with me! Come on, pull it together!"

"Uhhh… you have—a real gentle touch," he muttered.

Traush pulled a small communicator from his pocket and held it close to Ivan's face. "I took this from one of the dead guards, but it won't do me much good. All the comm frequencies I know would all have been deactivated years ago. Try and reach someone in the Resistance and tell them where we are."

Blood and spittle came out of Ivan's mouth as he made a sound Traush guessed was a laugh. "Don't be an idiot, Michael, I already told you I couldn't" Ivan said. "Like I said before, once I was captured, every code or frequency I ever knew would've been erased. They couldn't risk what I might tell them under a sayder probe. I couldn't reach them if I tried."

"I'm gambling someone made an exception," Traush replied.

"Yeah?"

"I don't think Lieutenant Marro would write you off so easily."

"Just because I'm her husband? I told you, she and I already discussed this. It might have torn her apart, but she would have written me off for dead and gone about her responsibilities."

"Maybe, but maybe not. You and she bent the rules and took a lot of chances being involved when the two of you were Hunters. My guess is that she's still bending the rules and taking chances for you, on sheer hope if nothing else."

Ivan made the same, sick gurgling nose that passed for a chuckle. "Sheer hope? What, on the slim chance a former Rensha would time travel to the present and bust me off a cruiser past a hundred soldiers?" He chuckled again. "No, not Kayla."

"Let's find out," Traush said.

He placed the stolen communicator gently onto Ivan's chest. Ivan eyed it, but made no motion to pick it up. His eyelids grew heavy and began to close. "Hey!!" Traush snapped, giving him another slap on the cheek. "Keep it together!"

"If—f I use this blasted thing," Ivan began, picking the communicator up, his hands shaking, "will you please stop hitting me?"

Traush couldn't help but to give Ivan a subtle smile. "Deal."

CHAPTER NINE

Ati finished his second beer and motioned to the bar tender for another. He had half a mind to order something stronger and get drunk quicker, but he knew it wouldn't do any good. Drunk or sober, he would remain miserable— aching for the daughter that was dead and guilty for not facing the one who was alive.

Just as he had the night before, he had returned to the hospital, waited around, and then headed for the bar. After an hour, he had almost talked himself into heading up to Éva's room, but just as he made up his mind, a Portal Hunter entered the building and he lost his nerve. It was his daughter's superior officer, Kayla Marro. She wandered by without a hint of acknowledgement and disappeared into a lift. No doubt she had come to see Éva, too. It made him sick to know that she could face her, while he couldn't. More than that, it angered him to know a Hunter would visit her at all. What right did they have? It was their fault she was in this predicament to begin with.

He couldn't stand the sight of them anymore. It was hellish to go to the Compound every day, cleaning up their messes, seeing them prance around like they were kings of the universe, all the while knowing that they had let his poor Éva down, and Greta, too.

"Curse them all," he mumbled into his glass. "Curse every last one of them."

"I'll drink to that," a voice came from the stool next to him.

Ati glanced over, only half interested until he caught sight of the man next to him. "You," he muttered.

"Yep, me," said the same bearded man he had met before. He even wore the same dark gray work jacket. "My name is Pavao, by the way. Sorry I didn't introduce myself the other night. I see you're still riled up about the Hunters. Well, I don't blame you. Traitors, every last one of them. You know the person who bosses them around isn't even a person. He's one of those filthy cow-ears."

Ati grunted an inaudible response and looked away.

"Yeah, but of course you know. You work at the Compound, don't you? I don't see how you can stand it."

"Isn't easy," Ati replied.

"I bet," Pavao answered then took another swig of beer. "Heard a rumor earlier today, one I thought you might be interested in."

"Can't say I am." Ati downed the rest of his beer and then motioned for another.

"Ah, I think you will. It's about the trial—Sergeant Jast's trial. Word is it won't even go forward. Rumor is they're working out an under the table deal and he'll get off Scott free."

"You're still on that, are ya?" Ati grumbled.

"Just thought you'd be interested. Like I said, part of the reason he's on trial is for trying to kill your daughter," Pavao pointed out. "If it were my kid, I'd be furious."

"But it ain't your kid."

"Yeah, true enough. I've probably got a dozen kids out there I don't even know about, but I'm sure she's not one of them," he said with a chuckle. Ati shot him a sideways glare. "Ah, heck, listen," Pavao went on, "I'm not trying to get you down, and I'm sure this kind of news isn't easy to hear, but I thought you should know. I mean, you have a right to know."

"If it's even true."

"Yeah, it may not be, but don't be too surprised if it is. I know people who know people," Pavao said as he wiped a bit of moisture off the side of his glass.

"Hm," was Ati's only response.

"It wouldn't be the first time something like this has happened," Pavao continued. "Yeah, these greasy cow-ears have been yanking our chain since before the Portal War. It's just worse now, now that the Empress is out of the way and now that they're running the show. They have their own ideas about justice."

"Hmmm," Ati grunted again.

"Yeah, but the great thing about justice is it isn't dictated by the government, it simply—is."

"That's a profound statement," Ati said with sarcasm. "But it doesn't mean a darned thing. If the government doesn't execute justice, who does?"

Pavao gave Ati a wide smile. "The people who care."

"And who would that be?"

Pavao didn't offer an immediate reply. He finished his beer, tossed some money on the bar, and stood up. Leaning over Ati, he whispered in his ear. "When you're ready to find out, come find me and I'll introduce you."

* * * *

The situation had deteriorated rapidly. Thirty minutes after Ivan tried to contact the Resistance the area was swamped with Gaoro troops, scouring building after building and patrolling the streets. Ivan had passed out five minutes after sending the signal, and Traush had not been able to wake him. He could still feel Ivan's pulse, but it was far too weak to matter now. Regardless of what happened in the next few minutes, Ivan would die.

There were a few empty storage crates on the far side of the shed, furthest from the door. Traush grabbed Ivan and pulled him behind the pile, then crouched down beside him with his rifle out and ready. It wouldn't be much cover. The crates were made from thin steel and were empty. A plasma round would punch straight through, but it was all he had to work with.

The sound of heavy footsteps came from just outside the shed. Two Gaoroes exchanged muffled words. There was a slow creaking nose. No other sound followed, then after ten seconds, the door creaked to a close and a pair of heavy boots marched off.

Traush breathed a sigh of relief and came out from behind the crates. He eased over to the window and listened, not daring to peek outside. The Gaoroes were all wandering off, further down the street. From what he could tell they were conducting a westward sweep. If they were, there was a chance he could sneak passed them by heading east. And then what? He still had no idea where the Resistance was.

That's irrelevant, at this point. I've got to get moving, he told himself.

With Ivan over his left shoulder and his rifle gripped firmly in his right hand, Traush eased carefully out of the shed and onto the street. He'd pondered leaving Ivan behind. It wouldn't do the former Hunter any good to be dragged along, but Traush's instincts prevented him from leaving him behind.

Down on the far end of the street, two Gaoroes checked one final building and then headed off around the corner. The coast was clear. The road to the east was long and straight and headed all the way to the Canal. From where Traush stood, he couldn't see any boats or harbors. It didn't matter, if he could make it, he could swim for several kilometers, putting much needed distance between himself and his current location.

Traush moved quickly, as quickly as he could while carrying an unconscious man. His eyes darted side-to-side constantly and his ears kept a careful listen for the sound of movement. He made it one block without any problems, then a second and a third.

Footsteps came from a side alley as he entered the fourth. They came without warning, too close to where he stood for him to make it down the opposite alley unnoticed. There were more footsteps coming from behind, sets of heavy feet running toward him. He glanced back in time to see four Gaoro soldiers barreling toward his position. He turned toward the closest building and started to run. Two more Gaoroes appeared, one out of each alley. Traush kept rushing toward the door. There were too many to fight in the open. He needed cover. When he was about five steps from the building, the door opened and another Gaoro stepped out.

"Hold it!" one from the alley shouted.

They all had weapons trained on him, though no one had opened fire. *They must want me alive*, Traush guessed. His ploy to make them think he possessed valuable information must have worked better than he thought, but it wouldn't matter. If they took him prisoner again, they would learn from their mistakes and he'd stand no chance of escaping a second time. There was no going back.

Traush dropped Ivan and whipped his rifle back in the direction of the four oncoming Gaoroes. His finger moved toward the trigger.

"Stop!!!!" a voice shouted. It was not a Gaoro voice, not even a male's voice.

Traush lowered his rifle and turned back toward the building. Standing next to the Gaoro in the doorway was Kayla Marro. She stared at Traush in dismay and then glanced down at Ivan.

"Ivan!" she cried out. She rushed over and knelt beside him. The Gaoro soldiers were all lowering their weapons. "He's alive," she said to the Gaoro next to her, "Barely. We've got to get him to a med-unit, right away."

"I'll get our glider," the Gaoro said and then hurried off.

Kayla sat in the street, dust and dirt covering her gray shirt and leather pants, cradling Ivan in her arms. She looked up at Traush. "Gunnery Sergeant Traush, I'd say you have some explaining to do."

* * * *

The back hatch snapped open as soon as the glider touched down. The Gaoroes that attended Ivan pushed his stretcher out into a dome-shaped warehouse.

"Clear the space, people! Coming through!" Kayla shouted as she hurried ahead of the stretcher.

Traush followed behind, keeping pace with Kayla but keeping enough distance so as not to get in the way. The sound of gears grinding together caused him to glance up. The opening in the roof that the glider had passed through was sliding closed. Traush hadn't noticed the roof doors when the glider had circled in for a landing. If he had to guess, it was probably holographic camouflage.

The warehouse's occupants were all human, save for the Gaoroes coming off the glider. The humans appeared tired and haggard. They wore patched clothing and some carried weapons that predated the Portal War. Only the Gaoroes were neat and clean, and they each carried the latest in plasma rifle technology. Yet no one gave the Gaoroes a suspicious or mistrusting glance. Instead, they reserved that for Traush.

"Get him down to the medical ward fast," Kayla ordered the Gaoro escort. "I want a full med team working on him right away!"

"Yes, ma'am," a Gaoro said, and with that, they hurried Ivan through a side door and out of sight, leaving Kayla and Traush behind.

Traush came up alongside Kayla. "I know you and he are close, but I have to tell you, Lieutenant, Sergeant Jast isn't going to make it," he said.

"Don't say that!" she snapped. "He's not dead until he's dead!"

Traush thought of a retort, a Rensha mantra about learning to face death, but instead he swallowed the words and said. "True, he's not dead until he's dead."

Kayla leaned forward and grasped her knees, taking deep breaths. Her face was pale, but emotionless. All the same, Traush could feel the inner battle as she fought to keep from breaking down. Finally, she spoke. "And it's not lieutenant anymore. Just call me Marro, or 'boss' if you insist on using rank."

"A crude, but fitting title," Traush replied.

Kayla pulled herself up straight and let out one last long breath with a tired sigh. "No matter what happens, I want to thank you for getting Ivan off that cruiser. I thought he would die up there. At least he's here with us, now."

"Not a problem."

"You never cease to amaze me," Kayla said with a shake of her head. "The legend of Traush goes on. You travel through time, free a high profile member of the Resistance against impossible odds, and manage to blow up a Gaoro cruiser in the process."

"Technically the Gaoroes destroyed their own ship, and the time travel was not deliberate," he replied.

"Right, you got caught in a feedback loop," she said.

"A feedback loop?"

"That's the nickname we gave it. The original portal staffs had a power cell that, if breached, would send a power surge into the summoner before shorting out the device entirely. It can cause a sudden surge of portals, mostly spatial and occasionally a dimensional portal or two, but I never heard of one creating a temporal portal until now. Makes sense, though."

"Another facet of the portals we don't fully understand," Traush responded.

"Not fully, but we've been working on it," Kayla replied.

"Ah, yes, Ivan told me that his future self and three others came back in time to stop Éva. You've tried replicating this process, yourself?"

"Trying is the operative word," Kayla explained. "It takes an advanced understanding of dimensional physics to pull it off, and we don't have a decent portal engineer on our team, not anymore. O'Reily is working for the Gaoroes and Mubarak's missing. That only leaves us with a few novices, though we do have one young man who has an uncanny understanding of the technology. He's doing his best to make sense of Dr. Klein's notes."

"You found Dr. Klein's notes?"

"Better than that, we found Dr. Klein," she said. "That was before I rejoined the Resistance. In exchange for his life, he helped the Resistance develop temporal portals. It worked, only something went wrong. Klein went missing again and several of our best people were killed. Ever since then we've been muddling through it, trying to recreate the process ourselves, but without Klein or Mubarak, it's been tough. It always seems there's something missing. Gabor's worked desperately to figure out what it is."

"Gabor?"

"The young prodigy I mentioned. He's only twenty-one, and has never been to a university, but he studied under Mubarak. It was phenomenal how much he understood and retained. I like to keep a close eye on him and make sure he stays safe. I can't imagine what we'd do if anything ever happened to him. Which reminds me," Kayla turned to a Gaoro soldier standing close by. "Where is Gabor?"

"He went on patrol with his sister. Said he needed the fresh air."

"Blast it! He knows he's not supposed to go out!"

The soldier chuckled. "Naturally. That's why he waited until you were gone before he left. Don't worry. They're due in any minute."

Kayla scowled and marched across the warehouse floor. "That girl knows better than to take her brother with her. You'd think of all people she'd be a little more careful," she mumbled.

Traush fell in step beside her. "You haven't yet told me why you have Gaoroes serving under your command," he said.

"Hmm?" Kayla looked up. "Oh, them. Not all the Gaoroes agree with their government's position. When the war between us broke out, a few voiced their objections and questioned the war on moral principles. In response, the Council started a witch hunt and had most of the objectors arrested. The rest went underground and later joined us. This group," she motioned around the warehouse, "is still on active duty with the GAF, but they moonlight for us. They each have a friend or family member who was persecuted for being an objector."

"Must come in handy."

"Very," Kayla agreed.

"But wouldn't common prejudice cause tension between them and humans in the Resistance?"

"Oh, loads," Kayla admitted. "That's why I restrict which of our cells they work with. Everyone here knows they're risking just as much as we are, and they appreciate it."

Kayla motioned toward the side door. "Well, come on. I want to check on Ivan, and you could do with a doctor, yourself. Those burns on your face look nasty."

"I've had worse, but yes, thank you," he started toward the door.

"Patrol coming in!" someone shouted.

Kayla turned back, the scowl returning to her face. "Good," she said, marching back across the warehouse.

The roof opened. A two-man glider came drifting down and landed in front of Kayla. Kayla stood there with her hands on her hips, frowning. The glider's passenger door opened and a young Caucasian man with dark hair crawled out. He gave Kayla a smile.

"Yeah, Mom, what's up?" he said.

"Don't call her mom," a woman's voice said from inside the glider. "You know she hates that."

"Gabor, how many times do I have to tell you? You can't go on patrol!"

"Well, I can't very well stay locked up here all the time, can I?"

"You know the dangers. You know what's at stake."

Traush walked slowly across the floor and watched the exchange with curiosity. There was something familiar about this man.

"Hey, who's that?" Gabor asked as he noticed Traush approaching. "A new guy?"

Kayla looked back at Traush and opened her mouth as if to answer the question, but she paused and her face went pale. "I—uh."

The pilot side door came open. Éva Katona leaned out and stared wide-eyed at Traush, her mouth gaping open in shock. Traush almost didn't recognize her. Éva had always been thin, but now she was thinner. Her usual dark complexion had paled and her hair had grown out as long as it was the first day they'd met. Even though she was still young, her eyes no longer betrayed any sense of youth and Traush glimpsed a hint of gray in her hair.

Éva came out of the glider and started toward Traush.

"You—" she said.

"Good to see you again," Traush said with a nod.

"Éva—" Kayla reached out to grab her by her arm, but she jerked away. Éva's surprised expression shifted into a hardened mask of hate. She picked up her pace and stormed toward Traush.

"You—MURDERER!!!"

Éva ripped a knife out from her belt and flung herself at Traush. He grabbed her by both wrists as she came down on him. Then, bending at the waist, he used her own momentum to toss her to the side and force her down onto the ground, burying a knee into her chest to hold her there.

She struggled against him with all her strength. Even as small as she was, it was difficult to hold her down. He gave her wrist a sharp twist. The knife came free and clanked on the ground. Spit flew wildly from her mouth and onto Traush's face as she shouted incoherent obscenities at him with all the force her lungs could muster.

Kayla hurried over to Traush "Éva!" she shouted.

"I've got her, but you'd better have her sedated while she's down," Traush said.

Kayla nodded and hurried over to a nearby med kit that hung on the wall.

Gabor stood in the center of the hanger, staring dumbfounded down at the two struggling on the ground. "Hey, someone mind telling me what this is all about?" he asked.

Traush looked up at the young man. "You're Gabor Katona?"

"Yeah. Who are you?"

"Michael Traush."

It took a second for Gabor to register. When it did his face went from bewildered, to surprised, to angry. He pulled out his sidearm and leveled it at Traush's head.

"Get off my sister. You're not going to kill her, too," he said. His voice was cold and deadly serious.

"Ah, so that's what this is about," Traush replied, understanding.

Kayla was standing next to Gabor, a syringe in her hand.

"Gabor, put the gun down," she said, calmly.

Traush met Gabor's gaze and held it. He could see the rage in his eyes, but he could also see the uncertainty. His pistol was pointed directly at his head. All Gabor had to do was squeeze the trigger, and there was nothing Traush could do in response, not while Éva was fighting desperately to get at him.

"Go ahead, shoot," he said without as much as blinking.

"Gabor." Kayla's voice was firm, yet not hard.

"Well?" Traush asked.

"You killed my sister," he spit out the words like they were poison. The pistol began to shake.

"Gabor," Kayla repeated. She placed a hand on his shoulder and reached for the gun with the other. "Give me the gun."

"I responded to a hostile situation with the force it warranted," Traush said. "The death of your sister was regrettable, and not intended. If that's something you can't live with then pull the trigger."

Gabor gritted his teeth and then bit his lower lip. His hands were shaking almost uncontrollably, but he kept the pistol aimed at Traush as best he could. Kayla placed a hand on his wrist, steadying it.

"I'm going to take this now," she said as her hand slipped delicately across his wrist and rested on top of the pistol. She gently pulled it from his grip, clicked the safety on and slipped it into her belt. Gabor was sweaty and pale. He stood there, empty handed, looking defeated. Kayla motioned to a pair of Gaoro soldiers standing nearby. They rushed up and grabbed Gabor, one by each arm.

"Take him back to his quarters," she said. "One of you, stand guard outside his room while he rests, in case he tries anything else rash."

Éva ceased her struggling and watched in dismay as her brother was escorted out of the warehouse by the two Gaoroes. Kayla walked over to where Traush had her pinned, knelt down and plunged the end of the syringe into her neck.

"Sorry, Éva," Kayla said as her eyes grew dim. "And my apologies to you, Michael. I should not have been so careless."

Traush released his hold and got back onto his feet. "Not your fault," he replied.

"I was just so distracted about what happened to Ivan, I forgot all about what you did to Greta. I know you were just defending yourself. I've seen what a person can do when possessed by those creatures, but regardless, it was their sister." She let out a tired sigh. "I can't believe how angry Gabor was. Éva was always temperamental, but Gabor? If I hadn't been here, he would have shot you."

"I don't think so," Traush replied. "There was hate in his eyes, but I could see no murder there."

Kayla looked away. "Maybe." Sadness seemed to overtake her. "But sometimes hate is just another name for murder."

* * * *

The face shield blocked out all sight and sound. Ivan had no idea where he was being taken, or what had happened to Kayla.

After Kayla surrendered her weapon to Major LeStrange, Ivan felt a sharp sting in the back of his neck and everything went dark. When he awoke, his hands were bound and the face shield was already in place. Rough hands grabbed him and started shoving him forward. He tried to walk straight, but with no sense of his surroundings he could barely take two steps without stumbling. Eventually, his captors grew restless, took him by the arms and dragged him along. When they arrived at their destination, he was shoved into a cold room and his bonds were fastened to a metal poll.

The minutes ticked on. For all he knew, he was alone, but that was only a guess. The room could be crowded and he'd have no way of knowing. All the same, he didn't think so. He could detect no vibrations or body heat.

Being both blind and deaf also distorted his sense of time. The minutes ticked into hours, or did they? He wasn't sure how much time had really passed. Maybe it just felt like a long time.

Finally, after what felt like an eternity, he could detect the subtlest of vibrations in the floor and then felt a hand touch the side of his head. Sound was the first sensation to return. He could hear someone standing in front of him, breathing. His sight returned a second later.

He didn't know the man standing in front of him, but he recognized him as one of the two who'd caught him by surprise at the hotel. He was in his thirties with dark hair, dark complexion, and a neatly trimmed beard. Someone else stood behind him. The second man was quite a sight. He was African with heavy scars on what little of his face was visible. Most of his head and face was covered with golden plating.

"You may go," the second man said to the first. The first left, making a grunting sound that Ivan could only guess was a response to the order.

Ivan glanced from side to side. It was a small room... not even a room. Pipes were everywhere and there was no furniture. He'd been sitting on the concrete floor the whole time.

"Where's Lieutenant Marro?" Ivan asked firmly, yet not heatedly.

"Safe, you'll be with her shortly, but I wanted a few minutes with you alone."

"Who are you?" Ivan asked.

"I go by the name of Raspin, but most people in the Resistance call me Boss, or Boss Raspin," he answered.

"Is boss just a nickname, or do you call the shots around here?"

Raspin's lip twitched up into a half-smile. "A little of both, you might say. The New Resistance doesn't have as formal a structure as the old, but I am the closest thing to the new Oran Cavar."

"I take exception to that," Ivan shot back, but careful to guard the anger in his voice. He wasn't sure if it was a good idea to upset this Raspin. "Oran Cavar was a true hero and I know he'd be proud of what we accomplished. He wouldn't try to stir up trouble and tear down everything we worked for."

"We worked for freedom, and after Cavar died all we did was trade one tyranny for another," Raspin answered, flatly.

Ivan gave a short laugh. "You really think the Civil Ministry was anything like the Empire? Where were you during the New Moon, in a cave?"

"Yes, more or less. I was kept locked under many meters of Earth under the Imperial palace in a small prison cell with no light, very little heat, and even less food. I know all about the Empress' cruelty."

"Then how can you compare the Ministry to her?"

"On the surface, the Ministry is a vast improvement, but the real problem is what lies behind both. The Gaoroes."

"Okay, fine, how can you compare the *Gaoroes* to her?"

"Once again, on the surface, very different, but you have to understand the full picture. The Gaoroes were the ones to make contact with the humans, not the other way around. They sent messages to two governments, the United Holy Republic and the Empire of the New Moon. Based on the responses, they decided to setup a meeting with the New Moon. Afterwards, they signed an exclusive treaty with the Empress, allowing her access to some of their technology and making her sole benefactor of an international trade agreement."

"Yeah, but the Republic tried to destroy their initial envoy," Ivan pointed out. "When that happened, they figured she was the only human they could trust."

"Ah, yes, but the Republic never took credit for the attack on the Gaoro envoy and there was never any conclusive evidence that they were behind it."

"What are you suggesting?"

"Nothing in particular," Raspin answered. "Just that the Gaoroes only wanted to deal with a single Earth government, in the interest of expediency. The attack became a convenient excuse for them to deal solely with the Empress. But even if the Republic *did* try to destroy the envoy, that doesn't change the fact that the Gaoroes equipped the New Moon with everything they needed to take over Earth. They knew what the Empress was doing and why, and they continued to trade with her and allowed her to rule the Earth, which in turn gave the Gaoroes control of Earth."

"What?"

"Think about it," Raspin paced the narrow space in front of Ivan. "They withheld key elements of their technology from the Empress and they also prevented other alien worlds from trading directly to Earth. The Gaoroes had something they could hold over the Empress' head. If she wanted to play a role in the greater intergalactic community, she had to do it the Gaoroes' way. But the Empress was able to break out of that trap when she discovered the portals, and that broke the Gaoroes hold on Earth. If the Gaoroes wanted to maintain their hold on Earth, that left them only one choice; destroy the Empire and devastate the planet."

"They were protecting themselves," Ivan countered. "She attacked them first. Goodness, she almost took over their entire nation."

"Yes, of course she did. She was a megalomaniac and the Gaoroes had no choice but to fight her off, but they did more than fight her off. And the Empress had to attack them if she wanted to establish Earth as a dominant power in the galaxy. It was both smart and pathological at the same time, but the Gaoroes didn't just defend themselves from a hostile threat, they took it a step further."

"How so?"

"It was the Siege. That's where they showed their hands. Every key leader in the Resistance knew that the plan was to neutralize Earth's defenses and have a combined Gaoro and Resistance taskforce take control of the planet. But the Gaoroes didn't stick with that plan. They bombed us and leveled many of our cities. A lot of people died, including members of the Resistance who were in the streets when the bombs fell.

"Once that happened, the humans were forced to rely on the Gaoroes' support to maintain order and rebuild our economy. So what did the Gaoroes do? They helped us build a new government, the Civil Ministry—another human institution that is beholden to the Gaoroes. Once again, the Gaoroes maintain their control on Earth."

"You're jumping to a lot of conclusions. The Gaoroes didn't plan the Siege out months in advance. Heck, it wasn't even their idea. We were the ones who stole the *Ark Royale*. We approached the Gaoroes and asked for their help."

"I know," Raspin replied. "On their own, the Gaoroes never had an effective counter response to the portals. But their endgame was always the same. The *Ark Royal* just sped things up."

"According to you."

Raspin's expression became grim. He stared down at Ivan, his visors glowing red. "I'd hoped that your current predicament would have given you a fresher perspective."

"You think kidnapping me at gunpoint is going to cause me to suddenly become sympathetic to your cause?" There was almost laughter in his voice.

"I'm not talking about this predicament," Raspin gestured toward the concrete walls. "I'm talking about your trial. I know what you did and why. Father Kim has joined us and he told us everything."

Hearing that, Ivan did laugh. "Well, if he's the kind of person you're recruiting, all I have to say is 'good luck'."

Raspin ignored the comment and continued. "You're a hero. When you stopped Corporal Katona, you saved not only Earth, but the entire galaxy. And how do the Gaoroes repay you? With charges of treason."

"The Civil Ministry is charging me, not the Gaoroes," Ivan said.

"Which is—"

"Just a Gaoro front group. Yeah, yeah, I get it," Ivan replied, dismissively.

"You don't believe me," Raspin said.

"Not particularly. It all sounds like paranoia to me."

"We have spies in the Ministry," Raspin said. "We watch and listen to what goes on. The Gaoroes were the ones to push for your case to go to trial."

That hit a nerve with Ivan, though he did his best to hide it from Raspin. He remembered Kayla's words about Borxos and the pressure he was putting on the hearings. As much as he hated to admit it that did play into Raspin's point.

"I'm not lying, Ivan. With a little digging, you can verify everything that I'm saying. Tell me, did you know that Ambassador Humrun was a part of the original envoy to Earth?"

"Yeah, that's no secret."

"And of course you know he was the Ambassador to Earth when Empress Drow was in power. It gets better. In addition to having the envoy to the New Moon as our envoy, we also have the prodigy of Admiral V'Moreth, the Gaoro who ordered the bombing of Earth, as the guardian of Earth's space," Raspin leaned close to Ivan. "Do they sound like people who have Earth's best interest at heart?"

Ivan drew his lips into a tight, thin line. He trusted their alliance with the Gaoro, but he had no counter argument for this point. Actually, he admitted to himself, he'd never given it much thought. Wasn't Ambassador Humrun technically responsible for the rise of the New Moon? He had negotiated the treaty with the Empress, arranged for the sale of weapons and other technical advancements, and Ivan was disappointed that Commander Borxos had pushed for hearings on treason. That had not endeared the commander to him, to say the least, even if he understood his reasons.

Raspin stood up straight and gave Ivan a smug smile. He knew he'd struck a chord, and that was good enough for now. Raspin knocked on the small, metal door that served as the only entrance and exit to the room.

"I want you to think about all this," Raspin said. "Mull it over in your mind, and then ask yourself if we are really paranoid, or if we're acting in the best interest of Earth. If you survive what comes next, you will be free. Go back to Cairo, watch and decide for yourself what is true and what is not."

"If I survive?" Ivan's eyes widened. "What are you going to do to me?"

The door opened and the other man stepped inside.

"Us? Nothing. But I can't promise what the doctor will or won't do." Raspin glanced over to the other man and gestured toward the door. "Take him to Vamperic."

CHAPTER TEN

The Resistance had fine doctors, Traush could not deny. The medical facilities were crude, but the Gaoroes who had secretly allied themselves to the Resistance had provided a decent selection of medical supplies. Naturally, it was all designed for use on Gaoro physiology, but with careful modifications it worked well enough on humans.

After two days, the plasma burns were healing nicely and bruises no longer hurt. He had rested and eaten well in that time, but despite the much needed treatment, he had the feeling of trading one prison cell for another.

It was never stated that he was restricted to the medical ward, but the doctors did what they could to keep him there. When he tried to move about to other parts of the ward in the hopes of checking on Ivan, the doctors told him he was not allowed into that section and would not give him any information on his current condition. In addition to the medical staff, Traush noticed that a pair of guards was always posted by the ward's outer doors. He wasn't sure if they would actively try to prevent him from leaving, but under the circumstances he decided not to test them and find out—not yet.

Aside from the medical staff's constant attention, he had been left alone since his arrival. 'Boss' Marro—as the others he encountered referred to Kayla—had not paid him a visit in those two days, nor had anyone of any significant rank. Fortunately, there was also no sign of the Katonas, either. Traush half expected one of the two to come and make an attempt on his life. He didn't fear either one of them. He was trained to deal with such threats. Rather, it worried him that he might be forced to kill another Katona if they persisted with their vendetta, and he knew that would not sit well with Kayla.

On the morning of his third day there, Traush decided to test the bounds and see if they were indeed holding him prisoner or just being cautious. Since it was clear the doctors did not want him to leave the medical ward, he waited until there was a shift change and then walked out the main doors and into the outer corridor. The usual two guards stood outside the door. As Traush stepped out into the hallway, they both turned and stared at him, saying nothing.

"Evening," Traush said with a nod.

The one on the right just stared back at him, without a word. The second guard gave him a curt nod. Traush paused, yet neither guard made a move toward him. Satisfied, he turned and strolled on.

The hallways were mostly empty. The hour was late. Everyone was either off on an assignment or in their bunks resting for the coming day. He passed only two others, both people he did not recognize. Neither made eye contact. One gave him a sideways glance while the other quickened his pace and hurried along.

The sound of footsteps could be heard marching along from behind, keeping an even pace with his every step. It was a single pair of feet. One of the guards had decided to follow him, he realized. Follow, but not restrict.

So they don't trust me, he mused. It was a natural reaction, he supposed, and arguably a wise precaution. After all, they had no scientific way of validating his story. Time travel was a rare event. Nevertheless, the blatant mistrust made him uneasy. Traush was used to having people question or suspect him, even (if not especially) his own colleagues, but to go about it in such an obvious and careless manner—no, that he could not respect.

Traush picked up his pace, and so did the footsteps behind him. He slowed down, and so did his pursuer. He resumed a steady pace, not suggesting he was hurrying, but giving the impression of moving with deliberate purpose. He came to a ninety degree turn in the corridor, ducked around the corner and pressed himself up against the wall. The footsteps approached, closer and closer...

"Looking for me?" Traush asked as his pursuer rounded the corner. It was the younger of the two guards. The man gave a slight, startled jump, but instantly recomposed himself.

"Sorry, no, I was just going on break," he said quickly, too quickly.

The guard started to walk around him, his pace slower than before and a nervous look in his eyes. As he passed, Traush's hand shot out and grabbed him by the arm. The guard froze, but did not resist.

"How much do you know about the Rensha training, about what we can do?"

The young guard gulped. "Not much," he admitted. "I was in the university during the war. I only joined the Resistance a few months ago."

"An academic? Yeah, that fits. Well, let me give you an educational bit of information. Rensha are trained to deal with any threat to the royal family or the royal estate—*any* threat. We know when someone is carrying a weapon with the slightest glance, no matter how well concealed, and we know how to deal with it, whatever 'it' may be. Deception is considered a weapon, and the Rensha are masters at detecting it. Anyone caught lying to or trying to conceal information from a member of the royal family in the presence of a Rensha is considered a danger and is dealt with accordingly." Traush leaned close to the young guard. "Are *you* hiding anything?"

He loosened his grip on the guard's arm and the young man pulled away. Without saying a word, he hurried off, daring only one glance back at Traush. As soon as he was well out of sight, Traush turned, doubled-back and headed down a different corridor.

Undoubtedly he'll report that encounter to Marro. It didn't matter, he told himself, he neither harmed nor openly threatened the young guard, and by scaring him off he'd bought a little unsupervised time to go roaming.

Traush wandered on for a few more uneventful minutes. The Resistance base was clearly an old glider hanger converted into a warehouse and then abandoned—probably during the Siege—until the Resistance found it and restored it to a functional facility. It was nothing more than a staging ground for whatever the Resistance was up to these days. What good such a ragtag band could do against the Gaoroes, he wasn't sure, but the odds didn't stop them during the Portal War, and they had won that conflict in the end.

Bored with his wanderings, Traush decided to head back to the medical bay. It was little effort to retrace his steps. As he reached the medical ward, he passed a door that had been shut when he first passed, but now was cracked open slightly. Voices came out. The first voice he did not recognize, but the other was Kayla.

"You've gone over the intelligence reports. They're genuine. Traush has scared the living daylights out of the Gaoroes," Kayla said. "He's not a plant. It's Traush, just like I said. Come on, I *know* Traush, Raphael. He was under my command during the war."

"I know, Kayla," the one called Raphael answered. "I never doubted you, but he's been gone three years. Where has he been? And why has he returned now, now of all times?"

"He already told us. Gabor reviewed the blood samples taken from the lab. He's not from this time, just like he said."

"But we don't know from what time," Raphael countered. "Gabor cannot identify the timeline just from examining a few blood samples, no one can."

"Klein could, if—"

"*If*, but he can't now, can he?"

"No, I suppose not." Kayla paused. "So, Raphael, you tell me, if he's not from the past, like he says, where do you think he's from?"

"Have you ever considered he may be working with the Portal Lords?"

Seconds of silence followed. Kayla could be heard pacing about. Traush moved closer to the door while trying to remain out of eyeshot. Kayla finally broke the silence. "No, I hadn't thought of that," she admitted. "It doesn't change anything, though."

"Doesn't it?"

"No. If he is working for the Portal Lords, at worst Gabor's plan would be a wash and we'd lose Traush, who— if you're right— is a liability, anyway. But if you're wrong and Gabor's right, we could end this war. Better yet, prevent it."

"You're assuming it's preventable," Raphael said. There was a mocking touch to his tone.

"When temporal mechanics are involved, anything's possible."

"Maybe, but even if it is, preventing this war may do nothing more than ensure our defeat." Traush could tell Raphael was getting agitated, or worried.

"You didn't object when we tried this last time," Kayla pointed out.

"And it didn't work then, so why bother with a second attempt?" Raphael was the one pacing now, Traush could tell by the way his voice moved toward and away from the door in a steady rhythm. "All that happened last time is we lost a couple of good men and your husband nearly died. Not to mention, if we never would have tried it, Boss Raspin wouldn't have—"

"There's no use in retreading old ground," Kayla countered, sharply.

"Isn't that what you're trying to do with Traush?" Raphael shot back.

"I've made my decision. It's my operation and my call. I'll go over the details with Gabor in the morning and, if he hasn't changed his mind, make the arrangements." Kayla's voice was growing louder and her shadow could be seen approaching the door.

Having heard enough, Traush moved silently and slipped back into his medical bay before Kayla stormed out into the hall.

* * * *

A holographic image of Dr. Vamperic's head floated above a flattened cube in Director Ferrgerr's hand. Gregory Mortan stood next to the director, holding his portal staff in both hands and studying the image with a deep frown. In front of Ferrgerr, on the other side of a laser grid, Fast Track and Tundra watched as the director played the message.

"…surrender to me the agents of justice you have in your care, or feel the wrath of Dr. Vamperic!"

The image shifted. It was impossible to determine where Vamperic was by his surroundings, but they could see a tall, cavern-like ceiling and plain, tan walls. He motioned to a large vat behind him. Steam rose out and washed over Ivan Jast and Kayla Marro who were suspended above it by a long rope.

"Now we know what happened to the lieutenant," Greg mumbled.

The message continued. "Included in this transmission is a set of coordinates. The three agents are to come to these coordinates alone and unarmed. If you send any of your Hunters—" He motioned again to Kayla and Ivan, "—these two will die. If any one of the heroes does not submit upon arrival, these two will die."

The holo-image pulled back in and focused on Vamperic. A gauntlet covered hand rose in front of his face and shook as he spoke. "Do not test me in this! I will be obeyed or you will pay for your insolence in blood! MUHHAHAHAHAHA!!!"

Director Ferrgerr flicked the hologram off.

"Is there anything else?" Tundra asked.

"No," the director answered. "The message plays on for another minute, but he does nothing more than laugh until the image fades to black. Very melodramatic."

"Or idiotic. Does everyone in your universe talk like this?" Greg asked the two through the laser grid.

"He's a villain, how else do you expect him to speak?" Tundra answered.

"Maybe not like a complete moron."

"Yeah, well, that might be a bit much to hope for from Vamperic," Fast Track replied with a smirk.

"You may find this situation amusing," Ferrgerr said, lowering his gaze directly at Fast Track, "but I assure you, I do not. Both these Hunters have served us with distinction, and the lieutenant is a highly valued leader in our organization. I do not intend to lose them to this criminal."

"We would not ask you to sacrifice any of your men for us," Tundra said. "If you had not detained us, we might have prevented this. Be that as it may, there is still a chance to save your friends, but you will have to trust us."

"Trust you? Why? How do we know you aren't working with Dr. Vampire?" Greg asked. "For all I know, this nut job took Ivan and the lieutenant captive as an excuse to get you two freed."

"As I have already demonstrated to you; we stay in this cell as a gesture of good will," Tundra said in a low voice, almost akin to a growl. "If we wanted to leave, you could not stop us."

Greg opened his mouth, about to retort, but Ferrgerr placed a hand on his shoulder. "Under the circumstances and with all the information we have gathered so far, I am inclined to take you at your word," Ferrgerr said to Tundra.

Greg scowled. "Director—"

"Sergeant, your concerns are noted," Ferrgerr said, cutting Greg off. "But as I said, under the circumstances I do not see many choices. The biggest problem I see is that we do not have three 'agents'. The third one is missing."

"No, he isn't," a deep, British voice came from nowhere.

A shadow formed in the corner of the cell. Greg lifted his staff and aimed at the dark mass as it took the shape of a man. Mr. Black stepped forward and stood alongside his two companions.

"Welcome back," Fast Track said.

"Did you find anything?" Tundra asked.

Black shook his head. "The doctor and my nemesis have concealed their tracks carefully. I have not been able to pick up their trail, so I thought I'd rejoin you and check on your progress. I see my timing is impeccable."

"As always," Fast Track added.

Black turned and looked at Ferrgerr. "You must be the person in charge."

"Of this facility, yes," he answered.

"Well, rest assured we will let no harm come to your companions. If Dr. Vamperic will free them, we will surrender to him willingly. Once he has us, we will find a way to turn the tide and take him and Mr. White captive."

"You two are being very cavalier," Fast Track glanced back at Tundra and Black, "but I don't like this one bit. Vamperic knows what we're capable of. He wouldn't expect us to surrender unless he had an ace up his sleeve. It's possible he may have found a way to neutralize our powers."

"It's a risk we'll have to take," Black said.

"It wouldn't be a risk if we knew where he's keeping the hostages," Fast Track replied. "I could be in and out with the hostages while you two distract White and Vamperic."

"A splendid idea. And do you know where they're being held?" Black asked with a reproachful glare. Fast Track didn't answer. "No, I thought not," Black said in a smug voice.

"But we might," Greg said. He snapped his fingers together and perked up. "I can't believe we didn't think of it. Yeah, we know exactly where they are!"

"You do?" Fast Track responded.

Ferrgerr raised an eyebrow. "Indeed?"

"The tracer on Ivan. He's out on parole. As part of his parole they implanted him with a tracer that lets the authorities locate him whenever they want. All we have to do is contact the police and get his coordinates. We can port a squad in and rescue them both."

Ferrgerr folded his arms and tilted his head toward the floor. "Hmmm, yes," he said thoughtfully. "It should work, though Vamperic may have accounted for that possibility and may have put certain safeguards in place. We should send two squads, just to be sure."

"You can send ten, but I am not sure how much good that will do you," Black said. "Vamperic is used to dealing with normals."

Ferrgerr raised an eyebrow. "Normals?"

"People, or aliens for that matter, who don't have powers," Fast Track interjected.

"Mr. Black is right," Tundra said. "We should come with you. Your Hunters can free the two captives and leave us to deal with Vamperic."

"That's not a good idea, Director," Greg argued. "They're too eager to help. I still say we can't trust them."

Ferrgerr said nothing for a moment, but then reached up and deactivated the laser grid. "Your concern is noted, Sergeant, but I have made my decision."

The three came out of the cell. Fast Track leaned back and stretched her arms. "Ah, free at last, free at least."

Ferrgerr took a step toward Mr. Black. The uncannily dark suited man was taller than Ferrgerr, yet when the two locked gazes they seemed almost eye-to-eye. "Understand this; you are only to engage Vamperic or anyone else from your world. Anyone from our world you will leave to us. And we will run the operation. Sergeant Spears will head up our efforts. You will coordinate everything with him. Is that clear?"

"Perfectly," Black said with an assuring smile. "Dr. Vamperic and Mr. White are our only concerns. Once we have them, we will leave you in peace."

"Good," Ferrgerr replied. "Then we have a lot to do in a very short period of time. Let's get to it."

* * * *

The noxious fumes rose out of the vat and washed over both Kayla and Ivan, stinging their skin and eyes and turning their stomachs with its pungent smell. It made breathing physically painful. Ivan tried holding his breath, but that did little good. Eventually, he had to take in air. The longer he held his breath, the more air he instinctively sucked in, and the more painful the experience. No, as long as they were tied, dangling above the boiling green liquid, there was nothing to do but suffer through each breath.

The vat beneath them was a free-standing cylinder approximately four meters tall. Its hollowed out center could hold half a dozen men if it were not filled with the strange, toxic ooze. It sat alongside a raised platform that looked hastily and cheaply constructed. It was composed of poly-plaster piping and sheets of thin metal held together by finely strung silver wires.

Both the vat and the platform were positioned along the interior wall of what Ivan assumed was a large abandoned silo. The entire space was encircled by cracked, tan walls that rose dozens of meters into the air. The floor was dirt mixed with ash. The silo's interior was completely empty, otherwise.

A long ladder extended from the dirt floor to the top of the platform. It had been from this ladder that Vamperic had drug his two hostages and tied them over the vat. He had then climbed down to the base of the silo, recorded his message and then begun to pace. Ivan heard the recording, but couldn't make much sense of it. Kayla hung behind him, oddly quiet. Finally, he asked her if she had any idea what this was about, and she told him everything.

"You're kidding me," he said when she was finished. "We're being held hostage by a villain from a holo-sat. A *holo-sat*? And *Justice for All*, no less!"

"You've heard of it?" Kayla asked, not bothering to hide her surprise.

"Yeah, well, I hadn't given it much thought in almost twenty years, but my grandfather gave me and my brother a few when I was a kid. I watched them, but I never saw one I liked. The holo-technology was very dated and the acting was horrific. I can't see how kids ever enjoyed that stuff," Ivan glanced over at the metal vampire pacing the floor below. "Huh. I thought he looked familiar. You sure this isn't some kind of joke?"

"It doesn't feel like a joke to me," Kayla said before yielding to a fit of coughing.

Ivan blinked away a few tears as his eyes began to sting even more. "No, you're right about that. It's a pretty bad one, if it is. It must be some kind of trick the New Resistance is playing."

Kayla coughed again. "That's unlikely. That would mean they have access to the Matrix and technology to simulate superhuman abilities."

"Unlikely? As unlikely as being held by a fictitious super villain?"

"SILENCE!!!" Vamperic bellowed at them from below. He waved his arms above his head as he spoke. "I will have none of your incessant chatter ruining this delicious moment, the moment that I, Dr. Vamperic, finally rid the universe of these meddlesome heroes. MUHAHAHAHA!!!"

Vamperic cackled on for several minutes and then resumed his pacing. Ivan and Kayla hung there in silence, doing their best not to lose consciousness or get sick. After what felt like an hour, Ivan couldn't take it anymore.

"So much for a nice, quiet evening at the Ramora," he said in a hushed voice. Vamperic did not seem to notice or hear him speak.

"Yeah," she replied in an equally soft voice, followed by another coughing fit. "I paid good money for that room. Shame it went to waste."

"Listen, Kayla," he hesitated. "I just want to say—about your proposal—it, well, I've been thinking, and I feel kind of stupid, looking back. I—I really wish I'd said yes."

"Do you?" Her voice was so quiet Ivan could barely hear the words.

"Yeah, I do. I thought I was protecting you by holding off, but now look where we are. I'm afraid we may have missed our only chance to be together for—well, for however short a time it may've been. I just—I just wish—"

"Don't start saying your goodbyes yet, Ivan," Kayla said, her voice was a little louder. "We can still get out of this."

"Oh, you know something I don't?"

He could feel her hands squirming against the bonds. "You notice what this gas is doing to the ropes?"

He flexed his wrists, testing them and trying to see what Kayla was getting at. "They feel solid enough to me," he answered.

"True, but they're getting wet," she pointed out.

Ivan flexed his wrists again. "Yeah, they are, but they're still holding."

"But they're getting slick, maybe slick enough to squeeze out of," she said. "Why did he even use rope? Why not titanium cuffs or gravity clamps?"

"They always used ropes or steel chains in the holo-sats," Ivan said as his memories of the old shows returned. "Even though they were filmed a hundred years ago, they were based on an earlier century—either the twentieth or the twenty-first, I always forget, but either way, it was pretty low tech. Ropes and chains were about the best they had."

"Let's be thankful that Vamperic didn't bother researching modern imprisonment methods. Give me a minute. I think I can do this."

She began pulling and twisting her wrists. Ivan could feel the ropes cutting tightly into his own wrists the harder she worked. "Wait, you sure this is a good idea?" he asked. "These bonds are the only thing keeping us from falling into that gunk."

"Just watch and learn." She continued wrestling against the bonds. Ivan glanced nervously over at Vamperic, but the armored villain just paced back and forth, staring at the ground and muttering to himself. He could feel Kayla's right hand beginning to slip free. "It's working," she whispered.

"Careful!"

She gave the bonds a sharp tug and her hand came free. With the right hand no longer bound, her left hand slipped easily out of the ropes and immediately she began to plunge into the boiling vat below.

"Kayla!" he called aloud.

Her arms snapped back behind her and wrapped around Ivan. The sweat and moisture collected against his clothing from the rising vapor made him as slick as the ropes. She slid two-thirds of a meter before she was able to stop her descent. Her feet were only centimeters from the boiling liquid.

Hearing Ivan's outcry, Vamperic jerked his head up and toward the two dangling captives. "What is this!?!" he bellowed.

"Oh, snap!" Ivan blurted. "Kayla!"

"Hold on!" she cried. Kicking her feet forward, she pushed against Ivan and began to rock them both back and forth over the vat. She repeated this motion, increasing the radius of their swing to almost, just almost over the lip of the vat.

"Narh!! !" Vamperic snarled. "Enough! Had you not resisted me, you might have survived. Now you both shall die!"

A solid red beam shot out of his hand and struck the suspension line just above Ivan's head. The entire rope turned a florescent red and then disappeared. Kayla and Ivan went tumbling down into the boiling liquid.

CHAPTER ELEVEN

It was a full day after his sojourn before anyone other than the med techs came to check on Traush. He remained content to stay in his assigned suite for the time being. The conversation he'd overheard between Kayla and Raphael—whoever that was—had him puzzled. *Portal Lords?* It had an ominous ring to it. Ivan hadn't mentioned anything of the sort in their internment together. Who were they, and why would the Resistance suspect him of working for this group?

The door next to his cot swung open as he lay there pondering these questions and Kayla Marro strolled inside. She glanced down at him, her expression hard and unreadable.

"We need to talk," she said.

* * * *

Kayla and Traush marched down the long underground corridors of the warehouse base. Traush recognized much of what they passed from his wanderings the day before, though it was just as uninteresting now as it was then.

"Intimidate anymore of our recruits lately?" Kayla asked, interrupting minutes of silence.

"Are you referring to the young guard you had follow me yesterday?" Traush responded.

Kayla gave him a sideways glance. "Marco. Yes."

"You shouldn't assign rookies to be my watchdogs," Traush replied. "He was far too obvious. Besides, with a recruit that green, if I'd wanted to hurt him he wouldn't have had a chance."

"Did you want to?"

"He isn't dead, is he?"

"No." There was a tone of caution in her voice.

"Then you have your answer," said Traush. "If you wanted me restrained to the medical bay, you should have locked me inside."

Kayla didn't say anything for a moment. "I just wanted to make sure you weren't disturbed."

"You mean you wanted to make sure I didn't run into the Katonas," Traush said candidly.

Kayla drew her lips into a tight, thin line. "Something like that."

"I can appreciate the dilemma this puts you in, but I can also respect their anger," Traush said. "For the last three years, Éva thought I was dead. She probably even thought she killed me, and that thought must have given her a certain amount of satisfaction. Now that I'm back, her bloodlust has returned."

"You didn't kill Greta. It was the Darkness," Kayla countered.

"I fired the shot," Traush admitted.

"Michael, I saw what someone is like under the influence of a shade. Greta was dangerous. I'm sure you had little choice. If she hadn't been possessed, she'd be alive today," Kayla said. "The blame is not yours."

"Maybe, but the Katonas obviously don't feel that way."

Kayla looked away. "That's my fault," she said. "After it was all over, Éva's mental health was, well, questionable and her memories of what happened were skewed. She thought she'd killed Greta, and the guilt was killing her. Her father told the director that you shot Greta, so I used that. I convinced her that her father's account was the accurate one. Since you were dead, what did it matter? Gabor already believed it, anyway. So her guilt turned into anger and she was able to cope much better after that."

"Understandable."

"Yeah, understandable, but it was a mistake. I honestly had no idea what happened to her sister, but I was afraid of what the grief was doing to her. I guess I thought anything else was better."

"And now you don't?"

Kayla shrugged. "In the short term, yeah, it helped. Now, looking back at who she was before and who she's become—" Kayla shook her head. "I don't know. I may have saved her life at the cost of her soul."

"Well, regardless, it will make it difficult for me to work with either one of them. Whatever you have in mind for me, it would be best if it had nothing to do with either of the Katonas."

"That may be difficult," Kayla said, stopping at a non-descript door. She punched three numbers into a key pad and the door opened. Inside was a round table large enough for six people. Sitting opposite the door, glaring up at Traush, was Gabor Katona.

* * * *

Traush sat at the round table, in the chair furthest from Gabor Katona. In the seats between sat Kayla and a middle-aged man of Latin decent who answered to the name of Raphael Varona. Traush recognized his voice as the same man Kayla had argued with the day before.

"Your arrival could really be a Godsend, Michael," Kayla began. Gabor scowled at those words, yet said nothing. "Frankly speaking, the war against the Gaoroes isn't going well. We've run into numerous—complications. If it wasn't for the growing unrest within the Gaoroes' own community and our newfound allies that have surfaced because of it, we wouldn't stand a chance. As it is, we're only treading water.

"Our plan up until now has been one of attrition. On Gaoro, the civil population has grown tired of the manpower, time, and resources that their government is pouring into the occupation of Earth, and the Prajic have started mustering their fleet again. Our hope is that a war between the Prajic and the Gaoro would force the Gaoro to withdraw some of their forces here to protect their home world.

"Our biggest problem is Admiral V'Moreth. He has risen even higher in the ranks and is now supreme commander of the entire military. He wants Earth and the humans contained. It's his top priority. I think he suspects us of being involved with the Prajic somehow. In any event, that's the excuse he uses to justify everything they pour into the occupation, and as long as he has any say, he won't give up the occupation, no matter how many worlds declare war on Gaoro."

"If the Gaoroes control the portals, how can the Prajic be perceived as a real threat?" Traush asked. "The Empress used the portals against their fleets very effectively. The Prajic were the first to retreat into a strictly defensive posture during the war."

Kayla and Raphael exchanged nervous glances.

"That's beside the point," Raphael spoke up. "The point is that we can't defeat the Gaoroes unless we make ourselves too much of a bother. But what constitutes as too much of a bother is a matter of opinion. V'Moreth may be willing to endure everything we shell out. We need a new strategy, and Boss Marro believes you're just what we're looking for."

Traush swiveled his chair to face Kayla. "Go on," he said.

"A couple of years ago we discovered the secret of time travel," Kayla said.

"Time travel? The Resistance? How?"

"It was Klein," Raphael said.

"Dr. Hermann Klein?"

"Yes," Kayla went on. "He decided to cooperate with us. The idea was to go back in time and change events that would result in a free Earth. Our plan didn't work, and Klein went missing, presumed dead. What few portal technicians we had took Klein's notes and tried to figure it out on their own. But Klein's notes, well, they're really advanced, to say the least, and our engineers, as talented as they are," she gave Gabor a reassuring nod, "—just aren't up to Klein's level."

"I see," Traush said. "I take it something's changed, something to do with me?"

"Yes," Kayla said. "You're not from this time."

"True, but how does that help us?" he asked.

Gabor cleared his throat and leaned against the table. "Every person and every object contains a kind of radioactive signature of temporal energy. We've only recently been able to identify this signature, but it exists. Everything that *is* has it. As an object ages its signature changes in conjunction to that time. That's how an object or a life form gets to a new place in the temporal timeline. It ages. Everything has to age. You, however, got here without aging. Your temporal signature isn't from this time. It's three years out of sync."

"Makes sense," Traush said, "but again, how does this help us?"

"I know how to create temporal portals, but I don't know how to direct them," Gabor went on. "If I knew the calculations behind a temporal signature from a specific time period, I could feed this information into the summoner and open a portal to that exact time, or one close to it. But we've only been recording data on these signatures for the last few months. I have no idea what one looks like from three years past."

"We've been running tests with blood samples our doctors took from you and we've started working out the formula," Raphael added.

Traush leaned back in his chair. "So you have the information you need from my blood sample. What do you need me for, exactly?"

"That's what I keep asking," Gabor said in a low, threatening tone.

Kayla gave Gabor a reproachful glare and then turned back toward Traush. "Someone has to go back in time and set things right and whoever goes won't be coming back. It makes sense that since you're from that time period, you should be the one to go. Given your Rensha training, you're probably the only one who can carry out this mission by himself, anyway."

Traush spread his arms wide. "How can I prevent all this? I may be a Rensha, but I am still just one man."

"Your job will be to save Minister Gramont while gaining evidence that Commander Borxos was behind it."

"How will that help, in the grand scheme?"

"It will give us leverage to win this war politically, without further violence," Kayla said. "Granted, we don't know if it will work, but Admiral V'Moreth has plenty of political enemies that would jump at this and use it to bring him down." Kayla shrugged. "It's the best we could come up with."

"Then you plan to send me back to when I disappeared?"

"Probably a couple of months later. Gabor thinks we have about a two month window he can project with the information he gathered," Kayla answered.

"Why two months? Why not from the moment I disappeared? How will I explain my absence?"

"I'm sure you'll come up with something," she answered. "The truth is, we don't know how this will affect the timeline. For the last three years you haven't been seen or heard by a single human being. You simply didn't exist. Once you go back, that changes."

"To maximize the potential of success and decrease the potential of unforeseen damage, we want to send you as close as possible to the moment when Minister Gramont was murdered," Raphael explained.

The desperation was plain. Traush weighed the plan in his mind. They must know it wouldn't work, yet as he looked from Kayla to Raphael, he could tell they were banking on it.

"Okay, if that's how you want to play it, I'll give it a shot," Traush said, at last. "So how exactly are you going to create this temporal portal? The Gaoroes have control of the Matrix."

"Yes, but some of our Gaoro associates can get us limited access," Kayla explained.

"But here's where it gets tricky," Raphael interjected. "Gabor says he can't modify a standard summoner to create such a precise temporal portal. He'll need to interface with the Matrix directly."

Traush turned back toward Raphael. "How is that my problem?"

"Because you'll have to break into the Matrix's core," he answered.

Traush tapped the table, suppressing a noticeable frown. "That may be a problem. I'm not even sure we could break into the Compound, but even if we did, there's no chance I'd be able to make it to the Core, not without some serious backup."

"We can get you into the Compound," Kayla said. "Our Gaoro contacts can port you in undetected, probably even into the secured areas. You'd have to take it from there."

Traush rubbed his chin. "Hmmm, might work."" He leaned against the table, toward Gabor. "Okay, I'll do it. But I'll need you to train me on how to interface your formula with the Matrix."

"No need," Gabor said. "I'm going with you."

"Out of the question," Traush said.

"I agree," Kayla said. "Gabor, you know how valuable you are to us, and you're not a foot soldier. Trust me, I know what it's like to break into the Compound when it's under enemy control. During the Siege, we took only our best, and several of us didn't come back, including Oran Cavar."

Traush could see the sadness in Kayla's eyes as she mentioned the former head of the Resistance. Oran Cavar was truly a remarkable man, Traush had to admit, and a formidable enemy for the Empire. Traush admired him even when he was a Rensha, and doubly so once he had a chance to meet him in person after joining the Resistance. He also knew that what she said about breaking into the Compound was true. Like Kayla and Cavar, Traush had been there.

Gabor wrinkled his nose in a sign of annoyance. He was young, and like many his age, Traush could tell he didn't like being treated like a kid. Reaching into his pocket, Gabor retrieved a small device that resembled a summoner. "Don't worry about that, Boss. I'll have this."

"It doesn't work!"

"It will in the Compound. It's encoded with a frequency that will allow me to auto-hack the Matrix for a single port—*if* I'm close enough to the Core, which in this case I will be." Gabor put it back into his pocket. "The Gaoroes want me alive, so they won't kill me, and I have no interest in being their prisoner. If the situation goes south, I'll port out of there faster than you can blink."

"It's still too big a risk," Kayla protested. "You can train Traush how to configure the portal himself."

"You're kidding me?" Gabor raised his voice. "The guy's a grunt. He couldn't understand it if I shoved it into his skull, which I would if I could!"

"He's not an idiot. Rensha were bred for intelligence, too," said Kayla.

"Boss," Raphael cut in. "I've got to side with Gabor on this. This mission is too important. He's got to be the one to configure the portal, and he's got to do it himself. Anyone else might muck it up." Raphael leaned close to Kayla. "We're talking time travel here. Do you have any idea what could go wrong if this isn't done just right? It could be a lot worse than last time."

The room fell silent. Kayla glared, with a hardened expression and cold eyes back at Raphael. Traush could tell she was preparing arguments and counter-arguments in her head, yet she offered none.

"Do you have any idea what could go wrong if Gabor is captured?" she said finally.

"Ms. Marro," Gabor said. "You realize if this works, everything that's happened since the Gaoroes took over would be undone. Everything would be different. That means your husband would never have been captured by the Gaoroes, and he wouldn't be lying brain-dead in an underground med-bay."

Some of the color went out of her face at those words. She looked away, the color returning with a flush of red. "Fine," she said at last, looking over at Traush. "Michael. You've got to make this work. You can't let us down. You can't let *me* down."

* * * *

"We're in position," Jonah Spears called into his wrist comm. Next to him were two other Portal Hunters and Tundra. The muscular, armored hero stood tall and proud in the center of the portal bay, directly in front of where the portal would open.

"Same here," Gregory Mortan called back over the comm.

"Ditto," a third voice answered.

There were three groups in three different portal bays, each waiting on the signal. Each group had with them one of the *Justice For All* members and three Hunters. It would be up to Jonah to take command and coordinate everything once they were on site, but for now it was up to Director Ferrgerr to issue the final order and activate the portals.

The three-tiered attack had been Ferrgerr's idea. Engaging in a three-tiered attack provided the Hunters with two advantages. To begin with, it kept the heroes separate until they were in the combat situation. Each group would send their hero through first. That way, if it proved to be a trap then it would be easier to get Jonah and his men out with a quick retreat before the trap could be sprung. If the heroes were sincere, then the attack from three angles would allow the taskforce to hit Dr. Vamperic hard and fast before he had any idea what was happening. Ideally, this would be a simple operation.

A holo-image of Director Ferrgerr appeared at the far end of the bay. "I'm getting a steady reading on Sergeant Jast's tracer," he said. "Remember, as soon as the portal opens, move quickly. We'll shut the portal down as soon as you're clear, as a precaution. Send a signal as soon as you have the lieutenant and the sergeant."

"Roger that," Jonah said.

"On my mark." Ferrgerr's head tilted down.

A four-by-six meter portal formed in the bay's center.

"You're clear. Go!"

"You heard him. Move! Move!" Jonah shouted.

Tundra held his arms wide and leapt forward, disappearing into the portal's silver haze. The two Hunters followed close behind. Jonah took up the rear. As soon as they were through, the portal snapped shut with a hiss.

* * * *

Ferrgerr watched from the command deck as a set of holo-images, one for each of the three bays, flicked off in sequential order.

"All teams clear," the operations officer called back. "Portals closed and secured."

Ferrgerr nodded. "Keep a close lock on their signal."

"Now we'll find out what this is all about," Flupd said.

"Perhaps," Ferrgerr answered.

The door to Command and Control opened with a swish. Flushed and sweaty, Ahmed Akhtar rushed inside. Ferrgerr raised an eyebrow and turned toward the red-faced youth.

"Cadet?"

"I-I'm sorry, sir," Ahmed stammered. "They said you were in here."

"Indeed I am. What is so urgent as to interrupt a control session?"

"A control—? Ah, blast! Don't tell me you sent the JFA with the Hunters."

"Cadet, I would mind your tone—!" Flupd began.

Ferrgerr cut the assistant director off with a sharp wave of his hand, his attention still focused on the cadet. "JFA?"

"Sorry, the characters from *Justice For All*, JFA. You didn't—?"

"We did. You have something you wish to tell me?"

"Sir!" a Hunter sitting at the control board shouted. "We just lost our trace on the team's summoners."

"What!?!" Flupd spat.

Ferrgerr walked over to the edge of the command deck. "Explain."

"We're getting interference. I'm not sure I can explain. It's the same type of spatial feedback the Matrix generates, the same kind Major Mubarak credits as preventing the formation of rogue portals within the Compound. I have a lock on Sergeant Jast's tracer, but not on our team's summoners."

"Get a portal open, now. Use the sergeant's tracer to pinpoint an opening."

The Hunter began working at the control then stopped, frowning. "It's no good. The feedback is blocking us."

"That doesn't make any sense," Flupd fumed. "No one's been able to reproduce the type of radiation given off by the Matrix."

"Someone has," Ferrgerr turned back toward the cadet. "Do you know something about this?"

"Uh, no, sir. Portal physics are not my strong point."

In a rare act of emotion, Ferrgerr scowled at the young man. "I'm well aware of your credentials, Cadet. You came here hoping to stop this mission. Why?"

Fidgeting nervously, the cadet took a step back. "It's Mr. White. I can't believe I'd forgotten all about this. It's been so long since I watched any of the 'sats."

"What about Mr. White?" Ferrgerr prodded.

"You see, in the show, Mr. White and Mr. Black are arch-enemies. There's this whole on-going story about how Black is trying to track down White, but can never catch him. White is always one step ahead. Supposedly their powers cancel each other out, and it will kill them both to fight openly, but it was never explained why, until the end of the fourth season. Some people thought this episode was really a hoax and that the next season they'd say it was all a dream and keep going with their rivalry, but the series was canceled, so we never learned, though I think—"

"Learned what?" Ferrgerr cut in.

"About Mr. White. It turns out he and Black were the same person. White would pose as Black to spy on the International Department of Justice, but in truth he was a bad guy all along. Didn't you say Black came through the portal with the others?"

"Agh!" Flupd spat. "I knew we shouldn't have trusted them. I knew—"

"Corporal," Ferrgerr called down to the Hunter at the control board, ignoring Flupd. "Get us two gliders and assemble all available Hunters. If we can't port in reinforcements, we'll have to do this the old fashion way."

* * * *

The portal popped open and Fast Track was through it in a flash. She could hear the three Hunters coming through behind her as the portal sizzled with their entry.

Timing was critical. If they were to take Dr. Vamperic by surprise, they had to act fast, and no one could act faster than Fast Track. She went immediately into hyper-mode. Everything around her came to a screeching halt as her sense of sight and sound began to register as quickly as her hyper-enhanced reflexes.

They were inside of a massive concrete silo. In the room's center Dr. Vamperic stood like a metal statue, frozen in the moment of her entry. His torso titled in their direction, indicating he was turning to face his unwanted guests. Behind him stood a large vat, the same one she'd seen in the holo-transmission. Ivan and Kayla were still above it, but they were no longer suspended by ropes. In fact, even with her senses in hyper-mode she could see them moving down, slowly but steadily down toward the churning green liquid.

They're falling! She realized. Despite her superhuman speed, she would never make it in time. They were almost at the mouth of the vat. That left her with one choice.

She leapt forward, took two steps and then vanished with a pop. With another pop, she reappeared directly next to the two falling Hunters. Despite teleporting, her momentum was not lost. She went flying forward in the direction she'd started, slammed into Ivan and Kayla at forty-five kilometers an hour, and wrapped her arms around them both. The three went flying over the vat and onto the platform behind it.

Kayla let out a piercing scream as Fast Track's arms caught her in the ribs. Ivan grunted loudly as they smashed against the platform and skidded across the metal surface. Fast Track was back on her feet before the two Hunters realized what was happening.

"*Shew!* That's what I call cutting it close! Are you two okay?"

Ivan tried to suck in a breath, but couldn't find his voice. Kayla spat out blood, grimaced and then collapsed.

"I think you broke my arm," Ivan finally managed weakly.

Fast Track gave the two a pouty expression. "Oh, you two are such whiners!" With a blur of red, she ran down the stairs and back down to ground level.

The other two portals vanished as Tundra and Mr. Black appeared with their Hunter escorts. The nine hunters and three heroes had Dr. Vamperic surrounded from all sides. He glanced from Tundra, to Fast Track, to Mr. Black, snarling at each one in turn.

"Treachery! Bah! It matters not! Since you did not surrender as I demanded, your two friends will die as I have sworn; only now each of you will perish with them!"

"No, Vamperic, I think not. You are beaten!" Tundra said, standing proud and tall, his voice booming throughout the vast, stone room. "You have no hope of escape and you cannot defeat us all alone!"

Vamperic threw his head back and laughed. "Who said I was alone?"

The sound of assault rifles charging could be heard from all sides. Hidden hatches all along the stone walls opened one by one, some on ground level, others higher up along the wall. Men and women of different ages and races, most dressed in little more than rags, leaned out and took aim at the Hunter's taskforce.

"Who the heck are these guys?" Jonah muttered.

"I don't—hey, wait. I think I recognize... Kris, is that you?"

A lanky, brown skinned man leaning out of the highest hatch flinched as Greg called up to him, but said nothing.

"Kris? Ah, nuts! Don't tell me—" Jonah began.

"The 'New' Resistance," Greg finished, shaking his head. "What the blazes are they doing helping this fruit cake?"

Tundra placed his hands on his hips and looked around at Vamperic's 'cavalry'. "This won't help you, Vamperic. You know these puny henchmen cannot hurt us with those toys."

"Maybe not, but perhaps I can," Black said.

Fast Track and Tundra both gave him a strange, confused look.

"What are you talking about, Blacky?" Fast Track asked.

Mr. Black took a step forward and came alongside Dr. Vamperic. Even Vamperic seemed confused by this gesture.

"I'm afraid I have been deceiving you, my good friends," Black said to Fast Track and Tundra. As he spoke, his skin and clothing began to shift. The texture flowed like liquid, yet he was still very much a solid, imposing figure. The blacks of his suit began to change to white.

"Oh, no!" Fast Track gasped.

"What madness is this!?!" Tundra roared.

"Your eyes do not deceive you, well, not any longer," Black responded with a sneer. "There is no Mr. Black. It was I, Mr. White, all along."

Jonah eased away from Vamperic and White, and motioned for the others to do the same. "This plan just went down the toilet," he said. "I'm getting us out of here."

"I think not," Mr. White said with a subtle smile. Reaching into his coat pocket, he retrieved a sphere-shaped object, held it up and clicked a small switch on its side. It came alive with gold and silver energy.

Jonah had no idea what the device was and no intention of finding out. He triggered the summoner on his staff. Nothing happened.

"Greg, my staff's malfunctioning. Get us a portal open, fast!"

"No luck," Greg said, as he tried to activate his summoner.

"There is no escape," White said. "While posing as Mr. Black, I learned many things about the Mistress' powers. The International Department of Justice once tried to duplicate her powers using technology, much as you have," White nodded toward Jonah and Greg. "But they discovered that the Mistress generated an energy field that blocked the creation of portals anywhere around her. Since this little device here is made from her life energy, it generates the same field. As long as it is active, you have no hope of getting away."

"This has got to be some kind of trick." Fast Track glared at White. "What have you done with Mr. Black!?!"

White grinned at her. "Are we that dense, my dear? Too afraid to realize what a fool you've been?"

"He's right," Tundra glowered. "It was so obvious, I can see it now. He played us like fools, and fools we were. It was he who killed Dianna and stole her powers. He released the Sea Hag to create a distraction, and even came up with the lie about chasing Mr. White so that we would not miss him when we went to stop the Hag."

White inclined his head. "Very good, Peter. It was a role I played so well that not even Dr. Vamperic knew the truth, until now."

Tundra pressed his right fist into the palm of his left hand. A cold chill filled the room and ruffled the folds of his bearskin cape. "But we are no longer the fools, White. You have removed the veil from our eyes too soon, and now it is time for us to take action and set things right."

"No, that time has passed. Can't you see? There are now two of us," White gestured to himself and Vamperic, "and two of you," he motioned toward Fast Track and Tundra, "and twice as many armed men with us than are with you. Now it is time for us to discuss your surrender." His grin broadened. "If you will do so willingly, I might even let a few of you live."

CHAPTER TWELVE

The roof was open, showing the night sky above, but there were no gliders in the hanger. They must all be out on patrol, Traush surmised.

It was his first time in the upper levels of the warehouse since he first arrived. His nose told him the air smelled better up here, but his mind told him that is was merely psychosomatic.

Two techs manned a small gravity lift and carried away parts for a glider and a stack of fuel cells. Kayla and a tall, stout Gaoro stood in the hanger's center. The techs gave Kayla a good-bye nod and started through a tall door that led to a storage area.

Traush hefted a heavy backpack over one shoulder, an assault rifle over the other, and strolled over to Kayla and the Gaoro. The Gaoro wore the uniform of the Gaoro Armed Forces with the rank of field ranger. Seeing Traush approach, he bent his left forearm to his shoulder—the traditional Gaoro salute.

"So this is the legendary Michael Traush," the Gaoro said. There was a hint of mirth in his voice, almost laughter. "It is truly an honor to meet you. I am Field Ranger Ru'Ruh."

"Field Ranger," Traush responded with a short nod.

Ru'Ruh grinned. "You've caused my Gaoro comrades-in-arms quite a stir."

"Indeed."

"Yes, they are trying to explain away the cruiser you destroyed as an act of sabotage. They say you brought a full squadron of men with you, and that you all died in the process."

"Some of that is an obvious lie," Traush said. "But that brings up a point, do they know I survived?"

"It's debated," Ru'Ruh said. "I wasn't even sure what to believe until I heard from Boss Marro. I will tell you this, dead or not, they won't under-estimate you again."

"We'll see," Traush responded.

A door on the far end of the hanger swung open. Gabor hurried through carrying with him an object that resembled a compact silver briefcase. Along its handle was a series of blinking lights. Traush had never seen a device like it before, but he had a pretty good idea what it was.

The door opened again and Éva followed after her brother. Traush tensed, but kept his body posture relaxed and non-threatening. She stopped a short distance from the door and exchanged a few hushed words with Gabor. When they finished speaking, Gabor gave her a hug and headed toward the others. Éva lingered behind, turning her attention from her brother to Traush. There was a deadly look in her eyes, yet Traush could sense something else behind the hardened gaze, something out of place. It seemed like an air of satisfaction, though for what he couldn't say.

"Just these two?" Ru'Ruh asked as Gabor came along side Kayla.

"Yes, I promised you I'd keep it as simple as possible," she answered.

"Well, the Gaoroes will know they were there, even if they don't detect their entry, so I don't know how 'simple' this will be, but I can manage it without the trace coming back to me," Ru'Ruh said. "However, that means it will be up to you to get out of there once you're finished."

"Don't worry, I've got that covered," Gabor said, fingering the small summoner he'd shown Traush at the meeting earlier.

"Good. Are we ready then?" Ru'Ruh asked.

Traush brought his assault rifle close to his chest. "I'm ready. Gabor?" He nodded.

Ru'Ruh pulled a communicator from his belt. "I'll send a signal requesting a portal for two. It contains a security encoding that will send you automatically to the Compound's lower level. The encoding will then filter back into the system and erase all traces of the port, but remember, if any human is seen down on this level, they'll arrest you on the spot—that is, if you're lucky."

"Understood," Traush said.

Ru'Ruh punched a series of commands into the communicator's tiny key pad. A three-by-four meter portal formed in front of them. "Best hurry," Ru'Ruh said.

Taking point, Traush leapt through. The hanger melted away and the familiar off-white, curved walls of the Compound appeared around him. He crouched low and took in his surroundings. All was quiet. There was no sign of anyone in the immediate area. Gabor hurried through directly behind him. Seeing Traush crouched in a combat position, he instinctively did the same.

"It's clear," Traush said in a quiet voice.

"Which way is the Core?" Gabor asked.

Traush studied the corridor. It was long, arching off to the right in one direction and coming to a set of sealed titanium doors off to the left. "I've never been in this section before," Traush admitted. "Those are the doors that partition the secured levels from the rest of the Compound, so obviously we head right. It should take us straight to the Matrix."

"Then we'd better get cracking."

"Yes," Traush responded. "We'd best."

* * * *

Mr. White fingered the globe in his hands—the essence that had once been a human being with the ability to summon portals, now condensed into a singular device. Dr. Vamperic stood in a defensive posture with his legs apart and his arms wide, glaring at Fast Track and Tundra. Neither of the heroes moved a muscle. Both ignored Vamperic and focused their attention, and their anger, solely at Mr. White.

Jonah, Greg, and the other Hunters kept their staffs aimed at Vamperic and White, but the sight of so many armed gunmen surrounding them seemed a more pressing dilemma. However, neither Jonah nor Greg dared shift their aim to the portholes that littered the room. One wrong move and the gunmen would open fire before they could get off a single shot. No, from Jonah and Greg, the question was whether to remain still and hope the super beings would take action first, or lay down their weapons and surrender before any of them were hurt.

"It's your call, Jonah," Greg said. "You're field commander."

"You sure you don't want to trade places?"

"Maybe with one of those guys up there," Greg gestured with a nod of his head to a couple of snipers nested high above them, rifles trained directly at their chests.

"Okay, fine, ask them if they'll trade with us," Jonah said.

"Cut it out! This is serious!" Greg shouted back.

"It is indeed," White said. "Personally, if I were you, I'd lay your weapons down slowly before I grow tired and order these fine people to kill you all."

"Okay, okay, just relax," Jonah said. "All right, Hunters, staffs on the ground! Nice and easy."

On the platform above, Ivan could hear the commotion below, but he couldn't see anything from where he lay. His mind and heart were with the woman lying bloodied beside him. "Kayla," he whispered, keeping his voice low. So far, no one was paying them any mind. He did not wish to remind anyone of their presence. Kayla made a low grown, tried to roll over to face him but grimaced in pain and flopped onto her back. "Kayla, are you okay?"

"Felt better," she mumbled weakly. "Just give me a second and I think I can stand."

"Better not try. We're in a real pickle." Ivan motioned toward a couple of the openings in the walls. Kayla caught sight of the gunmen and gave Ivan a short nod, indicating she understood.

Ivan took a moment to examine his own physical state. His left arm throbbed with a low, dull pain. He tried flexing his fingers. A sharper pain raced up his arm. His left side where Fast Track had impacted against him also hurt, though less intensely. *Pain or no, I can't just wait around until they decide to kill us*, he thought to himself.

Slowly and carefully, he pulled himself across the platform with his one good arm until he reached the edge. Directly below was the vat of boiling liquid. His captors stood approximately two-and-a-half meters beyond the vat with their backs to him. He could see Jonah and Greg and wondered if they noticed him. Craning his head, Ivan peered under the platform. It was dark. The platform itself and the large, metal vat were blocking all light sources. There was, however, a faint white glow coming from somewhere under the platform that shone against the base of the vat.

A gravity beam.

Ivan could tell the vat had been brought into the silo just for this occasion, and obviously they would need a gravity lift to transport such a massive object. He'd assumed the lift had deposited the vat and left, but it was actually there, beneath him, holding the vat in place. An idea came to him.

* * * *

The security cameras posed the biggest problem. Traush eyed each one cautiously as they moved along the winding corridors. He did his best to duck around and get by unseen, though he knew their visual range made it impossible and Gabor wasn't putting in half the effort, anyway. Their only hope rested in the scrambler he had taken from the Resistance's armory. It was a pocket sized device that would cause any camera within range to short out temporarily. There was some question as to whether it would work against the Gaoroes cameras. If they were using the original cameras installed by the Empress, it would, but if they'd been upgraded, there was no telling.

However, even if they did work, that posed another problem. The passage to the Core was not short. They had to pass at least a dozen cameras, each one being carefully monitored. If one or two cameras shorted temporarily, the Gaoroes might think it a small glitch and not care, but if they all shorted, one by one and each sequentially in the direction of the Core, they'd grow suspicious. Even if they still thought it nothing more than a technical problem, they would send someone to investigate. But all that aside, they had made it passed ten cameras without as much as an alarm or sight and sound of another sentient being anywhere in the area.

"It's too easy," Traush said, at last, his voice no more than a whisper.

"Don't jinx us," Gabor responded in a low voice, though not as quiet as Traush.

"I'm serious. The Gaoroes can't be this nonchalant about security. We can't have made it this far unless they wanted us to or didn't care."

"Come on, we're almost there," Gabor prodded.

They went on another ten meters. The eleventh security camera was in position, its red eye scanning the corridor. Traush paused then pressing against the wall, moved hurriedly passed it. Gabor followed suit. They came to a turn and Traush stopped.

"No, I can't accept this," Traush said with a frown. "We're going back. Activate your summoner."

"Are you kidding me?" Gabor was no longer whispering. His voice echoed off the arched walls. "It has to be close! Let's keep going."

"No," Traush said flatly. He held out his hand. "The summoner, please."

A look of rage overtook Gabor. "I don't believe this. We catch a lucky break and you lose your nerve. You, the mighty Traush! Scourge of the galaxy and murderer of children!"

"Keep your voice down!" Traush snapped.

"Why, there's no one here?" Gabor waved his hands about. "Have you considered that the Gaoroes simply are so overconfident that they hadn't bothered to properly secure the area?"

"Not a chance," Traush insisted. "Now, are you going to activate that summoner, or do I have to take it from you by force and do it myself."

"Fine," Gabor muttered the word as if it were profanity. He reached into his pocket and tossed Traush the summoner. Traush pressed the button for activation. Nothing happened.

"You said this was your way home. You said it would work," Traush waved the useless summoner in front of him.

"It will, but I have to sync it with the Matrix."

Traush tossed it back to him. "Then do it."

"No," Gabor said flatly, pocketing the summoner again. Gabor smirked at Traush and folded his arms in front of him. The silver briefcase dangled across his midsection as he kept a tight hold of it. "If you want out of here Traush, there's only one way." Gabor uncrossed his arms and motioned ahead. "It's down that hallway and three years back in time."

Traush didn't move, not even to blink.

"Well, what are you waiting for?"

"Activate the summoner," Traush answered, coldly.

"I said no, now let's get going," Gabor took a step forward but Traush blocked his path. "What, are you going to kill me like you did my sister?"

Traush was on Gabor in a flash. With one hand wrapped around his throat, he hoisted him off the ground and shoved him against the wall. "That's what this is about, isn't it? They know we're coming, don't they? You tipped them off knowing they'd kill me, but not you."

"You—paranoid—piece of—" Gabor gasped out between breaths.

The sounds of booted feet moving in their direction echoed from up ahead and around the corner. Traush threw Gabor onto the floor and pressed himself against the wall. Daring a quick, single glance around the edge, he saw four Gaoro soldiers, each carrying rifles, rushing toward his position. One of the Gaoroes had his rifle ready and opened fire the moment Traush peered out. Traush jerked back as the plasma bolt slammed into the wall. Wasting no time, he pulled a grenade from his belt and chunked it around the corner. There was a loud pop and then the swooshing of flames. The Gaoroes let out a horrific cry. Traush could even hear one being thrown into the wall with a thud, then all was quiet, save for the coughing of Gabor next to him.

Traush peered out again. All four Gaoroes were down. One had been ripped into pieces. Two more were definitely dead (or close enough as to not make a difference). A fourth knelt on the floor, covered in burns and hacking up several white, horse-like teeth. Traush stepped out, took aim and shot the Gaoro between the eyes

"Hmmm," Traush muttered, leaning over the body of the closest. "Standard guards. The Hunters always kept four armed guards around the Core's entrance. Looks like the Gaoroes did the same."

This section of the corridor was not very long and came to another turn. He walked slowly to the end, listening for the slightest sign of anyone else, and then stopped as he reached the door. The corridor came to a wide opening. There, in front of him, was the tall, circular, vault-like door that led into the Matrix's core. The guard station was fit for four, and each one empty. "Yes, I was right."

Gabor came staggering into the round room, clutching the silver briefcase and rubbing his throat with his spare hand. "Satisfied?" he said in a hoarse voice. "We're here, and you killed the guards. There's no trap."

It still didn't feel right, but they had made it. The only thing between them and the core now was a thick, titanium door. They had no hopes of cracking the security code, and the guards stationed outside would not have a key that would open it. Fortunately, Kayla had foreseen this and sent him with the necessary tools. Traush removed his backpack and pulled from it a round tube.

Even though he remained leery of their good fortune, at this point it seemed easier to see the plan through than to force Gabor into retreating. The young man was driven, and he wouldn't concede to return easily. He didn't have time to force his hand.

"All right, we're going to try it your way," Traush said, as he placed the cylinder-shaped bomb up against the door. "But if you cross me, you'll be joining your little sister today."

Gabor flinched at the words. His lips curled back and his mouth opened as if to offer a vile retort, but he closed it again, obviously changing his mind and biting his tongue instead.

"That should do it," Traush said as he keyed in the arming code. "Okay, back around the corner."

The two hurried back the way they came until they reached the pile of Gaoro corpses. Gabor regarded the burned and bloody remains with disgust, but Traush paid them no mind. Instead, he pulled the remote from the backpack and powered it on.

"Your boss sent us with two of these. Let's hope one is enough," Traush said. "Once this goes off, they'll know we're here for sure. Lucky for us they can't port into the Core, but they'll waste no time getting down here. You ready to configure the portal?" Gabor nodded and patted the case. "Okay, then. Cover your ears."

Traush pressed the button and a resounding boom filled the air. Even sheltered away from the blast around the corner, scalding heat filled the air and rushed passed. Gabor took a step back and threw his hands over his head.

Traush headed back toward the Core's entrance, keeping his rifle at the ready. The bomb had punched a hole in the door and incinerated its lower third. Shards of metal littered the floor.

"That should do it," Traush said as Gabor came up alongside him. "We can both squeeze through that. Just watch yourself. Those edges will be sharp."

Before he could take another step forward, the heavy, titanium door began to swing open a few centimeters, but no more. Traush waited to see if anything else would happen. Nothing did. *Must have taken out the locking mechanism.* More good fortune, it would seem.

"Come on," he said.

Even hanging open and loose, the door was extremely heavy. Leveraging his weight into it, Traush could open it another half meter. It wasn't much, but it was enough. The space beyond was dark, save for a multi-colored, strobe-like effect that radiated from the Core's many portals. Traush kept his rifle out and pointed forward as he began to squeeze through the opening then froze. Even in the poor lighting, he could see the dark outline of a cow-shaped head against the stone wall. He immediately took a step backward and right into the barrel of Gabor's pistol.

"Keep moving," Gabor said.

"Get back!! They're inside! They're waiting for us!"

"I know," Gabor said. "Good job on smelling out a trap and a motive. You're an intuitive guy. Too bad you didn't trust those instincts—not that it would have mattered. I would have never ported you out of here. Never."

* * * *

Jonah and Greg leaned gently toward the ground, their staffs hanging loosely in their hands. The other Hunters exchanged glances and then followed their lead, leaning forward with equal care and placing their staffs on the ground. White watched with satisfaction as he caressed the glowing orb in his outstretched hand.

Fast Track narrowed her eyes and focused on the glowing orb. In a blur of red and black, she shot forward. A loud crack echoed throughout the silo and Fast Track went flying backward across the open floor and slammed hard into the stone wall. She slid from the wall onto the ground and lay there, motionless.

"A reverse kinetics shield. A device created by the good doctor," White said. "If a solid object moves toward me with uncommon speed, the shield will repel said object with equal force."

Tundra gritted his teeth. "You are a true fiend, White! If you have harmed her, I will—"

"Do what, exactly?" White cut in. "Fast Track has been neutralized and your human friends have wisely laid down their weapons. You're alone in your defiance, my friend, and you are beaten."

A sudden, loud creaking sound came from directly behind White and Vamperic. They both turned just in time to see the metal vat lurch forward half a meter before coming to a stop. There was a deep, rumbling thud and then the vat began to tip over. Vamperic threw his hands above his head and snarled in alarm. White took two quick steps backward and inadvertently ran straight into Tundra. Tundra wrapped both arms around him in a massive bear hug and hoisted him up off the ground. White let out an alarmed gasp and released the shimmering globe.

"Move! Move!" shouted Jonah as green liquid poured out over the mouth of the vat and came at them in a wave. He snatched his staff up off the ground and threw himself to the side, just missing the green onslaught.

The green wave slammed into Vamperic. He roared as it washed over him, burning away the moth-eaten suit that adorned his armor. Two Hunters were not fast enough and were caught in the wave. They gave out hideous cries as their skin began to melt. The wave struck White and Tundra as well. The green liquid ate away at Tundra's bearskin robes, but otherwise it had no effect on either of the two.

Vamperic was still on his feet, his armor a mix of silver, charred black, and green slime. His moth-eaten suit had disintegrated completely. He seemed almost naked standing there without it. The large vat lay on its side directly in front of him, steam rolling out of its mouth. With another thud, something struck the back of the vat and pushed it forward. Paying it no mind, Vamperic wiped away bits of slime and ruined pieces of the outer armor while muttering angrily to himself. The vat struck him before he realized what was happening. It knocked him to the floor and rolled right over him with a loud crunch.

Ivan came barreling out from underneath the platform, riding the gravity lift that had kept the vat in place. He released the vat from the lift and let it roll on under its own momentum. The top end of the vat smashed into White and Tundra as they struggled, sending them both sprawling across the room.

White was back on his feet in an instant, unfazed by either assault. Tundra pulled himself onto one knee and glowered up at White, but White's attention was elsewhere. He glanced frantically from side-to-side.

"The sphere!" he shouted in desperation.

"You mean this?" Ivan leaned out of the lift and grabbed a portal staff belonging to one of the now-dead Hunters. He pulled the controls of the lift hard to the side and raced directly toward a pulsating globe lying in the center of the room. Wielding the staff like a polo stick, he swung, hit the sphere and sent it flying toward Jonah and Greg. "Greg!!!" Ivan called out.

"I got it!" Greg jumped to the side, reached and out grabbed the sphere.

"Shut that thing off!" Jonah shouted.

Greg turned the sphere over and over. "I thought this thing had a switch. Snap! If I could turn its glare down, maybe I could find it."

"Kill them!!!" White shouted to the surrounding gunmen. "Kill them all!"

Plasma fire rang out through the silo. A bolt hit Greg in the gut. With a hushed grunt, he fell to his knees. The sphere went flying out of his hands. White rushed toward the globe as it bounced along the floor.

"White! Face me!" Tundra's voice boomed out.

Mr. White ignored the challenge and ran toward the globe. A gust of freezing air caught him from behind with surprising force. The cold blast knocked White off balance and sent the sphere off in the opposite direction.

"No!" he cried out.

A gauntlet-covered hand grabbed him by the shoulder. Tundra turned White around and punched him hard across the jaw. White rolled with the blow and came back at Tundra, jamming his fist into his gut. Even through his armor, Tundra could feel the impact and had to struggle to keep from collapsing. White clinched both hands together and swung at Tundra's head, hitting him across the temple. The blow knocked him back, spraying droplets of blood from his nose onto his thick, white beard.

Ivan raced through puddles of acid, doing his best not to splash the dangerous chemical onto the Hunters scattered throughout the silo while trying at the same time to dodge the rain of plasma bolts. A series of bolts hit the top of the lift, but he was protected by a thin, steel roof. After the third bolt, however, the roof was nothing more than a few melted strands of metal. Using the staff, he fired shots wildly, hoping against hope one would hit a gunman and even the odds that much more, but whether he'd hit anyone or not was a complete mystery. The plasma bolts rained down in a continuous, steady flow.

Jonah ducked out of the way as a series of shots flew passed his head. He answered back by opening fire on two gunmen who were leaning out of the nearest openings. One shot caught a gunman in the shoulder while the second just barely missed. The second gunman fired back. A searing heat erupted across Jonah's ear as the bolt sliced into his helmet. He fired up at the gunman repeatedly while ripping off the melted and ruined helmet. There was a shout and the gunman fell back into the hole, out of sight.

More shots exploded at his feet and near his head. He had to keep moving, he knew. Standing in one place was just asking to die. As best he could, he fired up at the many targets and ran along the side, keeping away from the acid soaked ground. To his left he caught sight of a flickering ball lying in a green pool. Sparks and smoke rolled off it. The orb. The acid must be destroying it. Hopeful, he activated his summoner. Nothing happened.

A bolt of plasma blasted through his right thigh. Pain blinded him for a moment. He could feel himself falling. When his sight cleared he was lying on his side, half a meter from the green acid that crept slowly along. The orb was nearby, just two meters, but he knew he couldn't stand, and there was no way to get to it without crawling through pools of acid. Unless...

He still had a firm grasp on his staff. While holding onto its butt, he extended the staff as far as it would go. It was enough. The weapon's end touched the orb. He only needed to tap it gently in his direction.

A plasma bolt caught Jonah in his outstretched arm. He let out a profanity laced shout as his wrist went limp and his staff fell out of his hand. Another bolt blasted through his hip, just above the wound on his thigh. Choking down another series of profanities, he collapsed onto his back and lay staring up at the ceiling, waiting for the kill shot to come.

Tundra and Mr. White were literally locked in combat. The two had a tight hold on each other. White's fingers were wrapped around Tundra's throat and Tundra had his hands wedged between White's arms, trying to break free and put him back into another bear hug. Tundra poured on wave after wave of ice cold air onto White, but White held on with an uncanny determination.

"You—know—I am—the stronger!" Tundra growled between gasps for breath.

"Yes, I cannot keep this up much longer, I confess," White admitted, "not without another edge."

Mr. White's hands began to glow. A sparking white haze filled the air around Tundra's face. The haze grew with intensity until his whole face was lost in a blindingly bright aura. Tundra's head thrashed from side-to-side, trying to shake it off, but to no avail.

"Painfully bright, isn't it?" Mr. White mocked. "Don't you like how it penetrates your eyelids and fills your cornea with agonizing brilliance?"

Cold air pushed up against the ground and lifted Tundra into the air. White held on, squeezing his neck even tighter. Tundra spun around and around as he ascended, wind shooting out in every direction. White's fingers began to slip.

"Get—off me!" Tundra roared.

He brought both his fists down onto either side of White's head, knocking him off and sending him tumbling back to the floor below. Immediately the bright haze lifted from around Tundra's face.

Mr. White landed on his feet in a crouching position. He glared up at Tundra with a wicked sneer, though with less confidence than a moment before. Tundra let out a battle cry in Russian and soared down, ready to deliver a crushing blow. Mr. White became a blur of light and Tundra's fist struck nothing but acid soaked concrete. Before he had a chance to react, White reformed behind him and delivered a sharp jab to the small of his back. Tundra tried to turn to face him, but White was too quick. He grabbed him by the back of his neck, hoisted him up and then threw him against the nearest wall. The impact resounded with the loud clang of armor against stone. Tundra bounced off the wall and onto the floor. There were cracks in the wall from the force of the impact, yet he rose to his feet—barely. His knees trembled and he swayed to one side, but did not fall.

"Time to finish this," White said as he moved toward Tundra.

Ivan continued to dodge the barrage of plasma, firing wildly the whole time. He couldn't even be entirely sure at whom or what he was shooting at, at this point. He only hoped Kayla had taken his advice and stayed low. The graviflux lift was in full gear, gliding back and forth across the wet floor. Making another sharp turn, the lift came about and ran directly over a downed Hunter. Ivan cringed at the sound of crunching bones as metal tires bore down on the helpless Hunter. From the brief second he'd seen the Hunter, he'd appeared dead, or at least mortally wounded. Ivan tried to reassure himself that he hadn't killed the guy, but for all he knew, he had.

I didn't even get a chance to see who it was. Caucasian, so it wasn't Greg—could have been Jonah. Well, they can add that to my list of charges when they put me before the firing squad.

The graviflux lift jerked again as Ivan narrowly dodged another volley of weapon's fire. One bolt splashed against his windshield, incinerating the lower quarter instantly. Bits of red hot plasma sprayed against his chest, sending searing pain throughout his whole body.

The lift began to slide, loosing traction against the wet floor. He tried to compensate, but it only sent the tiny vehicle into a ninety degree turn in the opposite direction. Suddenly, a figure in burnt armor was standing directly in front of him. In his damaged armor, Ivan almost didn't recognize Dr. Vamperic. Both he and Ivan gave out an alarmed cry. Vamperic threw up his hands just as the lift came barreling straight toward him.

The two collided.   Vamperic was thrown up against the cracked windshield and the lift went into a three-hundred-sixty degree spin. Round and round it went. Ivan had the brakes on full, but there was simply no traction. He couldn't even tell in what direction they were spinning.

Something caught Ivan's attention out the corner of his eye. Even with the disorientation of the constant spin, he could see a flashing object lying off to the side. In one instant it would appear they were flying toward it and in another away from it.

It's that sphere, White's portal sphere!

Yanking the controls as hard as he could, he steered the spiraling lift in the direction of the pulsating globe. The lift spun faster, but they were getting closer and closer. Ivan leaned out, ready to grab the ball.

Vamperic grabbed Ivan's outstretched hand and pulled him nose to nose, his red eyes flashing with anger and fear. "Stop this contraption!!!"

Ivan tried to pull free, but Vamperic's grip was like a vice.   Time was running short. They were almost to the sphere. "Let go!!!" he shouted back. With his one free hand, he shoved the weapon's end of the staff against Vamperic's facemask and fired.

The discharge erupted against the metal mask and sent sizzling energy ricocheting in every direction.   Some of it caught Ivan on his chest and arm. Vamperic cried out and released Ivan. Ivan found himself tumbling out of the lift and toward a puddle of acid. The lift skidded on, slammed into the sphere and then collided against the wall. The sphere, caught between the lift and wall, exploded.

Dozens of portals opened all around where the lift had been a moment earlier. As Ivan plummeted to the floor, a portal opened and swallowed him whole. Then, as quickly as the portals had appeared, they closed simultaneously and were gone. Nothing of the lift, the sphere, of Ivan or Vamperic remained.

"Ivan! NO!!!!"

Kayla leaned over the edge of the platform, gaped down at the empty space where Ivan had been. Blood trickled out of her opened mouth. A nearby gunman turned as she cried out and leveled his rifle at her head.

An explosion shook the entire structure. The ceiling ripped away in a fiery blast, raining bits of rubble throughout the open, round room. At the force of the blast, several of the gunmen fell from their portholes. Small rocks, dirt, and dust covered Kayla like a blanket.

Mr. White took a step away from Tundra and covered his face from the falling debris. Peering up through his fingers, he could see the sky where once there had been a roof. A large glider floated into view and dropped long, dark bands of elastic that extended from the glider to three meters above the silo's floor. A wave of Gaoro troops slid down each one followed by a second wave.

The gunmen turned their attention to the incoming Gaoroes. The first round of volleys took out half the descending troops, but the second wave was ready. They blasted at the openings as they slid to the ends of the ropes and dropped to the ground. The acid sizzled against their feet, but their thick, armored boots were able to withstand.

A third wave of troops descended into the silo as plasma cannons from the glider's starboard side opened fire. The gunmen quickly retreated back into their holes, those that were able. A third were killed or wounded by the Gaoro's assault.

Mr. White watched in dismay as the room filled with alien soldiers. Tundra let out a boisterous laugh as White scanned the room for signs of surviving allies. "It seems the tides have turned once again, White, but this time not in your favor."

"This wasn't how it was supposed to go," he muttered.

"No, this is exactly as it should be, Traitor. You cannot escape justice, and justice will be served this day." Tundra drew back his fist and punched White square across the jaw. White staggered back and lost his footing. He tumbled down at the feet of a Gaoro soldier.

"Put your hands up and behind your head," the soldier said, leveling his rifle square against White's forehead.

"No, no I will not be defeated! Not now!!!"

White's entire body shimmered with a pure, white light. A beam of light shot out and struck the soldier, sending him flying across the room.

"Open fire!" someone shouted.

Over a dozen plasma rifles let loose, each one striking Mr. White. Bolts penetrated his back, chest, knees, and thighs. He began to ripple like water disturbed by a stone. The Gaoroes fired on and on. White's body contorted into strange, misshapen forms, but he got to his feet and remained there.

"What is this thing?" someone else shouted.

"Keep firing!!"

Tundra walked confidently through the rain of plasma and up to White. White's arms and legs rippled and bent like putty and his face contorted in anger. He glared at Tundra as the bolts ripped into his unnatural body. Tundra stood straight and tall, drew his lips into a firm, tight line, and pulled his fist back once more. When his fist made contact, White broke apart with a brilliant explosion. A rush of wind filled the air as blinding light erupted all around. Shards of white and black flew across the room in all direction. The closest Gaoroes were thrown back, but Tundra stood his ground as the blast washed over him.

The light dissipated and the silo grew quiet, save for the groans of the wounded.

"What was that?" one of the soldiers asked.

"A wrong set right," Tundra answered.

CHAPTER THIRTEEN

Five Gaoroes surrounded Traush in a semi-circle. Each one wielded a compact assault rifle no longer than their forearm and each one was pointed squarely at him. Gabor remained behind him with the barrel of his pistol pressed against the small of his back. A sixth Gaoro paced behind the others, keeping his eyes on Traush as he marched back and forth.

These six Gaoroes wore uniforms different than the four he'd just killed. The ones who had guarded the Matrix's entrance wore a light gray uniform with a logo similar to the Hunter's own logo. Obviously, that was an indication that they were assigned to the Compound. These Gaoroes, however, wore the same dark blue uniform that he'd seen all too often while being held on the Gaoro cruiser. They were naval soldiers, and the one pacing behind was clearly a naval officer.

At the back of the chamber, dozens of portals floated freely above a gaping chasm. They churned and moved, some growing smaller, others growing larger, as they drifted closer and then further from the thin, steel rail that separated the overlook from the cavern below. Traush had never seen the Matrix's core before. It was a marvelous sight, yet under the circumstances, he was not able to appreciate its beauty.

"So this is Michael Traush," the sixth Gaoro said. "You appear very lively for a dead man."

Traush offered no reply and was careful not to make any sudden motions. His hands were empty and his rifle lay on the ground two meters away where Gabor had forced him to drop it, but he knew that even unarmed the Gaoroes wouldn't hesitate to open fire if he made the slightest threatening move.

"Subcommander, I'd like to get started," Gabor said.

"Very well," the officer said. "A deal's a deal."

"And what deal is that?" Traush asked.

"I'm going back in time in your place, Traush," Gabor said. He returned his pistol to its holster, sat the silver briefcase down, and touched two of the flashing red buttons on the top. The case snapped open and automatically unfolded to reveal an oval shaped summoner hooked to a crude circuit board.

"You really think you're up to completing my mission?" *For that matter, why are the Gaoroes letting you?*

"Oh, I'm not going back to stop the minister's assassination. I'm going back to stop you," Gabor explained as he began to hook a series of loose wires from the circuit board into the summoner. "You really are the key I've been waiting for, but not the way Boss Marro thinks. You disappeared from your timeline seconds after my sister died. That means your temporal signature is very close to the moment I lost her, plus the few weeks you've been in this timeline. It's still close enough."

"Close enough for what?"

"Close enough for me to pinpoint the moment she died, then subtract about ten minutes," Gabor said. "I'll be waiting for you when you arrive at her apartment, and I'll kill you before you get a chance to strike."

"Don't be an idiot," Traush replied. "If you go into that apartment before I get there, your sisters will kill you. I can't believe Éva hasn't told you what she was like when she was possessed, what she could do, what she *did*."

Gabor scowled, but continued to work. "I know all about that. I'll take all the necessary precautions."

"It won't work," Traush warned.

"It's not your problem anymore. If you want something to worry about—," he motioned over to the Gaoro naval troops, "—worry about them."

"You're selling out the Resistance for what may seem like a noble act, but is really very selfish," Traush said. "You won't be able to complete my mission, and the Resistance's best hope of ending this war peacefully will be lost."

"That's where you're wrong," the subcommander said, cutting into the conversation. "Mr. Katona is actually ensuring a peaceful and beneficial solution for both sides, and so are you."

"I doubt that."

"You don't believe me?" The subcommander chided. "Ah, at gunpoint I doubt I'd feel much differently, but it's true. You see, there are some of us who believe this conflict with your people is putting us at unnecessary risk. With the Prajic on the move and with what we know about them now, we cannot afford a war on two fronts. Granted, the Resistance doesn't pose much of a threat, but it does pose a distraction, one we cannot afford. But unlike the Gaoroes who are assisting the Resistance in secret, we do not feel that it is in our best interest to leave Earth. Earth fought a war with us and lost. The new government signed a treaty with us. The treaty gave us dominion over the nearby spaceways and created a joint effort to develop and control the portals. This treaty is vital to the survivals of both our people."

"The Resistance would disagree," Traush said.

"Of course they disagree, but they only feel as strongly as they do because of Admiral V'Moreth and Commander Borxos' rash actions. The people I represent want to see the Civil Ministry restored. We want the humans to govern themselves once more and to have humans involved in the Hunter Project as they once were. Once this happens, many in the Resistance will be content and give up the struggle, including Boss Marro. The more radical elements within the Resistance will continue to plague us, but with greatly reduced numbers they won't be of any significance."

A hum resounded through the cavern. Traush glanced over and saw that Gabor had finished hooking the wires into the summoner. A thin, green beam shot out from a tiny dot on the oval surface and struck the closest portal floating within the swirl of the Matrix. The beam pulsated and, in rhythm with it, so did the portal.

Traush returned his attention to the subcommander. "Assuming any of what you say is true, how does capturing me help?"

"Gaoroes who think as I do are considered weak on matters of galactic defense. V'Moreth is using this rhetoric to keep us out of favor with the Gra Chamberlin. We need something to turn that around. Bringing the legendary Michael Traush to justice, now that—that would be something," the subcommander offered a twisted smile that seemed unnatural on his cow-like snout. "Your destruction of our cruiser has made you the highest profile criminal at large. When the Gra Chamberlin and the admiral learn that we caught you trying to destroy the Matrix, and just narrowly stopped you, they'll be indebted to us. That will give us the political leverage we need to make the changes necessary and help restore balance."

"Only I didn't come to destroy the Matrix," Traush said, "unless you plan to plant evidence to the contrary."

"No need. You brought the evidence with you." The subcommander motioned to the backpack.

"Ah, I didn't need two bombs, did I?"

"No, but Mr. Varona made sure to equip you with a second, so it would appear as if you came with terrorism in mind," the subcommander admitted.

"Clever," Traush said. "So Varona and Gabor worked this out with you?"

"Yes. As you humans say 'checkmate', Mr. Traush. But don't worry. Your death will serve your people all the same."

"My death? So you'll rig the trials to insure I get the maximum penalty, too?"

"Trials?" the subcommander lifted his hairy eyebrows and grinned. "They'll be no trials. When we found you, you resisted arrest and we killed you on the spot. That's what we'll tell them, anyway." The subcommander looked over at his troops as he addressed them. "Take careful aim, and remember, don't make it look like he was executed by a firing squad. Shoot out his knees, ribs… so forth. Thott, you get the headshot."

The five Gaoroes raised their rifles level with their snouts and took aim. Traush let his body weight tip backwards. As the plasma bolts went flying toward him, he went somersaulting in the opposite direction. He could feel the sting of plasma cutting into his flesh, but his mind blocked the pain as best he could and he rolled sideways, toward Gabor. The five Gaoroes tracked Traush and squeezed off a second round. More bolts ripped through the air, but this time he was ready. His body twisted and contorted as he did a second back-flip. He could feel the heat of the bolts soar passed, but not a one hit its target.

Traush came down directly behind Gabor. The young engineer knelt motionless over the pulsating summoner, frozen with fear as he gaped over his shoulder at Traush. Giving him no time to respond, Traush grabbed Gabor by the neck and hoisted him up, placing the young engineer between him and the firing squad. He held Gabor in a tight headlock, restricting—though not cutting off—his air flow.

"Cease fire!!!" the subcommander shouted, waving his hands at the five soldiers.

"Drop your weapons or I'll snap his neck," Traush said, his voice cold and deliberate.

"And what will that accomplish?" the subcommander asked. "If you do that, we'll just gun you down on the spot."

"Then it better not come to that. Guns down!"

"Mr. Traush, we can't let you go. It simply isn't an option," the subcommander said. His voice carried the tone of irritation, but Traush could see beads of sweat forming along his brow. "You're a soldier, born and bred to die for a higher calling. This is it. You will help your people and we'll give you a clean death, one that any Rensha would be proud of."

"I'll pass." Traush ripped the pistol from Gabor's belt and opened fire. He dropped the subcommander and two of the soldiers within the first second. The other three froze, unsure of what to do. He dropped another. The remaining two opened fire. Traush shoved Gabor out of the way and threw himself in the opposite direction. Hitting the ground, he rolled out of the oncoming volley, came up and fired twice more. He caught the closest Gaoro in the neck, dropping him as well. The second shot hit the other in the arm. The soldier cried out and recoiled, his rifle still firing, but now firing shots that went wild. Traush pulled the trigger one last time and struck him between the eyes.

Gabor lay on the ground, staring at Traush, horrified. "Are you going to kill me now?" he asked.

Traush got to his feet and dusted off. "It may surprise you, but no," he answered. "I've killed more people than you can imagine with my own hands, but I'm not a murderer, and I didn't murder your sister. Something powerful controlled her—a force we've never come to comprehend, and hopefully will never see again. If it helps you to grieve, go on hating me, but don't sell your soul to that hate."

Traush bent down over the summoner and checked the controls. He didn't know enough about this type of device to know if it was operating properly. "Is it configured for the temporal jump?"

"Yeah," Gabor managed weakly.

"Then we need to move the date, put it two months ahead like Marro told us," Traush said. "How do I do that?"

"You can't. It's a complex formula. It would take about an hour for me to configure."

Traush could detect no deception in his voice or in his eyes—plenty of hate, but no deception. He swore under his breath and tried to figure out his next move.

The echo of hurried, booted feet came thundering from outside the chamber. Traush glanced back at the damaged door that hung partially open. More Gaoroes were coming. Were they more naval officers, or had Portal Security realized something was going on? It didn't matter, not for Traush, but it would for Gabor. If it was security, they'd detain him, torture him, and extract all his secrets.

Traush pointed to his coat pocket. "You'd better switch on that summoner of yours and get out of here." Without waiting for a response, Traush bolted forward and charged straight for the pulsating green portal. The beam from the silver case continued to shine on, feeding its unusual properties into the portal. Traush poured as much speed into his stride as possible, closing the distance between it and him. The sound of metal against stone reverberating throughout the chamber as the Core's damaged door swung open. Traush didn't dare look back. The distance closed—eight meters, six, four...

There were angry shouts in Straffies, words Traush didn't understand, though their meaning was clear. He flung himself toward the portal, soaring over the chasm ledge and straight for the portal's mouth. Bolts of plasma flew all around him, seemingly coming from everywhere. A hot rush of searing pain tore into his lower back as one of the bolts found its target. The blast sent him spiraling out of control, tumbling head over end. Vertigo and the shock from the pain made it impossible for him to tell where he was falling. He no longer knew if he was aimed at the temporal portal or plummeting into the depth of the chasm. There were portals drifting all around. Without warning, a sparkling mist came up and swallowed him whole.

* * * *

The sun shone merciless in the sky. Ivan sat alone on a small patch of sand, shielding his eyes and waiting. The island he found himself on was no more than ten meters in each direction, and nothing but sand and a bit of rock. All around was the sea. There was no sign of land, ship, or glider in any direction, only water and sun. He was soaking wet, but even so, he felt hot and exhausted. With a sigh, he fell back against the beach and stared up at the cloudless sky.

A hiss sounded next to him as a gold and silver portal took shape.

"About time," Ivan muttered. A Hunter stepped through, flanked by two judicial officers both carrying stun sticks and pistols. Ivan sat up. "What took you so long?"

"Where is Dr. Vamperic?" the Hunter asked.

Ivan tapped a hollow suit of metal that rested next to him. It was charred, scratched, and cracked open down the chest piece. The mask that had once seemed so fearsome laid sideway covered in sand. "That's all that's left of him," Ivan said.

The Hunter marched up to the armor suit and prodded it with his staff. "Where's the body?"

Ivan tipped the armor on its side. A pile of black ash spilled onto the tiny beach. "That's all that's left," Ivan explained. "The portal dropped us in the ocean, about twenty meters out. I had no trouble swimming to shore, but Vamperic sunk like a rock. Eventually, he came strolling up onto the beach. As soon as he was out of the water, he dropped and started thrashing about, tried covering up the exposed skin and shouting something about the sun. He burned to a crisp within seconds. Never seen anything like it. Can't say I'm sorry. I don't think this island was big enough for the two of us."

The Hunter gave Ivan a curious look. "No... I suppose not."

The two judicial officers came up alongside Ivan. "Are you finished?" one said to the Hunter.

"Yes, we can head back if you're ready," he answered.

"Sergeant Jast, we're taking you back into custody," the second judicial officer said as he stroked his stun stick.

"Let me guess," Ivan said. "I'm late for my court-martial."

* * * *

The brilliant display of color was replaced suddenly with a dim haze. A dark gray surface rushed up to meet Traush as he plummeted out of the portal and landed head first onto hard concrete. He let out a grunt and rolled onto his back. His body had gone numb—whether from the impact against the concrete or from the plasma wound in his back, he wasn't sure. Either way, the numbness was welcome.

It took a second for the vertigo to pass and for Traush to regain a sense of his surroundings. The air was hot and dry. He was outside, lying on a sidewalk, staring up into a cloudless, blue sky. The shade of a tall, nearby building covered him from the harsher rays of the sun.

The numbness began to fade and the pain returned. *Pain is only what you make of it.* The Rensha mantra came to mind, and he repeated it several times, mouthing it wordlessly, before trying to stand up. Slowly, he rolled onto his side. Waves of agony hit him, but he repeated the mantra once more and pushed himself up, just slightly.

Just then, he heard something he had not expected, and it made him wonder if he was going mad. It was his own voice, only he had said nothing. It was not a recorded sound. It was too natural for that.

Where am I?

He lay in between two buildings, approximately six stories tall. The walkway he had fallen onto led back behind the buildings in what appeared to be a storage area. Ahead there were more buildings, identical to these two. He recognized them at once.

This is Corporal Katona's apartment complex.

From where he lay he could see the winding stairwell that led up to Éva's unit. There, on the third floor landing, he saw himself descending the stairs followed by a group of policemen.

It worked. Gabor's calculations worked. Traush felt a wave of relief knowing he'd fallen through the right portal. When the plasma round struck him, he just knew it had thrown him off course and into a different portal. There had been others to disappear in the Matrix before. Oran Cavar, the former head of the Resistance, had been in the Core when Admiral V'Moreth gave the order to start bombing the city. One of the blasts had hit the Compound and caused Cavar to lose balance and tumble into the swirling maze of portals. No one had seen him since.

Traush tried to push himself back onto his feet, but his legs would not obey. The wound to his back was more serious than he'd realized. He tried moving his ankles and toes, with some degree of success. *Not paralyzed, at least.* All the same, he could take no immediate action. He watched helplessly as his other self reached the top of the stairs and as the police officers took positions near the door. In less than a minute, those officers would be dead and Traush would be hurled three years into the future.

He opened his mouth to call out a warning, but then closed it without a word. *No,* he told himself, *better let this play out.* He'd heard the story from Ivan. If he did nothing and let this thing unfold as it had before, Ivan and a future Ivan would stop Éva.

"Move! Move!" Traush watched as the police officers stormed inside the apartment. Weapon's fire followed. Traush knew they had all just been killed. His other self moved close to the door, holding his staff out in front of him. Taking aim, his other self fired at something in the apartment.

I just collapsed the portal, Traush recalled.

A woman let out an angry cry and the other Traush rushed into the apartment and out of sight.

"Incredible," a voice said, less than three meters from where Traush lay.

Traush started to reach for a weapon and roll onto his back, but he had lost his pistol when falling through the portal and rolling onto his back caused him so much pain, he almost blacked out.

"Easy, Michael, easy. You're hurt. Try not to move more than you have to," the voice said again.

A man stood at the far end of the short alleyway near the storage doors, hidden in the shadow of the two tall buildings. He was medium height, with a muscular, though not impressive, build. Despite the heat, he wore an overcoat with a hood pulled up around his face. He was African, Traush could tell from what little skin was visible, though the man's voice was too gruff to distinguish any regional accent.

"You know me?" Michael asked, hoarsely.

"Who doesn't know the infamous Michael Traush?"

"And who are you?"

The man looked away and up at Éva's apartment. There was nothing to see from where he stood. Inside, the other Traush was fighting for his life against two deadly, demonic women.

"So it's true," the man said. "You really have been to the future."

"What are you talking about?" Traush asked, trying to act bewildered at the man's comment. In fact, he was. How could anyone know he'd been to the future?

The man looked down at Traush. His face was hidden in the black shadow of his hood, but Traush thought he could detect a smile. "I saw what you just saw. I saw you, running up those stairs with armed officers behind you, while you lay here in this alleyway watching. Two Traushes in the same place at the same time? There's only one way that's possible."

"Saying I just time traveled here is a pretty big conclusion to jump to," Traush responded.

"Maybe, but it's true," the man said. "You've seen the future. You know what's going to happen in the few short years to come. You know what the Gaoroes are going to do to us, and you've come back to stop it."

"Who are you?" Traush tried to put as much force into his voice as he could.

The man started toward him. "Someone who also wants to stop what is coming. Someone who knows some of what you know and is in a position to help you complete the mission Boss Marro sent you on. My name is Raspin."

Beams of indirect light pushed away some of the shadow that hid his face. The man's mouth and chin were badly scarred. He was wearing a golden helmet that covered much of the rest of his face, and his eyes shone with a faint ruby glow.

"You're from the future?"

Raspin let out a hollow, raspy chuckle. "No, not quite."

Traush tried to push himself up further. Raspin came up alongside him and knelt down. "Easy. Don't push yourself. You're hurt bad, but not as bad as all that."

"I need to get to a hospital," Traush replied.

"That wouldn't be wise," Raspin said. "Corporal Katona's father is going to pin his youngest daughter's death on you. You'll be wanted for murder. Don't worry, I'll send for some of my men. We'll get you out of here and to someplace safe. I know some physicians who can do top notch work." Raspin tapped the gold dome that covered most of his head and smiled. "I should know. We'll have you back on your feet in a couple of days. Then we can talk. You and I, Michael, we're going to change the course of humankind—forever."

CHAPTER FOURTEEN

The door to Kayla's hospital room swung open. Instinctively, Kayla tried to sit up to greet her visitor, despite the shooting pain that coursed throughout her midsection. "Director," she said, seeing her superior officer approach her bedside.

"Please, do not get up," he replied with a wave of his hand. "I thought you'd want to know, we located Sergeant Jast. He's safe and back in custody."

"Thank God." She lay back down, slowly and carefully. "What happened?"

"He was inadvertently transported to a small island in the Pacific along with Dr. Vamperic. Vamperic did not survive the experience, but the sergeant is well enough."

"The Pacific? How on Earth did he get there?"

"The spherical device he destroyed contained what can only be described as a mini-Matrix. When it shattered, the portals inside were released and spread across the room. Sergeant Jast and Vamperic were sucked in before it collapsed. If it wasn't for the tracer still embedded in his body, we would have had no way of finding him."

"That's twice the tracer saved his life," Kayla said with an ironic smile.

"Yes," Ferrgerr agreed. "It makes me wonder if putting one in all Hunters wouldn't be such a bad idea." Kayla's smile disappeared and she stared, stone-faced up at Ferrgerr. "Perhaps not," he added.

He turned and started for the door. "Well, I must report back to Command and Control. I hope you will feel better soon, Lieutenant."

"Director, you said Sergeant Jast was back in custody."

"That's correct," Ferrgerr said, pausing at the door. "His trial was scheduled to begin two hours ago. The authorities were understandably concerned when he failed to appear."

"But given the circumstances, they can't seriously hold this against him," Kayla replied, trying to hide her fear and anger.

"I am sure they will sort it out. Good day, Lieutenant."

* * * *

Cadet Akhtar was given the honor of escorting Tundra through the Portal Compound. The other Hunters were leery of the tall Russian's presence. Many of them had fought against him when he first arrived and the rest had heard the stories, yet Cadet Akhtar had a completely different attitude. It was the single most mesmerizing moment of his life.

After giving Tundra a tour of the facility, the cadet took him back to the portal bay where two other Hunters waited. Between them lay the remains of Dr. Vamperic's armor.

"The director told us to give this to you," one of the Hunters said, poking the metal suit with his staff.

Tundra threw it over his left shoulder and placed his right fist proudly against his hip. "This is not exactly what I expected to bring back with me, but it will make a fine trophy," he said in his usual, booming voice. "At least we won't return empty handed."

"It feels empty," Fast Track said, limping into the portal bay escorted by a medical technician. She no longer resembled a water sports athlete. Some of the acid had drained over to where she lay unconscious during the battle, destroying her hero's costume and leaving a nasty scar along her leg and thigh. Thick silicon wrappings covered the wounds, but they did not hide the bruises that marked her arms and face, nor the misshapen appearance of her nose. Her other leg was bound in an aluminum cast. The cast supported some of her weight, but only with short, quick steps.

"Ah, Fast Track, it is good to see you back on your feet," he said.

"You call this 'back on feet'? I can barely walk. I can't even move fast enough to teleport," she grumbled.

"You will recover, my dear, in time," he answered. "Dr. Vamperic and Mr. White, however, won't."

"I suppose that is something," she admitted.

Director Ferrgerr entered behind Fast Track and came over to Tundra. "The Civil Ministry and the Gaoro diplomatic office extend their appreciation to you both for helping us rescue two of our own and for stopping two potentially dangerous criminals."

Fast Track snorted. "'Potentially'?"

Ferrgerr gave her a sideways glance and went on. "Potentially, yes. We do not know what they intended to do with the sphere, but portal technology in the wrong hands can cause untold damage."

"Indeed!" Tundra boomed. "With that technology I shudder to think what they might have accomplished. They would have used it against your world and ours. It is we who should be thanking you."

"Don't thank me, yet. I am not entirely sure we are repaying your assistance with kindness." Ferrgerr turned toward the bay's control panel. Major

Mubarak worked busily entering a series of calculations into the Matrix's interface. "Well, Major?"

Mubarak shrugged. "I can pull it up, that's not the problem."

"Uh, what is he talking about?" Fast Track asked.

"The major believes he can send you back to your dimension, not without risk, however," Ferrgerr answered.

"The risks are acceptable," Tundra said, holding his head up high.

"They are? What risks are those?" Fast Track asked.

"I was able to recover the exact frequency the portal was on when both Dr. Vamperic and you appeared in this portal bay," Mubarak explained. "But there are two problems I see. For starters, the portal is nothing but a spatial portal. We know you didn't come from our Earth. You have to be from either another dimension or an alternate timeline. This portal is neither. The second problem is we can't pinpoint where the other side opens to. It goes literally nowhere, or nowhere I can trace. Theoretically, this will work, but for all I know I'm about to port you into a black hole, or out of existence entirely."

"Oh, that's just great. Just great," she muttered.

"You don't have to do this," Ferrgerr said.

"We must go back, Director. We have duties and responsibilities on our own Earth," Tundra replied. "If this is the only way, then so be it. The International Department of Justice faces danger every day. We will face this. Besides, I have every confidence in your major."

Fast Track looked over at Mubarak for a sign of reassurance. He merely shrugged and then pressed a switch. A gleaming silver and gold portal appeared in the center of the bay.

"Well, if you're ready then," Mubarak said.

"We are," Tundra answered. He reached over and placed his right arm around Fast Track. "Come, my dear, it is time for us to go home."

Fast Track's face paled noticeably as Tundra helped her to the portal, but she offered no further objection. They paused at the portal's mouth. "Here goes nothing," she said. With that, they both stepped through.

As soon as they were through, the portal collapsed. Mubarak gave out a muffled gasp. "What is it, Major? Did they make it?" Ferrgerr asked.

Mubarak began working the controls. "I can't tell. As soon as they entered, the portal lost stability. That could mean anything. I'm still not getting a reading from the other side. Either way, they're gone."

Ferrgerr stared silently at the place where the portal had been seconds earlier. "Hmmm," he muttered, then turned and walked out of the bay.

* * * *

The young Gaoro aid waited patiently outside the Prime Minister's office, admiring the stonework along the walls. The heavy oak doors that separated the lounge from the Prime Minister's suite opened and Malena Isben came marching out, carrying a thin metallic sheet in her hand. The young aid rose to his feet.

"The ambassador sent you?" Malena asked.

"Yes, he said you had something for him."

She handed the metallic sheet to the Gaoro. "Tell him it wasn't easy, but I got it done."

"Is this the original?" he asked.

"Of course not," she replied quickly. "I already sent the original to the Ministry of Justice. The announcement will be made tomorrow morning."

The aid gave Malena a short bow. "Thank you, ma'am. I will inform the ambassador at once."

* * * *

Ivan sat on the front row next to his attorney, staring up at the high justice's bench. Earlier, only the high justice had been absent from the courtroom, but now all three judges were missing. The other two had entered the courtroom ten minutes ago, but were promptly ushered out to the high justice's chambers by an aid. Ivan could tell by the look on the two judges faces that they weren't expecting the summons, and there had been no sign of them since.

Ivan waited with as much patience he could muster. He shifted in his seat, constantly crossing and uncrossing his legs, leaning back, sitting forward. The restlessness would not leave him. It was the first day of the actual trial. Considering that his bail had been revoked, he was feeling less and less optimistic about the outcome. If they were penalizing him for being held hostage by a madman, could he expect any further leniency? The judges' disappearance from the courtroom only increased his anxiety.

He leaned toward his attorney. "Is this normal?" he whispered.

"Hmmm?"

"Making us wait like this?"

"It's uncommon, but not unheard of," his attorney answered in a hushed voice. "Don't worry. It's probably just a procedural matter."

Ivan slumped in his chair and sighed. He tried to distract himself with other thoughts, but it was useless. In his mind, he could hear them reading the guilty verdict over and over again.

Glancing back, he peered around the room to see who was in attendance. Kayla sat nearby. Ivan couldn't help but notice how rough she looked. Signs of bruising were visible on her arms and face, her hair was out of place, and she looked tired, very tired. Regardless, she was a welcome sight. He hadn't seen her since their rescue and he wasn't sure how badly she'd been injured during the battle.

There was no sign of Greg or Jonah. Both had survived the battle, he'd heard, but like Kayla, he was given no information beyond that. He hoped they were okay.

The rear door opened as a lanky judicial officer came inside, escorting Director Ferrgerr. The two exchanged hushed words. The judicial officer then nodded and left.

Ferrgerr took a seat next to Kayla. Ivan could tell by Kayla's expression that she was surprised to see him. She opened her mouth to say something to him, but never had a chance to speak.

"All rise!" a voice boomed.

The side door to the justice's chambers opened and all three judges filed out, High Justice Gowon in the lead. Everyone stood as Gowon stepped onto a small platform and ascended to the top bench. As they waited for Gowon to take his seat, Ivan noticed that the high justice was carrying something with him. It was a thin metallic sheet cut to about fifteen by twenty centimeters. There was an official seal on the top edge, but Ivan could not make it out from where he stood.

Once Gowon reached his bench, the bailiff motioned and everyone took their seats. The high justice took the sheet and inserted it into a console. There was a flash of light as the computer accepted the insertion. The courtroom fell silent as the judge read what was displaying in front of him. Finally, he cleared his throat and leaned forward.

"Will the defendant please rise," he announced.

Ivan glanced over at his attorney, who nodded and gestured for him to stand. As he got to his feet, Ivan felt a sudden tightness in his throat. The trial hadn't even begun. Was he about to announce a sentence without as much as a hearing? Ivan remembered what Kayla had told him about the political nature of his case and feared the worst.

"He's just going to read the charges again," his attorney whispered in his ear, as he stood beside him.

"Sergeant Ivan Jast," the high justice began. His voice resounded throughout the court. "I have received a document from the Office of the Prime Minister, which has also been reviewed and approved by the Ministry of Justice. In conjunction with a request from the Gaoro envoy, represented by Ambassador Humrun, I would like to ask Ruthr Ferrgerr, Director of Portal Security, to come forward to make a statement."

Ivan's head jerked back in the direction where Ferrgerr sat. The director rose to his feet without a sign of surprise and made his way to the front of the courtroom. Facing Ivan and his attorney, he folded his hands behind his back and began.

"Sergeant Jast, during your recent abduction by a terrorist group as of yet unidentified, you committed several acts of heroism above and beyond the call of duty, especially in light of your pending hearings. Due to your quick thinking, you managed to thwart an ambush set for the unit I dispatched to rescue you, and during the conflict that ensued, you destroyed what has been deemed an item of contraband that posed a serious threat to portal security and the security of this planet. On behalf of the Civil Union of the United Earth and as your commanding officer, I am pleased to announce that you are hereby pardoned of any past crimes and reinstated on active duty."

All the blood rushed to Ivan's head. He had to grab hold of the table in front of him to keep from falling over. His attorney gave him a firm pat on the back and shook his hand, though Ivan hardly even noticed.

The courtroom erupted. There were applause and cheers, but there were also angry shouts and cries of foul. Mostly, the room was roaring with voices shocked by what they just heard.

Director Ferrgerr stood looming in front Ivan. He hadn't even seen the director walk up. Ferrgerr held out a hand. "Congratulations, Sergeant."

"Thank you, sir," he answered weakly.

"If you feel that you are able, I would appreciate it if you would report in at o-eight-hundred tomorrow."

"Yes, sir, I will do that."

A judicial officer marched over to him and motioned toward a side door. "If you'll come with me, we'll remove the tracer," he said.

As the judicial officer led him toward the exit, Ivan looked back over his shoulder at the throng of people who had gathered. There were both happy and unhappy faces, though at the moment everything seemed a blur and he couldn't honestly say if there was more of one than the other. There was one face, however, he could spot clearly through the sea of confusion. Kayla Marro remained in her seat, watching Ivan as he went. She contained her smile well, but Ivan could see it, and he could see the tears that swelled in the corner of her eyes. He gave her a reassuring smile and a wave and then hurried after the judicial officer.

* * * *

Malena Isben and Minister Al-Falahi sat in the comfortable, plush chairs of the lounge adjoining Ambassador Humrun's office. The ambassador sat in the seat next to Malena sipping a white wine vintage that she had brought for the occasion. In the center of the room floated a holographic image of Director Ferrgerr, reading this statement to the packed courtroom. The scene quickly cut to the evening reporters who began to offer commentaries.

"A happy ending to a potentially disastrous event," Humrun said with satisfaction.

"By averting disaster, are you referring to the lives Sergeant Jast saved?" Malena asked.

"No, I'm talking about the political disaster that would have followed if the sergeant had been found guilty," Humrun replied. He lifted his glass toward Al-Falahi. "I appreciate your role in averting this disaster, Minister."

"It was not a political decision, ambassador," he responded. "I reviewed the facts. The sergeant acted heroically. He deserved accommodation. These are not the acts of a traitor. There was no need for the trial to continue."

"Be that as it may, my thanks." Humrun downed the contents of his glass.

"Yes, well, it's getting late," Al-Falahi said as he checked his watch. He rose from his seat. "I had best be off. Thank you for your hospitality, as always."

"My pleasure," Humrun replied with a smile.

An aid saw the minister to the door and escorted him outside. Humrun watched him go.

"The minister is a fair man, but he's no politician," he said after Al-Falahi was gone.

"No, he's a political appointee. There's a difference," Malena said. "He wants to do what's right, which is how he got the job. He's not comfortable with these backroom dealings. If you want to keep him as an ally, you won't rub his face in it."

"But such dealings don't bother you, Ms. Isben, even though you are also an appointee," Humrun noted in a casual tone, as he refilled his glass.

"No, of course not. I work in the heart of the most cutthroat place on Earth. You learn the trade if you want to survive."

"Quite." Humrun said, taking another sip. "Well, as with the minister, I appreciate what you did."

"You can save your thanks. I had no intention of seeing a war hero lynched just because it's what the Gaoroes wanted. That's not justice."

"Ah, by Gaoroes I take it you mean Commander Borxos. After all, it was my suggestion to—"

"—to use the fact that Ivan Jast saved the lives and helped stop two dangerous sub-dimensional beings from doing God only knows what. Yes, I know, Ambassador, but your motives weren't entirely selfless, either."

"Oh?"

"Commander Borxos is no friend of yours. I suspect there is more between your rivalry than a difference in policy regarding the Hunter project, but in any event, you used the sergeant as a piece in your little chess match." She gave him a hard, knowing stare. "But understand that I am not a pawn in your little game. I got the Prime Minister to sign the pardon not for you or your rival. I will not be used. Never forget that."

* * * *

Ivan leaned back on the king size bed and waited. His heart was racing. He wasn't sure if it was from fear or excitement. The past few weeks had been the most intense of his life since the Siege, and in some ways even more intense on a personal level, yet none of that anxiety or exhilaration matched what he felt now. Kayla should be arriving any moment, and when she did, he would make a formal proposal.

Telling someone you want to marry them while dangling above boiling acid just doesn't count, he told himself with a grin.

Since she had technically already proposed to him, he didn't know why he was so nervous. He guessed it came from the knowledge of how much his life was about to change, and for once not under dire circumstances. It would be a strange thing to be a married man. Ever since his brother's arrest and his father's murder, he'd been on his own, just living from day to day. When he was drafted into the Army of the New Moon, he became little more than a slave. The idea of family seemed like a distant memory. Now it was about to become a reality once more.

Soft footsteps could be heard outside, coming down the hall. Ivan sat up and planted his feet against the carpeted floor. As the door handle began to turn, Ivan tensed. Flash backs of Major LeStrange and his men surprising him came to mind. Ivan had reserved this room for him and Kayla at an out-of-the-way, much lower profile hotel, but lower profile or not, how was he sure this hotel didn't have members of the Resistance working here, as well? They must have had people working at the Ramora. It was the only way they could have known where they would be, but no one knew just how far the Resistance's network went. For all he knew, he could easily be in the corner of another trap, only this time he didn't have a tracer in his arm to lead the Hunters to him.

The door opened. The familiar silhouette of Kayla Marro stood in the entrance way. Ivan let out a sigh of relief and went over to her. "Hey there," he said as he embraced her.

Kayla flinched at his touch and pulled back sharply. "Ow! Careful!" she said.

"Oh, sorry. Still sore?"

"If that's what you call having your ribs held together by steel netting, yeah," Kayla glanced nervously back into the empty corridor outside. "We'd better get inside."

"Sure," he motioned for her to enter, "but I really don't think there's anyone around here we know. Besides, we're not going to be a secret much longer."

Those words got no reaction. Kayla stood in the center of the room, staring at the wall. Ivan came up behind her and began massaging her shoulders. He suddenly felt even more nervous than moments before, but did his best to force the anxiety away.

"Hey, what's wrong?" he asked.

She turned toward him and gave him a faint smile. "Oh, nothing. It's just—these last few weeks have been very taxing."

Ivan brushed his fingers gently up and down her arm. "You don't have to tell me. I knew it would work out, though."

"Did you?" she said playfully.

"Well, truth be told, I was pretty surprised by the pardon," he admitted. "I'd hoped for maybe a commuted sentence, or a slap on the hand—anything but an accommodation."

"You're a hero again," Kayla said, "but then to me, you always were." She leaned forward and kissed him.

He drew a hand up against the back of her neck and held her for what felt like a long time, careful not to inflame her injuries. After what felt like several minutes (though he knew it must have only been a few seconds) she pulled slowly away. He bowed his head forward and rested his forehead against hers.

"I love you," he said.

"I know. I love you, too."

"So, do those friends of yours still have that marriage license lying around?"

Kayla stiffened. Ivan took a step back and tried to make eye contact. She glanced uneasily from side to side. "What? What is it?" he asked.

"Ivan—" she started. Ivan felt his heart skip a beat. "You know how much I love you," she said, finally. She looked at him, but her eyes refused to meet his.

"I sense a 'but' coming on."

"Ivan, you just got reinstated. Your career's back on track. It was a close call, but it's back on track."

"Right," he replied, speaking the word as if it were not true.

Kayla finally met his gaze. "Remember what I told you earlier, about your trial?" she asked. Her words were slow and deliberate.

"What in particular?"

"About it becoming political," she said. "There are people in both the Civil Ministry and the Gaoroes who were very happy to see you pardoned, but there are others who feel cheated."

"Commander Borxos, you mean."

She nodded. "He's a powerful man."

"He's not even a man," Ivan countered. "What does he have to do with us, anyway?"

"They'll be watching you closely," she explained. "Remember, my family has been involved in politics a long time. I know how this goes. He won't be able to let this slide, but now that you're a free man and a public figure he can't touch you, not without really good cause."

"So you're saying if we get married, he'll have me arrested for fraternizing with a superior officer."

"He'll ruin you, ruin us both," Kayla said. "I don't care what he'll do to me, but I won't be the reason your life falls apart."

"Kayla, you're the reason my life *hasn't* fallen apart," he put his hands on her shoulders and drew her close. "Without you, what would I be? We both agreed it was worth the risk to be together."

"We take a risk to be together every time we meet, but getting married isn't a risk, it's a losing battle," she replied.

Ivan pulled away from her and paced over to the door and then back to the foot of the bed. "It was even more of a risk when you asked me to marry you. Why the heck did you even bother, if this is how you feel?"

Kayla curled her lips down into a frown that reflected both sadness and anger. "The risk was higher for me. You were already in a bad spot."

Ivan stopped pacing. "You didn't think I was going to get off, did you?"

Kayla hesitated, as if searching for the right words. "No," she answered flatly. "If you hadn't tipped that vat over and smashed that sphere, they would have nailed you to the wall."

"Thanks for the vote of confidence," he replied with a sarcastic tone.

"Ivan, I have every intention of marrying you, just not now," she said. The anger had left her. She walked up to him and placed her hands on his shoulders and stared into his eyes. This time, it was he who looked away. "Ivan, look at me. I love you. If you're asking me to marry you, the answer is yes."

Ivan's eyes snapped over and locked with hers. They were wide with surprise. He felt his heart skip a beat again. His frustration rolled back into anxiety once more. "You mean that?"

"Yes, I will marry you, but not right now."

The mounting frustration returned with a flash.

"I'm doing this because I love you, and I don't want anything to come between us. You're in good standing once more. If we wait, you might be able to push and get onto a fast track to become an officer. You might make lieutenant in six months, a year tops—*if* we're careful. Once you're promoted we can be married right away."

"Wouldn't that look suspicious?" he asked with a touch of bitterness in his voice.

She ignored his tone and replied with a shrug. "Probably, but it won't matter. They won't be able to stop us or penalize us, and if Commander Borxos or any of his allies haven't touched you by then, something else will most likely preoccupy their attention. The world moves fast in the political arena."

Ivan chewed this over in his mind. The disappointment was difficult to bear. He felt as if someone had punched him in the chest and looking at Kayla's pleading eyes only made it worse. And yet, there was something else. Behind the gnawing disappointment, he felt a sense of relief.

"All right, we've waited this long, I guess a few more months isn't that big a deal," he said.

He leaned forward and gave her a short, half-hearted kiss and then turned for the door. "This was probably a bad idea anyway, meeting like this."

"You're leaving?" she asked.

"I'm on duty in the morning. I really should go home and get some rest," he opened the door then paused and looked back. "Wouldn't want to be late on my first day back. It might give the commander something to jump on."

With that, he stepped outside and shut the door behind him. Kayla stood staring at the closed door for a moment and then sat at the foot of the bed. The ache in her ribs started to throb and she felt suddenly very alone.

* * * *

Attila Katona sat alone at the back of the bar, an untouched beer in his hand. All around were the sounds of loud voices and the sour smell of cheap liquor, but he didn't notice any of it. He merely sat, staring blankly at his beer

"Rough day?" a voice said.

Ati glanced up. Pavao stood there holding a beer bottle. "Mind if I sit down?" Without waiting for an answer, Pavao took the seat across from him, uncapped his beer and took a swig. "Quite a crowd at the courthouse yesterday, wouldn't you say?"

Ati grunted an inaudible response.

"So, I heard you were looking for me," Pavao said. "Is there something I can do for you?"

"You talked about justice," Ati muttered.

"Come again?"

"Justice, the other night when we were talking, you said justice wasn't up to the authorities." he went on.

"Yeah, true. If a wrong gets set right, does it matter who did it?" Pavao took another swig.

Ati turned his head toward the bar. A holo-image of two political commentators floated just below the ceiling. The den of the usual after hour crowd made it impossible for him to hear what they were saying, but in between the two commentators was another holo-image of Ivan Jast with the words 'Pardon: Fair or Foul?'.

"Not to me, it doesn't," Ati answered. He turned his head back toward Pavao. "I've got one daughter lying in an insane asylum and another lying in a morgue, all because of these blasted Hunters. No one's paid for what's happened to my little girls, and someone's got to."

Pavao sat his beer down on the table. "Couldn't agree with you more."

"You said—" Ati paused. "You said you knew some people."

"People who could get justice," Pavao finished.

Ati said nothing at first, and then just nodded.

Pavao placed his arms behind his head and leaned back, grinning. "Oh, yeah. I sure enough do, and with your help, I'm certain we can get justice for both your girls. Oh, yeah, I do not doubt it."

* * * *

The last few days had been hard. They were the hardest Peter LeStrange had experienced since he'd joined the New Resistance. It was bad enough that they'd wasted resources, time, and even personnel on the debacle with Dr. Vamperic, but Raspin's refusal to meet with him privately since the plan went south added insult to injury. He didn't want to point out Raspin's failure in front of the others, but he was dying to speak with him and find out why on Earth he ever thought dealing with a trans-dimensional madman was a good idea.

"Well, at least one thing has gone as planned," Peter LeStrange said with a sigh. He marched down the long flights of stairs of the Indigo Towers descending into the basement. As always, the stairwell as dark and quiet, save for the echo of his own feet and the feet of the man who walked beside him.

"Yeah, it was a piece of cake. It just took time and a little priming," Pavao said.

"You're certain of his conviction?" LeStrange asked.

"Yeah, certain enough," Pavao answered. "Honestly, the guy hates the Hunters worse than we do. I don't think Mr. Katona would give a single one a glass of water if they were on fire, save for his daughter, but that's not a problem anymore."

'She might return to active duty," LeStrange said.

"Ah, the girl's off her rocker. We'll have plenty of time. Any idea what Raspin wants him to do?"

"No," LeStrange answered. "He just wanted someone else on the inside."

"Sounds fair," Pavao said, nodding. "Now, mind you, Mr. Katona is a proud man but a little spineless, if you ask me. Sure, he'll help us, but don't ask him to put a gun to Ferrgerr's head and pull the trigger or anything like that."

"I'm sure that's not what the boss has in mind," LeStrange said.

The stairs came to an end. A long and poorly lit hallway stretched on in both directions

"Well, I've got things to take care of," Pavao said. "Send the boss my regards."

Pavao headed off to the right. LeStrange turned to his left and headed down the far end of the hall. After crossing about ten meters, he could hear muffled voices up ahead. *Sounds like he's got a crowd with him this evening—again.*

One of Raspin's men was leaning against the wall next to a rusted door. It took LeStrange a second to remember the man's name. *Rascal.* Rascal had a wiry build—short and thin, but not unhealthy. His hair was brittle and in disarray. While not formidable, like many in Raspin's inner circle, he had a cold calmness about him and soulless eyes that regarded everyone with seeming disdain. As LeStrange came closer he could see that he was holding a knife, which he swung back and forth between two fingers.

Rascal watched LeStrange approach. Without saying a word, he punched a button on the wall and the door swung open. Laughter and light greeted LeStrange as he entered the room Raspin had dubbed as his 'private office'. It wasn't an office, really. Undoubtedly, when the building was functional, it had been a storage area approximately six-by-eight meters. Most of the room was filled with lamps that emitted a bright, natural light. One corner of the room, however, was left mostly in shadow. It was there that Raspin sat in a cushioned, high-back chair with faded upholstery.

The room was full with other key members of the Resistance as well as Raspin's usual mysterious entourage. There were eight people total. Three were field officers, like himself: Raphael Varona, Gen Yadama, and Jessica Crowne. Krause, the interrogator, was there, as was Father Kim. Standing next to Raspin was the familiar yet unidentified man with a muscular build. He still had the red scarf around his face and hood pulled up, but even now LeStrange could not shake the feeling he'd seen this man before, before he'd become Raspin's personal guard.

In the room's center sat a long, rectangular table. It was common place for charts and maps to be strewn about its surface. Today it was empty. Father Kim sat at a chair at its foot, with a pronounced smirk. Everyone else in the room, save for Raspin's mysterious guard, was chuckling. *I obviously missed the joke,* LeStrange thought to himself. The mirth irritated him. He was already furious with Raspin and their present situation, and seeing no one else appear concerned just poured salt on the wound.

"Ah, Peter. Good to see you," Raspin said as LeStrange entered. "How did it go with Pavao?"

"Fine," LeStrange answered curtly. "He says Attila Katona is in his pocket, and we can count on him, up to a point."

"And what point would that be?" Raspin asked.

"We can count on his hatred of the Hunters, but we can't count on his bravery."

"That makes sense," Raspin answered. "He's not a soldier, and it doesn't matter. He won't need a great deal of courage for what we'll ask of him."

"And what might that be?" LeStrange asked his tone so direct as to demand an answer.

Raspin's ruined lips twisted into a smile. "Wait and see."

LeStrange felt his temperature rise as a rush of anger came on him suddenly. "'Wait and see'? You mean the same kind of wait and see you asked us to do with Vamperic!?!" LeStrange placed his palms against the smooth surface of the table and then curled them into fists. All thoughts of courtesy or formality were lost in that moment. The hint of mirth disappeared from everyone's face. "That worked out *soooo* well, didn't it!?!"

"Actually, yes," Raspin answered matter-of-factly. "I was very pleased with the outcome. It couldn't have been better."

LeStrange slammed his fists against the table. "Are you insane? We lost good men, risked exposure, and came up empty handed—all because we made a devil's bargain with that lunatic. It was a disaster! How can you say it couldn't have gone better? It could barely have gone worse!!"

"Ah, Peter, Peter. As Christ once said to your namesake, 'ye of little faith, why do you doubt?'"

At those words, LeStrange had half a mind to turn the table up on end. He had to strangle his rage. Raspin took a step out of the dark corner and into the light. "You obviously didn't understand what the plan was. It was executed flawlessly, thanks in part to you, of course," Raspin said with a nod of the head. "To start with, we didn't come up empty handed. We needed to convert the Seven Seals into a series of more compact nuclear weaponry, but we lacked the understanding of nuclear technology to do it ourselves. Vamperic did what we could not. He provided us with a smaller device that we can use with greater effectiveness."

"Only one, and it's just a prototype. We don't even know if it will work," LeStrange countered.

"Oh, it will work, and we'll be able to make more, lots more. I already have engineers going over the prototype and creating a blue-print for producing others. And as to the incident in the silo, yes, we lost a few good people, and that is unfortunate, but this is war. People die."

"They died needlessly," LeStrange said. "His plan to kidnap a Hunter was utter stupidity. We're lucky it didn't turn out worse."

"Oh, no. That, too, went accordingly to plan."

"So you planned to just waste our time and men on Vamperic's personal agenda?"

Raspin didn't seem the least bothered by LeStrange's strong retort. "Vamperic was a dangerous man, he and White both. We needed him, but only for a while, and then we needed to be rid of him. Once Vamperic gave us the prototype, he served his purpose. I selected Sergeant Jast as our target of choice, because I knew he had a tracer. That shouldn't come as a surprise. He was out on bail! Of course he had a tracer. I knew as soon as Vamperic announced he had the sergeant as a hostage, the Hunters would be all over him in an instant. And if for whatever reason they weren't eager to rescue someone facing charges of treason, I knew they would rescue Lieutenant Marro."

LeStrange couldn't believe what he was hearing. "You used the Hunters to clean up our own mess."

"Precisely," Raspin said. "I knew we couldn't kill Vamperic ourselves, and it would have been pointless to try without flushing out Mr. White. But the Hunters had already made an arrangement with three super beings that had come to stop Vamperic, the same ones Vamperic had hoped to exchange the hostages for."

"By using Jast as the bait, you lured everyone out in the open," LeStrange said, understanding.

"Ridding ourselves of an unwanted ally, and killing a few Hunters in the process," Raspin said. "And even better, we made Sergeant Jast a hero, thus getting him reinstated."

LeStrange wrinkled his brow. "Why does that matter?"

Raspin strolled back over to his chair and sat down. "Sergeant Jast still has a role left to play, and in order to play it we need him right where he is, a loyal and valued Hunter."

"I don't understand," LeStrange replied. Judging by the expression of a few others in the room, he could tell they didn't either.

"No, and I don't imagine you do," Raspin responded curtly. "And that doesn't matter. What matters is it's so."

LeStrange took it all in. Raspin's explanation turned everything upside down. It was brilliant, yet hopelessly reckless. The thought of it made him lightheaded. He went over and sat in an empty chair by the wall.

"Raspin, that was a big gamble," LeStrange said. "So many things could have gone wrong—so many things. With more time, we could have figured out how to reverse engineer the Seals ourselves. The risk—"

"The risk?" Raspin snapped. "Our enemies have dozens of fleets, millions of troops, ample supplies, and control of the portals. Risk is all we have. Besides, the plan was flawless. The risk was far less than you believe."

"It was a brilliant plan, Raspin," Gen Yadama said, giving Raspin a short bow. Turning his attention to LeStrange, he shook his head. "Really, Peter, you shouldn't be so critical. When has the boss ever led us wrong?"

LeStrange felt his temper spark at that, partly due to the condescending tone, but mostly because he was right. Plans as outrageous as this shouldn't succeed, yet anytime Raspin was behind it, it did.

"I have to say I agree with the major, it was a risky plan," Raphael said, "but what's done is done. The important thing is it worked."

Father Kim spoke up. "Of course it worked. By choosing Ivan Jast he insured it would work." A grimace flashed across his face. "As much as I hate to admit it, if Jast could survive the Darkness for as long as he did then he could survive this Dr. Vampire madman."

"Vamperic," LeStrange muttered.

"Whatever. The point remains," Kim shot back.

"So, what are we going to do with the nuclear weapons once we've constructed a few more?" Raphael asked. "Shouldn't we conduct a field test?"

"There are plenty of neighborhoods still in ruins," Jessica Crowne pointed out. "We could place one of the bombs there and see how much it levels."

"Don't be ridiculous, Crowne," LeStrange said. "The Gaoro naval forces will detect it in an instant. Even if they can't trace who set it off, they'll realize what happened and will triple or quadruple their efforts to find out who was responsible."

"I thought you planted the idea in Minister Gramont's head that the insurgency had the Seals?" Jessica asked. "Would they just blame them? I thought that was the whole point."

"Yes," LeStrange admitted, "but once they launch their investigation, it's only a matter of time before they learn the truth."

"But meanwhile the Gaoroes will do us the favor of finally eliminating the rest of that New Moon trash," Gen countered.

"Sure, but we still don't know what happened to Dr. Klein," LeStrange pointed out. "If the Gaoroes and Civil Ministry get too gung-ho and start flushing out the rest of the New Moon's rat nests, they might find him before we do."

"I doubt it," Father Kim said.

"You doubt it? Why?" LeStrange asked.

"He isn't on Earth," Kim said.

"We're not entirely sure of that, yet," LeStrange said. "All evidence does point that way, but—"

"But nothing. He left Earth months ago."

LeStrange rose from his chair and went over to the table. "How do you know this?"

Kim shrugged. "In the future, it's common knowledge. About a year after the Darkness emerged Ivan and Kayla Jast found Dr. Klein and recruited him to help the Dawn fleet. As it turned out, he'd been hiding in Prajic space most of the time, I believe it was on an outlying world—Raggi. Yes, that was it."

"But that's only in your future," Raphael pointed out. "You already admitted that since Dark Hour has been averted, everything's different."

"Don't you get it?" Kim spat as he spoke. "He wasn't hiding on Raggi to escape the Darkness. He arrived there only three months after the Siege. He went to Raggi because it was the furthest from Gaoro\Earth space he could get."

LeStrange blinked. Had he heard right? Had the annoying, self-righteous, delusional priest just given them Dr. Klein?

"Raggi," Jessica mouthed.

The sense of shock in the room was palpable. Everyone gave some visible sign of surprise except for Raspin and his unnamed guard. Raspin sat there with a smug, confident smile.

He knew, LeStrange realized. *That's why he had us recruit Kim in the first place, Raspin knew that he knew.*

"By gods, it makes sense," Gen declared. "Why didn't you tell us this earlier, Father?"

"No one ever asked," Kim said.

"I'm not sure how much that helps us," Raphael interjected. "Raggi's a long way off. We can't port there and no human or Gaoro ships are allowed in Prajic space."

Raspin pressed his feet against the floor and leaned his chair against the wall. "It will be tricky. We'll need a special team for this. Peter, I want you on this one."

"Me? I thought you wanted me to run ops on the Command infiltration."

"Pavao can handle this one on his own," Raspin replied.

"And what about Brandon? He's not going to be happy about this. He's been heading up the search for Klein for months," LeStrange pointed out.

"He'll understand. This mission takes special skill. I want you to handle this personally, but you'll need help; someone who's traveled the galaxy and knows how to disappear completely, when necessary."

"You have someone in mind?" LeStrange asked, afraid to hear the answer.

Raspin tilted his head over toward his guard. "What do you think, Michael? Are you up to the challenge?"

The guard nodded. "It would be better if I did it alone, though."

"Yes, you are a true solo artist, but this time I think you'd do better to play a duet."

LeStrange couldn't help but to remark that even the man's voice sounded familiar. "And does Michael have a last name?" he asked, finally, meeting the guard's cold eyes.

He pushed back his hood and pulled the scarf away from his mouth. "Traush," he answered. "I assume you've heard of me."

The room went deafly quiet. Even Father Kim was taken back. "That's impossible," the self-proclaimed priest stammered. "Michael Traush is dead. He died before Dark Hour."

"The future is different now, Father," Traush answered.

"Yes," said Raspin, "and once we are finished, it will never be the same again."

About the Creators

Shannon Smith

Shannon Smith has an artistic family. His wife engages in numerous fields of art, including both drawing and photography. His younger son is a self–taught pianist. Shannon's older son is an avid graphic artist, whose work includes the logo and digital artwork of this book. Shannon studied graphic design at Abilene Christian University, but has focused most of his creative energy in to developing projects with Blue Inferno. Currently, in addition to his work with Blue Inferno, Shannon owns and manages a gaming store in Sherman, Texas.

David Furr

All of his life, David has been involved in creative projects of one kind or another, even at a very young age. In college, David released two short run comic books, while studying television and film. Since then, he has collaborated with Shannon on numerous projects, including Portal Hunters. In addition to his job and his creative pursuits, David also volunteers with a summer Bible camp in Miskolc, Hungary every year. His time in Miskolc has inspired him to study the culture and the language, something that he commonly references in his writings.

Coming Soon

Portal Hunters: Book Four

Gods & Monsters

by David Furr and Shannon Smith

www.ingramcontent.com/pod-product-compliance
Lightning Source LLC
Chambersburg PA
CBHW051240170626
46809CB00004B/1414